iii

"Sunshine On Leith"
Words and Music by CHARLES STOBO REID and CRAIG MORRIS REID
©ZOO MUSIC LTD.
Courtesy of Neue Welt Musikverlag GmbH

Any similarities to persons, living or dead, except for the purposes of satire, are purely coincidental.

Cover by Billy Christie

ISBN 9798577884437

The album "Sunshine On Leith" by The Proclaimers… if you haven't heard it, you really should…

# Links In The Chain

**Links In The Chain**

Billy Christie

Independent Publishing

Munich, 2020

# Contents

# Chapter 0

The waves whispered their rumours, hushed each other and lapsed into momentary silence, like old biddies pausing mid-gossip as the object of their disparagement approaches. They spoke in huddled tones of the boats, bobbing at their moorings, flaccid in their lack of purpose; they susurrated opinions on the bygone optimism of their purchase: a life of leisure, a life of toil, a life. They hissed and breathed of a body, a body they bore in turns, in grey solemnity to ragged shore line, to join a flotsam of unburnable wood, unwoven rope and decomposing kelp. They gasped as the body rolled and moaned. Its arm fell across the pebbles, without muscle, without ligament; the existence of bone was only confirmed by the hinge at the elbow.

His hands bobbed, detached in the water by his sides, rising and falling with the languid waves or his grateful breath, both.

Be still. Shut down. Stop. Silence the pain. Leave it. Float, float. Fade. Lean in, embrace. Drift and fade, drift and fade. The waves persuasive, pervasive, promising release, pestering him to join their endless murmurings. He could surrender. He was spent.

It would be easy, so easy. Just, let go.

But not yet. The almost extinguished spark of self-preservation glowed still, refusing to wink out completely. Where he was... that was one thing... from a given 'there' to the current 'here'... that, he could map out. Every journey has a start; its identifiable, certain, nameable, blameable start.   But try to find the final 'jumping off' point... a decision... an indecision... a moment's hesitation... the fork in the road that leads to this ruin or that redemption, a connection made or missed; that wrinkle in time, where events might have unfolded this way or that way.

To place the finger on the moment... to find the pulse, feel it quicken... or for that matter, feel it falter...

# Chapter 1

Ross was so unaccustomed to seeing letters on the mat, and so little of the hall floor was visible, that it was only as he passed the front door for a second time, après-shower, drying his hair on a small hand-towel, that he spotted the envelope. He picked it up and recognized that the return address had a Dumfries postcode.

Salvation in written form; she missed him so much that she wanted him to head south for a few days… meet the family… the future was looking up. A bit of home cooking… civilized chat by the fireside… sure, they'd need to be quiet 'on-the-job' but that was fine. Ross didn't harbour any illusions about his abilities in the sack and Miranda wasn't particularly vocal in her appreciation of his ham-fisted efforts, more's the pity.

Ross was already thinking of who would be his best man on the inevitable big day when he reached his room and sat on the bed to luxuriate in opening the letter.

"Ross," (uh, oh… not good. No "my dearest", no "my darling", no "you savage wild stallion", not even a "dear").

"I'm sorry to write to you like this; I know it's cowardly but there is no other way right now."

Breathing ceased to be an automatic body function.

"We have had a few good times together and that will always be special to me."

Ross felt his perspective momentarily shift sideways, as though his place in the world's order was no longer steady. If he had been standing up, he would have fallen over. He didn't even read the words; they arrived in his brain, but he was sure he hadn't read them. Time jolted forward by a few seconds. Adrenaline rushed around his body and turned sour.

"This isn't what I need right now. It's not you, it's me."

The standard escape clause. Ross was sure it was him, and probably her as well... and most likely some of his father... but mostly him.

The questions started. What could he have done differently? Should he have been more assertive? Less assertive? Should he have been taller? Shorter? Mentally stronger? Physically stronger? Tried going to the gym?

The rest of the letter was skimmed through. The usual platitudes... it's for the best... still be friends...

It didn't touch the sides.

Ross lay on his back and let his arms fall. He realized he would present a more convincing and pathetic tableau vivant of the broken heart if he was in the foetal position so he curled into a ball instead and started to whimper.

As complacent as he had been about Miranda in the past, she was now his one true love: the girl he would have married if his father hadn't got in the way; the girl that would have borne his children, if she could bear his father; the girl that would have been his girl, if he hadn't been his father's son.

Ross had no choice. He had to get his dad out of the flat and back to his mum, if only to prove to Miranda that he wasn't as weak and pliant as she clearly thought him to be. But how? Ross hated confrontation as much as his father did.

He rolled to face the window, caught sight of his own reflection and cried, unremittingly and without shame.

And so the cycle began: a continuous, two-day, round-the-clock indulgence of self-recrimination, self-doubt, self-loathing, starvation, sleeping, crying and significant amounts of self-abuse. From time to time, he would partake in more than one discipline simultaneously with varying degrees of success; weeping while masturbating proved quite effective, partly because the interrupted breathing of a full body sob brought on a state of erotic asphyxiation, partly because the shudders that wracked his body reduced his control. Instead of the rapid, economical motion of a proficient manual manipulation, speed, grip and aim were all compromised making it feel like Miranda was doing it… it precipitated yet more crying.

On the second day of the sulk-a-thon, Ross was running out of self-pity, but he couldn't leave the pain alone. It was like being unable to keep his tongue from a damaged gum following a painful tooth extraction. He needed something to take his mind off her. Necessity being the mother of invention, Ross raked through a box of his dad's junk marked "Car Stuff – Miscellaneous" till he found what he needed: a flexible attachment designed to secure a mobile phone to a car windscreen.

Back in his room, he clipped his phone into the retainer and lay down. The other end, he secured to his bedside cabinet and bent the phone round till it was directly in front of his face. Now, he was truly ready for the healing to begin. Any amount of internet porn would be right there, and he'd still have both hands free for punishing that part of his body that had begged him to get involved with Miranda in the first place.

His tears hadn't quite abated, but he was a little more in control. He used the occasional bouts of crying to justify a virtual session with one of the many "Women of the Web". There was no fresh Kleenex left, and of course, neither he nor his father were prepared to go and buy any, so Ross had to resort to recycling. A laudable and ecologically sound idea, until he made the mistake of grabbing a tissue from the wrong pile of used ones to blow his nose.

As luck would have it, Ross did not have a mobile phone contract; he was on pay-over-the-odds-as-you-go and had all too quickly blown his entire credit on downloading porn. Buying more credit would have meant breaching the impenetrable boundary of the front door. It's the one thing that saved him from electronically stalking the girl he couldn't think of as his ex, but that didn't stop him from mentally constructing scenarios. In his mind, he would make it clear that he was an independent spirit that couldn't be tied down to one girl anyway, and she'd see the error of her ways; the Miranda of his imagination would be convinced of his undying love and she would tearfully beg him to take her back.

He would talk to her as a dear friend, nothing more; so mature in the ways of the world that he had almost forgotten they were ever an item... she would feel like she had to prove to him and herself that they had indeed been an item, and she would come crawling back.

He would lay down the law and she'd be so cowed by his manly strength, his Rhett Butler stance, that she'd Scarlett O'Hara into his arms once more.

As most men never learn, the world doesn't work that way. The feature that distinguishes conversations with a real person versus those with an imaginary substitute is that the living, breathing version usually doesn't say what you expect them to say.

*She* had left him.

She *had* left him.

She had left *him.*

She had *left* him.

*She had left him.*

No matter where he put the emphasis, it was clear: he was loveless and lost. Ross resolved to do what any self-respecting young man would do in the circumstances.

Get drunk.

Get laid.

Both items on his to-do list involved leaving the flat.

Could he get drunk? Precedence said yes... all too easily. Could he get laid? He'd managed before, but he had no idea how. It was usually predicated on being just drunk enough to lose his inhibitions. Take it too far though and he ran the risk of falling asleep, or worse still, becoming so disorientated in unfamiliar surroundings that he would probably make some subtle faux pas.

Ross still mentally slapped himself every time he remembered staggering out of a strange bed (still clothed), lifting the toilet seat to pee before being woken by the lights coming on to reveal he had actually raised the lid on an antiquated record player. He had already achieved a rate of flow that could not be stopped by effort of will or even a tourniquet when he looked down to see he'd delivered a gushing review of a vinyl edition Kanye West album, a review which most critics could only dream of merely writing. The pen is mightier than the sword, but sometimes the penis is mightier than the word.

Get drunk? Get laid? Get real.

# Chapter 2

"Get out!" Ross yelled into the sink. "Go on! Leave me alone!"

"I just wanted to see what was wrong," his dad said, backing out of the bathroom. "You've been moping round with a face like a wet weekend in Falkirk."

"Just give me a minute, OK?" Without turning round, he kicked the door shut. The slam satisfied his need to make a noise.

Ross should have been grateful. This show of concern was the closest thing to compassion his dad had demonstrated since a week previously when he'd turned up at the bottom of the stairs, pleading to stay for a few days and demanding help to carry 'a few bits and pieces'. Gratitude was the last thing on Ross's mind; he craved solitude.

By the time he was confident he could speak without choking on the words, his dad was once again fastened to the armchair. Ross eased himself into the living room and stood directly behind his father. He exhaled slowly through his mouth, stared at the back of Michael's head.

The red hair was close-cropped. The skull rose vertically from the neck; it lent his father an aggressive air. "So what's the problem?"

Michael asked. He didn't turn. He didn't show any willingness to be distracted from the TV.

What the hell? A bit of sympathy might be what he needed. Ross breathed deep. "Miranda ditched me."

"And you're snivelling away like a baby?" So much for sympathy. "Go and talk to the lassie." He spoke more quickly and loudly than expected, like rushing to get in the punch-line to a joke before someone beat him to it.

"What? Like you and mum?"

A pause... Michael seemed to deflate, he continued quietly. "Yes, well... that's different. We've been married for years. Nobody expects us to talk anymore."

"So what happened? What did you do, dad? Why won't you even call her and say sorry?"

"Me? Why should I apologise?" countered Michael.

"Whatever it was you did, I'm sure she'll forgive you."

Only now did Michael disengage his eyes from the screen. He laid his hands in his lap and stared at them. "I didn't do anything... nothing." He bowed his head in contrition. "That's the problem. I didn't do anything."

"Do you mean helping round the house? Even mum wouldn't have thrown you out for that."

Ross sensed his father was about to open up. He moved round to rest his hand next to his father's on the arm of the chair. The once-textured surface was worn smooth; it had already served Michael and Theresa for years before Ross had inherited it for his first attempt at leaving the nest.

Michael stared forwards again, rheumy eyes reflecting the TV in miniature, more moist than usual. He gently turned his gaze first to Ross's chin, then to meet his eyes. It was childlike, vulnerable. "She didn't throw me out... I walked out. She's been seeing someone else."

Ross flicked his attention from left to right across his father's face, seeking truth. Michael believed what he was saying himself, even if Ross didn't quite. "What? Since when?" Ross couldn't think of

18

anything else to say. It sounded callous to his own ears, like the timing was more important than the infidelity itself.

"I don't know. I think it's one of the teachers at the school, but, honestly, I don't know for sure." Michael staggered a breath in.

"How do you know, then?" It sounded too much of a challenge. Ross knew that after he'd said it. "Mum wouldn't do that." He added trying to repair the damage he'd just done.

"And what would you know about it? You're never there. You only live half an hour away and you never come to visit. Don't you think we..." he faltered "I... might like to see you from time to time?"

Ross knew he shouldn't take the opportunity for a dig; the road to Milngavie was a two-way street, but his father only visited Glasgow when he wanted something from his son, usually a bolt-hole from Theresa's temper. "What are you going to do, dad? Have you talked to her about it?"

"I can't do that. If I'm right, that's 25 years down the shitter. If I'm wrong, she'll say I don't trust her. She'll never let me forget it." He laid his face in his hand. "Look, son." Michael tried for a brave smile and failed. "Don't fuck your life up like I have. If you and Miranda are meant to be, go and tell her that. I'll hold the fort here." There's nothing more pathetic than the walking wounded drawing attention to their own martyrdom by pretending to put someone else first. Ross was no stranger to this trick himself. He was sure he had physically flinched at Miranda's name, but didn't think his father had noticed.

"Maybe if I'd paid your mum a bit more attention she wouldn't have..." Michael wound down, couldn't bring himself to say what she would or wouldn't have done.

Ross glanced back at the door. What could he do? Maybe if he set a strong example, his dad would follow suit. "OK. You're right. I'm going to go call her." Ross straightened up, didn't bother with a jacket, and marched out. He was glad of the excuse to escape.

In the stairwell, he paused. He had no intention of calling Miranda, but he couldn't bear to look at his father right now. Ross was the lovelorn one but he couldn't even do that right. He was supposed to be the angst-ridden adolescent, and here he was being upstaged by his father. There was no justice.

If his mother was cheating on his father, what was Miranda doing right now?

She had left him… more than likely to perform lewd acts on some muscular border's sheep-shearer. Things she had never wanted to try with him. They were probably at it right now… laughing together in the brief interludes between bouts of sweaty, energetic, cavity-searching, eye-rolling, back-scratching, ground-shaking, bruising, gymnastic, voluminous sex. Laughing at that poor sap Ross… God, how could she ever have let him near her?

Ross needed a pub.

# Chapter 3

Each step Ross took ticked off another yard towards Byres Road.
Each step marked another beat of the song stuck in his head;
permanently on internal playback, a song of loss and pain, of sticks
and stones.

Cosseted in his misery, the traffic lights at the junction of Great
Western Road didn't even register; he stepped blindly into the inner
lane.

A cab driver honked his disapproval then eloquently added a few
sage words of advice and questions as to Ross's sanity and parentage.
He rounded off with a stirring rendition of "if I wasn't driving right
now, I'd already be smashing your face to a bloodied pulp" scored for
car-horn, headlights and middle-finger. To the delight of the
audience, he lowered his window and encored by questioning loudly
whether Ross was indeed a particular piece of female genitalia, "or
what". In the context, the coitus-related adjective chosen to prefix
the gynaecological comparison seemed to be a bit of a tautology.

*Fair point*, thought Ross. It's exactly how he felt.

And still The Proclaimers played a private rendition of "Sunshine
On Leith" in his head. Suitably chastened by the Cab Driver of The
Apocalypse, Ross had stepped backwards onto the uneven pavement

to wait for the protection of the green man. Without the pace of his feet to keep time, his internal soundtrack was stuck on one line, a record needle bounced off kilter by a scratch to find its previous groove, causing more damage with every skip, deepening the cut with each repetition.

This track would never sound the same again. "My heart was broken... my heart was broken..." Enough. The Reid Brothers could ply their misery on some other hapless bastard.

Ross pulled his MP3 headphones out of his shirt pocket, jammed them across his head, and tapped the play button. "Your beauty and kindness made tears heal my blindness..." Was someone taking the piss? The MP3 player was already cued half way through exactly the same song... exactly where he'd left it himself during the previous night's self-flagellation session.

He reached up to his left ear piece. His questing fingers sought the 'Random' button. Ross's one recent self-indulgence in the world of gadgetry had been a pair of Steinweiser headphones with built in MP3 and Blue-Tooth. No more wires... no umbilical to a separate player... no display screen... no idea what button he was pressing.

The soothing pre-recorded voice told him that he'd pressed 'Repeat'. Just before the band could once again remind him that he wasn't the only one who'd been hurt, Ross tore off the headphones; he couldn't imagine that anybody else had ever suffered a loss like this. Only he knew true misery. It was nonsense though; he hadn't even realized he had anything he would regret losing until Miranda's letter spelled it out for him.

Ross stabbed the OFF button and stuffed the headset back in his pocket, almost hard enough to break them; almost, but not quite. He had enough self-control left to remember just how much this unit had cost him. Saved from his reveries by a gap in the cars, he plunged across. What did men traditionally do in his situation? Ah yes... a drink. That was the original plan.

His brief jog slowed to a more sustainable pace as he reached the pavement, his footsteps once again measured the time and distance as he ticked off the pub possibilities offered by the West End of Glasgow. There was plenty of choice but none worth choosing:

Bobar: Too poncey.

The converted church he couldn't remember the name of: Too pricey.

Ubi-Chip: Too full of couples.

Jinty's: Too boil-in-the-bag Irish.

Curlers: Possibility, but he'd been there with Miranda.

Tenents: Bad reputation, too threatening.

The Aragon: Too small.

The Judges: Too far away.

QMU: Disenchanted saturnine wannabes, don't look at me 'cause you'll get in the way of everybody else noticing me; I want to make sure that as many people as possible know that I don't want to be noticed. Disaffected in a middle-class, daddy-will-still-pay-my-credit-card-bill-if-I-ask kind of a way. Might get a chance of a ride if some black clad girl wants to teach her parents a lesson, but will have to put up with a tirade of self-invented problems and how misunderstood she is. No way. No shag was worth that. No matter how hot Goth-chicks look in yellowed lace and threadbare velvet.

Ross didn't walk the slope-shouldered reluctant meander of his misery. To all outward appearances he strode along with purpose, each step stabbing into the pavement, venting a little anger with every strike of his boot heels, leaving little footprints of wretchedness behind; soft, cloying dog-turds of despair that someone other poor sod could tread in and get stuck to their shoes instead of his.

# Chapter 4

By University Avenue, Ross wasn't exactly happy, but the ache of his self-pity had dulled. Maybe the rhythm of his walk had helped clear his mind. Maybe it was the simple act of doing something, anything, that gave him a sliver of a hope of redemption. Maybe it was just being out of the apartment and seeing people other than his immediate family.

He'd walked farther than he'd realised. Without a fixed destination in mind, his feet had just kept moving. This time waiting for the crossing lights, Ross noticed it wasn't much farther to Krister's place.

Krister, Ross's lab partner, confidant, drinking buddy and overly privileged rich-kid was usually good for a laugh… and if not a laugh, then loan of a tenner for a beer or two; a debt that would often be tactfully forgotten by both parties.

Crossing the junction at a diagonal, it was only a couple of doors past the lights to Krister's ground floor flat. The lucky bastard had everything easy; ground floor, bought by his parents, peppercorn rented to Krister, misrepresented to HM Tax Office. Each storey of the converted tenement had been subdivided and subdivided again till some of the flats were little more than a room and cupboard sized kitchen. The Georgian high ceilings remained meaning that most of the rooms were taller than they were long.

Krister had often joked that if he could find a way for people to sleep upright, he'd get another four rooms out of his place and sublet them. Or, if he could advertise for short-arses, amputees and those with curved spines, he'd put a mezzanine level in and stack'em like Pringles. Then he'd pause and raise an eyebrow… waiting to see if you thought he was joking. It was Krister's usual way of testing the waters for his more morally dubious schemes. Ethics were something that happened to other people, but he was adept at pretending long enough to camouflage all manner of transgressions and unpleasantness.

In a multitude of alternative realities, Krister Bonn was a celebrated advertising executive, a politician, a psychopath, a whole range of professional liars and con-men… and still he could make sure that when it all hit the fan, he'd walk away whiter-than-white while the luckless bystanders were liberally coated. It was one of the things that made him so disgracefully likeable.

Ross pressed the door intercom. Two years previously, the name "BONN" had been penned on a strip torn from the top of a newspaper, weatherproofed with sellotape and temporarily overlaid on the bottom buzzer. The ink had long since faded from its original blue biro to a pale stain; the paper yellowed and the name utterly unreadable.

Kris had once responded to Ross's enquiry on the subject, "If it's someone important, they'll know where I am. If they're not important, what right have they got bothering me?" Prompted or not, Kris would occasionally repeat this reasoning with a nod at the intercom. He liked portraying himself as raffish scoundrel, a slight hint at a nefarious past. He didn't miss many opportunities to reaffirm himself in the eyes of others that he thought could be impressed.

The buzz of the door lock cued Ross to shoulder the door open. Typically Kris wouldn't even lift the intercom to check who was there before pressing the key shaped button. Ground floor, first on the left, the door was just ajar enough to stop its weight reengaging the lock.

"Kris?" called Ross as he stepped from the echoing communal hallway onto the polished floor boards of the flat.

"Ah, Ross The Toss." Kris replied. He'd already made it back to the living room and was looking over his shoulder, twisting out past the arm of the sofa towards Ross. Krister couldn't quite turn round far enough to fully make eye contact.

"Krister The Sister Fister."

"She wasn't a sister... she was a mother superior. I've got standards," retorted Krister. He had a range of replies to this customary salutation ranging from the merely tasteless to the utterly disturbing.

Formalities over, Ross removed his trainers by standing on the heel of each in turn and left them where they fell at the threshold. He leaned his back on the door to close it and paused there for a couple of seconds. Jolting himself fully upright by thrusting his backside against the door, he went to join Kris.

"S'up?" The rest of the world had grown weary of "s'up", but Kris persevered.

Ross wasn't prepared for this. He didn't like for Kris, or anybody, to think he was ever at a loose end. If he admitted he was wandering disconsolate and heartbroken, he'd be exposing himself as some kind of vulnerable sad-act. He'd be disappointing Kris and somehow, that would be worse.

"Eh, I was thinking we should maybe start planning this project." He improvised. "Just make sure we're not overlapping or missing anything."

Kris looked askance at Ross.

"Ross, what's the due date?"

"Eh, October sometime?"

"Right... and what month are we in now?"

"Eh... wait a minute. I know this one. June?" Ross hazarded.

Kris lifted both hands to push his Buddy Holly glasses back up his nose. He didn't want to relinquish his vicelike grip on the game controller to which he was currently attached. "Right you are. Which means we have… anyone? Anyone?"

He un-paused the game. Death, mayhem, destruction, all the key ingredients of a successfully wasted afternoon, spat from the screen across the narrow sitting room. The culmination of decades of semiconductor research and billions-worth of investment, computing power the moon landings could only have dreamed of, pandering to the addiction of a bored twenty-something year old. Sustaining and nurturing, bathing his mind, cradling his hypothalamus, drip-feeding electronic dopamine.

"Three months." Ross beamed, deliberately childlike.

"Three months, as the crow flies. You got it."

"Well… yes, but I just thought…"

"Don't think. You're not good at it," Kris interrupted, "Standard operating procedure in this situation, as you well know, is to do sod-all about it till about 36 hours before the deadline, then either:

a. Rush around in a blind panic trying to fake the results we should have been assiduously working on, or

b. Get a sick note from the doctor to pull an extension."

Ross paused to consider the options, not entirely sure what "assiduously" meant. He was under the impression that it referred to trees which lost their leaves in winter, but in the context, he wasn't absolutely certain. Wisely, he kept quiet.

"So… who's for option b?" asked Krister. "It's always been my favourite number."

By way of an answer, Ross collapsed into the sofa beside Kris and followed a likely looking cable to locate the spare games handset. It led beneath a ring binder, its plastic coating picked off at the edges. Doodles and scribbles adorning the surface varied in shape and intensity according to Kris's mood at the time. Delicate cubes reflected a relaxed, introspective dreamlike state. Furious, tightening spirals of overlapping biro hinted at a less controlled persona, each circuit of the pen obscuring the last.

In a bygone era of studious fervour, before the novelty of university had worn off, Kris had filed his loose-leaf paper in binders such as this. Nowadays, a binder was more likely to support loose-leaf tobacco, resin, roaches and rolling papers, providing a conveniently flat surface.

Ross hit the START key on the handset. Ordinarily this would open a window asking which character would be his criminal avatar, but nothing happened.

"Sorry, mate," Kris explained. "I've got a solo-mission going. You can't join till I restart in multimode."

"Well, restart it then. Don't be a fucker all your life."

"Ach, Ross. I've never got this far before. Can you not wait? Go and make a cup of tea or something." There were unnatural pauses between his words. Kris couldn't or wouldn't concentrate on anything except slaughtering cops and driving over prostitutes.

Ross sat and watched the screen in sullen silence for a few moments before looking round at his friend.

"Kris... Miranda... she..." He heard his own voice weaken and waver. He thought he'd be able to do this. "Kris... I... she dumped me." Ross felt his eyes moisten.

"Uh-huh." Kris was too wrapped up in reversing a Camaro repeatedly over the prone body of a bullion delivery man. But he did risk a brief sideways glance over the corner of his glasses the moment he knew Ross was looking back at the screen.

"Em... can you not save the game or something? I could do with a bit of company."

"I'm here, amn't I?"

"Only in body..."

Kris tipped the controller, even though this had no effect, as he swerved the stolen car back onto the digital streets of LA.

"Kris, please."

"Ach, stop your foul whining. Let me just get to the next check point then. We can go grab a pint."

# Chapter 5

Half an hour later (a further three game checkpoints, and two changes of shirt by Krister), they were installed on the high stools at a barrel/table in the beer garden of Jinty's Almost-Irish bar.

"So what happened?"

"She sent me a letter. She didn't even have the…"

"What did it say?" Kris interrupted.

"The usual shite. We can still be friends, she needs space… needs to decide where her life is going… all that bollocks."

"Is she seeing someone else?"

Ross reluctantly looked up from his cider. He'd been aligning and realigning the base of the glass with the pattern on the beer mat. He raised his eyes to meet Kris's. "I don't know. She didn't say… but she wouldn't, would she?"

"Maybe. Maybe not. If she's trying to spare your feelings she wouldn't."

"If she was trying to spare my feelings," Ross forced, "She wouldn't have fucking dumped me, would she?"

A couple at the next barrel glanced over. Someone else's romantic misfortune is always good entertainment. Soap-operas are built on this simple truth. To emphasize the point, Kris turned and played air-drums and sang the intro to Eastenders. Hint taken, the voyeurs pretended they had been chatting amiably between themselves the whole time. At least it raised half a smile from Ross. Kris could be a bit obnoxious, but he had his uses.

"So…" Kris continued. "To summarize: you were punching above your weight. She dumped you… it was bound to happen eventually. The sun is shining, we're in a beer garden, we have pints… although yours is a cider so it barely counts. Life isn't that bad." Kris raised his glass, partly to demonstrate what a pint looked like, but also as a toast that Ross failed to return.

"It gets worse. Dad has taken root on the sofa. I can't even get peace in my own flat right now."

"Is that why you turned up on my doorstep like a little lost kid?"

"Yeah, I guess so." The simile was pretty apt. Ross's feet couldn't reach the ground from his barstool and swung disconsolately back and forth as he talked. Standing, he barely reached Kris's shoulder, and Kris was no giant.

They both supped at their pints to fill the lull in conversation.

Kris broke the silence. "Jesus, it's almost warm. Might even risk getting the shirt off."

He shrugged out of his shirt revealing a factory-faded, pre-aged "Pixies" T-shirt underneath, and some serious tattoo work.

"Are you not going to get that finished sometime?" Ross waved his pint in the direction of Kris's arm.

A sleeve tattoo of a 1950's style comic strip started behind his wrist and wound its way in pseudo-print-pixel vivid colour to disappear under the pallid green of his T-shirt. It wasn't any particular comic book extract; Kris would not have deigned to support anybody else's ideas with his body. The design was more of a pastiche of the hero comics of the era; unfeasibly hourglass shaped women stifling a scream with a delicate hand, lantern-jawed narrow-eyed leading men in Trilby's, low browed thugs, pistols and elegant cars.

"It is finished. It runs up and across my chest too." Kris used his left hand to caress from his right shoulder and down across his pectoral indicating the extent of the piece. "And part way over my back."

"No, I mean the speech bubbles. None of these guys are saying anything."

"Ah… see… that's part of the plan." Kris explained. He leaned in, ready to impart information that might be classified, or even dangerous if it fell into the wrong hands.

"It's a total babe-magnet. They see the tat… ask about the speech bubbles, like you just did. Then I tell them I haven't decided what all my little people should be talking about." There was something vaguely unsettling about the way Kris said "my little people". That group might be limited to the story-board characters on his arm, or then again, it might not.

Ross folded his arms, tipped his head back and to the side. He could see what was coming.

"So, I ask for suggestions… then I pull out a pen and they can write what they like. Eventually, they graduate to my chest… by which time my top is off and I'm half way there."

"Yeah, cunning," said Ross, without enthusiasm.

"And the next morning, I can wash off whatever drivel they've left behind as soon as they're out the door."

Sure enough, the gaggle of girls standing in the smoking zone were discussing Kris's arm and alternately looking over. The tallest of the three took a metal pot the size of a shot glass from her handbag, unscrewed the top and crushed the remains of her cigarette into the already brimming container. She strode confidently over to Kris's table. It was no longer Kris and Ross's table; Ross was irrelevant background. "Nice ink. Can I have a closer look?"

"Sure. Help yourself."

The girl gently grasped Kris's hand across the palm to control his movements. She stroked a finger up the inside of his arm, pausing in the crook of his elbow to glance at his face, and continued her exploration to the sleeve of his T-shirt. "Love it. I've got two tats myself," she confided. "But nothing like this."

"Whereabouts?" Kris asked, more out of habit than anything else.

"One on my ankle and the other just above my arse." She waited to see if Kris would be turned on by the word "arse"; it was a polar opposite from her innocent West Country accent. Some guys liked it.

"A hummingbird down here," she pointed towards her foot. "And a black and white butterfly here." She turned and stuck out her behind provocatively. Her beige trousers were tight enough to be worth pondering the contents, but not so tight as to give the game away all at once.

"Ah, tramp-stamps? Nice."

"Very funny," she chided, but Ross could see that the gentle ribbing was working. She was interested. Damn Kris to hell. "So, can I see the rest of yours?" she continued.

Damn Kris to hell again... and all the way back.

"Look, I'm sorry... what was your name?"

"Laura. Yours?"

"Kris."

They shook hands, still ignoring Ross.

"I'm sorry, Laura, but I'm not really into girls that smoke."

She looked a little crestfallen but recovered magnificently and straightened her neck, shimmied her head. The action was half way between a denial and a twitch.

Ross saw his chance. "Kris, I'd have thought you'd be all for girls that smoke."

"How's that?" asked Kris.

Laura seemed to suddenly realize there was someone else at the table and looked round for clarification.

"'Cause at least you know they're used to sucking on something small and unpleasant smelling."

"Aye, very good," conceded Kris, but laughing all the same. He was still giggling as he raised his pint and looked over the rim to watch Laura walk back to her mates. They both held their arms out and mimicked fighter aircraft hitting the ground... crash and burn.

34

Ross was surprised at himself. Despite the layer of misery, he was maintaining a veneer of normality. He could almost feel the separate compartments in his mind, one failing to deal with the Miranda situation, the other succeeding in dealing with the here and now.

"Still... nice arse though." Kris's opinion, not Ross's. "Maybe if I do her from behind I don't need to smell the fag ash."

"Aye, and she won't need to see your ugly face either. Everyone's a winner." Ross took a sizeable gulp of his cider.

"Hmm... fair point," said Kris. He seemed to be genuinely considering the prospect.

Laura, her back pointedly turned to Kris and Ross, was shaking her head. She and the chubbier of her two friends slung their handbags over their shoulders and made their way into the overcrowded bar.

Krister's eyes locked on target and tracked. "Roscoe... ", he pondered at leisure. "You're an educated gentleman. Explain this. Why do girls always go in pairs to the pisser?"

"It's so if the seat is manky, they can hold each other up. One stands on the other's feet and takes her arms then lowers her down so she can hover."

Kris gave the reasoning due consideration, sipped his pint then lowered his glass. "Bollocks is it."

"Anyhow," he continued. "I'm going for a slash as well. Do you want to come and hold me up?"

"Nah, I'll stay here and get the girls to form an orderly queue pending your return."

Kris swaggered off, making sure as many of the patrons as possible could get a look at his body art.

Alone, Ross tried to look like he was waiting for a friend to return from the toilets, rather than a sad-act who drinks solo. It's not an easy message to get across, but he checked his phone for non-existent calls, checked his watch, made sure the staff didn't clear Kris's almost empty pint glass, checked his phone again.

He was head-down rereading old text messages from Miranda when Kris sneaked up behind him.

"Two pints. Proper beer this time... not that fruit juice you were on earlier."

"Cheers man." Ross pushed his empty out of the way and centred the fresh drink precisely on his beermat.

Kris glanced over Ross's shoulder at the phone. "Are you still pining on that?"

Caught in the act, Ross closed his phone, straightened to put it back in the hip pocket of his jeans, then folded back into his previous slouch. "I was just checking... you know... see if I missed anything... or if I said something wrong."

"Look, Ross. You said you wanted to talk about the project." Kris raised an eyebrow. "Or was that just an excuse?"

Silence from Ross.

"Yeah, thought as much." Kris took his seat and leaned back, a tradesman appraising a difficult task. "Anyhow," he continued. "Why not? We need to do it sometime, and something else to think about might just about stop your bottom lip sticking out."

Ross sighed and tried to squint down at his own bottom lip. He pulled it hard with his thumb and forefinger instead and let it snap back to position. "A'right," he said. "Where do we start?"

"What was the topic again?"

"Were you not at the last lab group before the exams?" It was a fairly pointless question. Kris only turned up to lab groups if it was raining and he happened to be in the neighbourhood in need of shelter.

"What's the point in both of us going?" he asked. "That's efficiency for you."

"No Kris. That's laziness for you. I go... you stay in bed."

"And what's your point?" Kris was unashamed, even proud, of how he could coast his way through uni. It probably stemmed from the fact that if he really screwed up, his parents could afford to bail him out. Unfairly, this relaxed attitude seemed to pay off.

It was a losing battle. Ross let it go. "We've got to write and document a bit of software to analyse financial market movements and see if there really is a naturally occurring oscillation." To illustrate the point, Ross dragged his finger through a pool of spilled beer to draw a wave pattern.

"See…" he continued. "If there is a kind of technical action-reaction, we should be able to isolate the underlying frequency of that."

Ross glanced at Kris to see if anything was either sinking in or registering as familiar. Neither. Kris's face was unreadable. "OK. Think of it this way. If the price of gold starts to drop there will be a percentage of investors who want to sell up immediately and get out while they're still in profit. If that number is big enough, the price of gold will fall even farther as the market saturates. Capice?"

"Yeah, OK."

"Right. But, at some point, the price gets so low that people start to think it's a good idea to buy in again. Demand outstrips supply and the price rises again. Yeah?"

"So the price swings up again. So what?"

"So the price swings up until it gets too expensive to buy… current owners get jittery and worry about the price crashing again… or, maybe they just decide they've made enough and don't want any more risk. So, they sell… supply beats demand… price drops… and the cycle begins again."

Kris retraced Ross's sine wave. He looked momentarily thoughtful but it was likely he was already trying to decide how to minimize his expected effort in the joint project.

"But," Kris argued. "Hasn't this been done to death before? I mean, gold has been tracked since they first dug it up. Do we really need to do all this again?"

"True. Gold has been done to death. But if gold is the baseline, all other markets can be seen as a function of gold movements…"

Kris triumphantly spotted a flaw. "Yes. But, surely there are so many influences and knock-on effects that seeing any kind of pattern is impossible." He drew a second wave in the spilled beer, mirroring the first. "I mean. If the man that sells his gold has cash on the hip, he might buy something else… maybe real-estate. Maybe silver… maybe he'll just invest in powder and shove it all up his nose."

Ross nodded and opened his mouth to explain that this was indeed the case but…

"Anyhow," Kris cut his friend off. "If it was me, I'd go out and rent myself a dozen supple and pliant young ladies, a paddling pool and about 100 litres of warm olive oil." He drained the last of his beer, deliberately rattling the glass against his teeth; it illustrated how the very thought of slithering around with a bevy of beauties was overloading his limited capacity for control.

"Aye. But… that's where the challenge is. We need to…"

"Challenge? You're right. Do you think I should be less ambitious? Maybe 6 girls and 50 litres of olive oil?"

"No, I mean we need…"

"How about jelly instead then? At least I have a chance of getting a grip. I don't think I'd get any real traction in oil."

"Kris." Ross waited to see if Krister was going to continue. He often kept mining once he thought he'd struck a vein of humour.

Kris caught Ross's eye and forcefully snapped his mouth shut.

"We are supposed to use Fast-Fourier transforms across a whole range of data to separate out the noise. Then overlay individual data sets to see if there is a buy-sell pattern, or any kind of timing, or… or… or whatever."

"Bo-o-o-o-o-oring." Kris rolled his eyes and faked a yawn.

"Tell you what, Ross. You stick to your Furry-transforms. I'll see if I can find something else furry to stick to." He glanced across at Laura and her friends. His rule about girls who smoke was definitely becoming more of a guideline.

"Kris. Do you even know what a Fast-Fourier transform is?"

"Eh… yeah. It's the thing in a car that charges the battery, yesno?"

Ross knew Kris was taking the piss. Irritatingly, he was pretty good at maths without seemingly putting in much effort. He sighed and let his head droop. "This means I'll be doing all the work… again… doesn't it?"

"No." Kris denied, managing to sound genuinely offended at the affront to his diligence.

"No. I know what they are. It's how you break down a noisy signal into component sine waves. But, to be honest, I'm buggered if I remember how to do it. If I see an example, it'll come back to me."

"Well, thank God for that. We're saved." Ross ladled on the sarcasm.

"But there's more to it than that. We need to match the right sets of data to be able to spot the patterns. If people are pulling out of gold buy silver and we're looking at tin, we won't find anything interesting." Ross regretted the choice of the word 'interesting' but it was too late.

"'Interesting'... a matter of opinion. So..." Kris challenged. "What do you suggest?"

Ross paused, trying to decide whether it was worth explaining more, or keeping Kris interested. The two options were probably mutually exclusive. He hedged his bets and went for the latter. "I suggest," he paused, "another pint. It usually helps the thought processes." Since the Romans had worshipped at the shrine of Bacchus, the fallacy of this logic had never been called into question for long. It was fairly self-fulfilling. Per consummatio ad adsumptio... Per vino ad nauseam, or something like that.

Ross raised his empty glass and one eyebrow.

"Does Margaret Thatcher burn in hell? Of course, my good man." Kris pinged his already empty glass with a fingernail.

"Actually, she's probably running the place by now," mused Ross. "Satan is most likely tugging his forelock and begging forgiveness as we speak... trying to explain why there're still any working pits..."

"Pints." Kris drew Ross's attention back to the highest priority task, tapped the barrel-top twice, and pointed at the pub door.

Alcohol: purchase, consume, repeat...

"So, what d'ye reckon, mate?"

"I reckon... you're talking bollocks, Kris. It'll never work."

"I'm telling you it will."

"There's no way in hell that..."

"I'm telling you, she's gagging for it. I'm going for it, it'll work," guaranteed Kris.

"Look, before you get a kick in the nuts for your trouble, can you forget trying to get her," Ross nodded in Laura's direction, "on all fours? What are we going to do about the project?"

"All fours, eh? Which end am I taking?" Kris raised his glass again. He saw the look in Ross's eye and paused briefly to touch down on Planet Sober.

"OK…" Kris conceded. "How's this for a plan? Remember my folks have a wee holiday place up in Glen Fanaidh Balaichen?"

"Aye, you mentioned it," agreed Ross.

"Well, I don't think they let it out this month. I was thinking of heading up there. Get a wee bit peace and quiet… that is, if I don't end up getting a wee piece tonight." Kris sucked air over his teeth as he surveyed Laura's backside once again.

"Or maybe I'll use my piece to keep her quiet, eh?" He stuck his tongue into his inner cheek cause a phallic bump on the outside, just in case Ross hadn't got the point. Kris continued, "Why don't you grab a sleeping bag and a laptop and come to the cottage with me? If the weather's half decent, we can set off tomorrow morning. We can start the assignment, a bit of hill-walking, take a few beers with us. You know…"

Ross considered the offer. "It's a cunning plan, but with two small draw backs."

Kris waited for clarification.

"First," explained Ross, unsteadily focusing on his raised index finger. "My dad has taken up permanent residence in my place and I can't leave him on his own. He'll have the place burned down or something."

Kris had only met Michael a couple of times, but nodded at this note of caution.

"Second…" Ross placed the index finger of his other hand next to the first; it was easier than relearning how his hand worked. "I don't have a laptop."

"No problem… that part's easy. We can dump all the project crap onto an external hard-drive. I'll use dad's PC at the cottage; you use the laptop he just got me."

*Yes, of course he did*, thought Ross. *If he adopts me, can I have one too, pretty please?* "OK... did you leave your porn on it?" Ross meant it as a joke, but only just.

"But of course. That collection has taken years to build up. That's my back-up wank fodder, in case of emergencies."

Alcohol: purchase, consume, repeat...

"Right... where was I?" asked Kris.

Ross wavered, part intoxication, part reluctance to watch Kris scoring yet again.

"Oh yeah," Kris realized. "I was about to go and get better acquainted with the Lovely Laura."

"And I was about to watch you go down in flames, mate."

"Nice one... she is ginger, after all. I could use that... thanks Ross. Go down in flames... go down in flames..." Kris pondered the possibilities for a smart-ass chat-up line.

# Chapter 6

Ross stared despondently at the tide marks of foam that marked each swallow he'd taken of his beer. Through the candyfloss of alcohol swaddling his brain, he vaguely remembered hearing somewhere what caused the infamous "breaking of the seal" effect; that self-inflicted bodily handicap suffered by drinkers the world over... i.e. that the first pee heralds a repeat visit every half an hour or so. It has nothing to do with the volume of liquid consumed; the bladder uses a hormone called ADH (or was it GBH or ADHD?... whichever)... the bladder uses this hormone to send a message to the brain saying "I'm full... do something about it, or so help me, I won't be held responsible for the consequences."

However, as a medical student friend had explained, a cruel twist of evolutionary fate means that alcohol interferes with this notification mechanism. Once there is sufficient alcohol in the blood, the hormone message gets stuck on repeat play... no matter how little fluid is left. The net effect is that there is a perpetual and insistent need to visit the little boy's room, or girl's room, or nearest tree, bush or fast food cafe for relief.

Ross could no more ignore the desperate pleas from his body to 'drain the vein' than he could bodily pick his father up and throw him out of the window of his flat. A pint of cider, 5 pints of something yellow and fizzy that he couldn't identify and two drams of whisky would brook no argument. Since the weak summer sun had eventually slithered below the tops of the surrounding buildings, the drop in temperature wasn't helping much either.

"Mate… I'm going for a slash. My eyeballs are floating here." He declared.

"Yeah, do it." Kris replied, but it was pretty obvious he was paying no attention, fixated as he was on Laura.

Ross scooted forwards off the bar stool, dropping the short distance to the paving slabs where he swayed slightly. Weaving his way through the crowded beer garden, it was by no means a certainty that he could make it in time.

Finally and gratefully squeezing through the partially obstructed door to the gents, he was already unzipping his jeans as he reached the urinal. Timing was critical. He held the elastic of his boxer shorts down with his left thumb and flipped "Ross-junior" over the waistband, just as the torrent let fly. The overpowering smell of second-hand lager clashed with the sickeningly sweet aroma of the hygiene blocks cluttering the metal trough. In the moment of tranquil meditation that came with the release of bladder pressure, Ross pondered how the deodorising effect of the lemon-fresh cubes could somehow serve to heighten the nasal assault of a day's worth of stale piss.

He shivered deliciously and, not for the first time, mused on what caused that to happen. One theory was that his body temperature was rapidly lowered by the loss of a litre or so of warm pee, but Ross had never had that confirmed. Whatever the reason, he'd sometimes confessed to himself that this one shuddering interlude of pleasure was better than sex. It felt great, the more beer he drunk, the more often he could do it, instead of the other way round… plus he didn't need to talk about "where this relationship is going" afterwards.

Happy in his relief, a man suddenly finding himself at peace with the world, Ross engaged in one of his favourite sports. He used his high pressure yellow stream to chase the urinal blocks up and down the trough. He would count himself a winner if he could hose one from one end to the other and back again before running out of liquid. It would be a victory of sorts on an otherwise outright loss of a day.

Shuffling sideways to catch up with his quarry, hydraulic pressure still holding steady, he was about to begin an unprecedented second lap of the metalwork when he briefly lost his footing on the raised dais. Ross caught his fall with his toe as his right heel suddenly found itself in open space with no support. He lurched forward and overcompensated, banging his forehead on the tiled wall.

The momentary disruption to his balance shocked his left thumb free of the waistband of his underwear; the elastic snapped back up, painfully pinging the underside of his knob and roughly disrupting his aim away from the citrus cubes to a nearly vertical arc. Tipped forward as he was, the golden stream still maintained sufficient pressure to liberally spray across his lower face before his boxers recaptured his briefly liberated penis. Unable to stem the flow, Ross reluctantly dragged his gaze to where the crotch and thighs of his jeans were already turning a deep, sullen blue. Droplets of beer-scented urine dripped gently from his nose and chin to continue their diverted journey into the sewer system. By comparison, wetting his jeans was getting off lightly. His shoulders sank. The moment of happiness shrivelled and expired; Ross realized that the world just wasn't ready to deal him a fair hand.

As he watched the dark patch spread farther and he felt the liquid warmth pervade his legs, Ross contemplated his options with a resigned detachment. At least the bar was crowded enough that nobody would be able to see his jeans; it was pretty much standing-room only. And the dusk outside meant he could probably make it home without too much embarrassment. If he washed his face, he could just slip away into the twilight.

Face rinsed off, Ross edged out into the bar and towards the nearest exit. None of the other patrons paid him any attention. *Typical*, he thought. *Even soaked in piss nobody notices me.*

In the sodium glow of the lights of Ashton Lane, he could see Kris already integrated at Laura's table. Bastarding bastard of a bastard's bastard. Ross was sure that even if Kris could tear his attention away from his intended victim, he wouldn't see Ross leaving as long as he stuck to the shadows; head-down, pissed, pissed off and pissed on, Ross made his way home via the darkened back-lanes of the West End of Glasgow.

Breathing heavily at the top of his stairs, Ross knew he was taking unpleasantly large lungfuls of his own vaporised urine. That and the cold chafing of wet denim on his thighs reminded him his jeans were still soaked. He unlocked the front door as discretely as possible and headed straight for the bathroom. He kicked off his shoes, unsure if they had survived unsoaked. He congratulated himself on remembering to put his headphones somewhere dry; they were advertised as waterproof anyway, but he still hadn't ever quite believed it enough to try. Climbing fully clothed into the shower, his hand turned on the water without any further conscious instruction.

The booze still richly pervading his blood stream once again tricked his body into relieving his bladder. He did so, right there in the shower, without even attempting to release his traitorous penis first. It couldn't make things any worse, could it? He was too maudlin and too drunk to care.

It took some moments before Ross realized he had stopped urinating as the warm shower-water was confusing his beer-addled senses. He turned and stood a full five minutes longer with the spray directly on the back of his neck, thinking of how often life could kick him in the balls before it stopped hurting anymore.

He unbuttoned and peeled off his shirt, followed by his jeans, underwear and socks and let the sodden mass drop to the base of the shower unit. The drain, previously mostly clogged with a mat of hair and a suspicious off-white mucus, was now fully blocked with clothing and the water slowly advanced up his ankles. Ross idly

46

watched as the rising tide covered the harvest of mildew that festooned the shower curtain and approached overflowing the shallow basin. He contemplated letting it run out and into the bathroom just to see what would happen.

Realism overcame nihilism when he figured out that all that would happen would be that he would have to clean it up. Reluctantly, Ross turned the tap and stood naked and dripping. The plastic curtain, no longer displaced by the flow of water, now hung as slimy as a cow's afterbirth and clung clammily where it enveloped his flesh.

There were no clean towels, of course, and only a meagre hand-towel, already suspiciously stained and inflexible, hanging by the sink. Ross, modestly holding the towel across his groin, slithered on wet feet to his bedroom. He was chilled by the breeze from his open window that toyed with the water droplets still adhering to his naked skin.

Pulling out fresh jeans and a T-shirt to wear, Ross continued grabbing clothes from the drawer. He watched himself stuff a week's worth into a backpack. The part of his mind that still held onto a glimmer of hope for better things to come had staged a mutiny and was now fully in control. He would take Kris up on the offer and join him in 'Balaichen tomorrow. Fuck it. He'd set off right now. He'd take his gear and head straight back to the pub. Kris wouldn't mind him crashing at his place tonight so they could make an early start the next day. He vaguely remembered this proposal being made an hour or so previously.

Ross toyed with the idea of just disappearing. Maybe it would give his old man food for thought if he just left. But it was more than likely that Michael wouldn't even notice. No, it would be more effective if he left a note. Nothing too specific, just enough to make sure his dad knew he was gone, but vague enough to perhaps trigger a little paternal guilt trip.

He didn't want to say where he was going or with whom. Ross was under no illusions that his dad would attempt to find him or get in touch, but he liked the idea that McDade Senior might try to imagine where his son could be. Perhaps he might even get the hint that Ross would rather be wandering aimlessly with no fixed abode than share his flat with his father any longer.

In the end, he settled on "Back in a week or two, Ross" scrawled in biro on the torn-off top of an empty cornflakes packet. He folded the card and cleared a space for it to stand upright on the kitchen counter where it might stand a chance of being discovered eventually.

Checklist: clothes, toothbrush, book, headphones, sleeping bag. He would wear his hiking boots back to the bar. Nothing else sprang to mind... oh yeah, Leatherman, torch, warm jacket, insect repellent... nope. He could buy some tomorrow morning, or maybe Kris had some already. That was definitely an essential though. The Highland mozzies could reduce a strong man to tears.

Ross snapped out of his reverie. He was already packed. He was already drunk. He had nothing to lose. He felt the door lift slightly on its hinges as its weary Yale lock engaged behind him. He didn't bother pushing the light switch; the timer was carefully calibrated to switch off just as he reached the lowest landing where there was no other source of illumination. He was used to groping round in the dark, feeling his way along the wooden bannister, and could pretty accurately tell which floor he was on by touch alone; the higher up the building, the fewer hands had rubbed at the varnish, the less bare wood was exposed.

Edging his way towards street level, lower, step by step, he thought of his father who'd rather leave his own home than deal with the situation head-on. And when Ross faced a similar dilemma, didn't he take the path of least resistance as well? Here he was vacating his own place.

Who could he usurp? There must be a chain of sad-acts, each more pathetic than the last, each one just a little lower in the pecking order, some kind of sequence that could be mapped out. Somewhere, somebody must be more pathetic than he was, but Ross was damned if he could believe that. There could be nobody more likely to walk away from confrontation than Ross.

In the darkness he stepped off the bottom level only to find his foot hit the floor instead of space. He'd prematurely hit the lowest level, disrupting his sense of where he was.

Twenty minutes later, Ross was approaching Jinty McGinty's Irish-ish Bar once more. In the dim-light of the lane, he could make out Kris and Laura sharing some confidence or other; their heads were tipped together, Kris's dark spiky hair mingling with Laura's auburn curls.

Laura's two friends seemed neither impressed nor included. They stood with arms folded, shoulders turned inwards, occasionally pulling their heads back and raising an eyebrow in disapproval. As Ross got closer, he could hear the two outcasts opinionating caustically to each other on the morals of coming out for a drink with a friend who ditches them at the first chance of a bit of cock, no matter how miniscule it was bound to be. Their commentary was intentionally loud enough to be audible to Laura, but she stalwartly gave her full attention to Kris.

Ross waited in the shadow another moment to take a breath, and stepped forward nonchalantly. "Kris mate… d'ye need another one?" Ross nodded in the direction of Kris's pint.

"Naw… this one'll do me for now." He put his arm briefly round Laura's shoulder and squeezed. She giggled appreciatively; Ross placed his arm back on the barrel top.

"Unless…," he turned to Laura, "you've got a twin sister or something?" He shrugged, raised his eyebrows, turned his palms upwards and his mouth downwards. Typically, he'd left it open to interpretation as a joke if Laura was offended, or a serious suggestion if it turned out she actually was up for being one slice of bread in a sausage sandwich.

The other girls tutted loudly.

Kris looked back to Ross. "You were gone a while though. What happened? Did you end up taking a dump? Must have been an epic struggle. Is it safe to go in there?"

"Oh, you noticed I was gone, did you?" Ross asked.

Laura's two erstwhile friends smirked in agreement. He'd scored a point there.

"Not really, no." Kris wasn't fazed. "Are you going to get the beers in then?"

He wasn't trying to belittle Ross, no matter how it felt. He was boosting himself in the eyes of Laura. If that meant treating his friends like second class servants, that's what he would do. Ross had known him long enough not to be offended. Kris did this kind of thing subconsciously and there was no real malice in it.

"OK. Keep an eye on that, yeah?" He slipped his backpack off his shoulder and onto the ground at the foot of Kris's stool. "What are you for?"

"Pint of Euro-piss. How about you, my dear?" Kris didn't think anything of extending someone else's round to fund the girl on his own arm.

Laura lowered her fluorescent vodka mixer from her lips and gave a brief shake of her head, mouth too full to speak. Kris appreciatively watched her tighten her cheeks and swallow. Ross turned to the other girls, both narrow mouthed with indignation at being upstaged in Laura's immediate social circle. He put the picture together in his head quickly enough. The two girls, although not unattractive, were a clear league below Laura's class. They would hang around with Laura in the hope of benefiting second-hand from some of her social cachet; Laura would tolerate this pair for whatever gain was available until something better came along, when she'd suddenly forget they had ever existed.

Face facts, Kris and Laura were cut from the same cloth. Gazing into a sickening future, if this pair ever had kids, the little mutants would be more self-centred than a gyroscope. Kris would probably send them to work down mines or up chimneys anyway.

"Aye, but who does he think he's kidding?" The shorter of Laura's erstwhile companions, Mags, had eventually succeeded in climbing onto a bar stool and was leaning precariously forward onto the barrel top to collude with Ross. "I mean, what's all this about?" She pinched both earlobes and waggled them. Kris, deliberately or not, had

50

definitely got on the wrong side of this girl. She was criticizing the spacer holes in each of Kris's ears, two hoops of ecologically harvested wood stretching the lobes, creating large fleshless voids. He liked to feed his in-the-ear headphones through them, claiming this was to ensure they didn't fall out; the reality was he liked the squeamish reaction it provoked. It was another weapon in his arsenal of girl-traps.

Mags continued, "Is that so his mammy can drag him home on bath night, or what? Or is it so she can hang him up to dry afterwards?"

But Kris's body modification didn't end there. In addition to the spacer hoops in the lobes, Kris sported a row of three smaller examples through the top of his left ear. From the right angle, he reminded Ross of one of those old-fashioned rotary telephone dials his dad had shown him. Kris felt free to permanently adapt his appearance safe in the knowledge that it wouldn't really affect his future. Most individuals who were serious about making some kind of career would agonize over the correct choice of interview tie, just on the off-chance that it could swing the balance. But not Krister... he was guaranteed a place in daddy's firm... if he couldn't find something else that held his interest more than a week or two first.

As the glasses emptied, Ross found himself nurturing a bit of a soft spot for Mags. Maybe it was the booze doing his thinking for him, or maybe it was the idea of a cleansing hate-fuck, get Miranda off his mind, or maybe it was that she was articulately voicing suspicions he himself had silently held about Kris. She was definitely an angry young lady though, and getting seriously prettier by the pint.

Kris suddenly looked round, holding everybody's gaze in turn, then slapped his hand on the barrel top. "Hungry. Must eat."

It was either a statement of his condition or a command to the assembled masses. Either way, Ross was suddenly lip-dribblingly aware of the cardamom, garlic, curry, chili, chicken, lamb, oil-drenched dream that was seducing him from the Ashoka restaurant not thirty yards away. A mere thirty yards, but probably thirty pounds away too. Chutney, poppadoms, nan-bread... rice, tandoori, madras...

His stomach, with nothing but drink to digest for the last few hours, was in violent agreement with Kris, "Hungry. Must eat."

Mags shattered the spell. Ross could almost see the jasmine-coloured steam, formerly a coquettish beckoning finger of aroma, dissolve and fall unsavoured to the ground. "No' me." She snapped. "I'm away home." She used the barrel to help herself descend from the stool. Ross realized she was seriously leaving.

A slick chat-up line, the offer of another drink, a request for a phone number... all failed to materialize on his lips as he watched her teeter on vertiginously high-heels and clip-clop across the cobbles and out of sight.

Elaine sighed, thrust her hands in her jacket pockets and half-walked, half-jogged to catch up.

Ten minutes later, equipped with kebabs, extra hot-sauce, added grease, minimal salad, the remaining three wandered south down Byres Road. Speed was limited by the need to navigate drunkenly and concentrate on not losing any of the so-called meat.

"Em... Ross?" Kris questioned. He was deliberately talking with his mouth wide open and full. "Don't you, in fact, live in the other direction?" He widened his eyes at Ross, twitched his eyebrows twice in the direction of Laura.

"Yeah, but you said I could crash tonight so we can get away early tomorrow?"

"Did I? I don't remember that."

They continued their meandering path in silence for a few moments.

"Em... Ross... I can't help noticing you're still with us."

Ross briefly stopped walking to navigate a long and stringy piece of fat, joined together with strips of meat, into his mouth. He had to tilt his head back to achieve this so forward motion was dangerous, if not impossible. "Yeah," he managed, finally. "But, I'll just pass out on the sofa. I can't be arsed heading all the way home and back again tomorrow. I've got my stuff and everything."

"Ah, that's what the bag's for… " Kris seemed to only notice it just now. He deliberately bumped into Laura's shoulder. "OK, but look… don't blame me if the squeals of animal lust coming from my room keep you awake."

Laura raised an eyebrow, but didn't comment.

"Don't worry about it, Kris." Ross sanctioned. "I can cope with the 30 seconds or so. Just as long as you don't spend 15 minutes apologizing afterwards as usual."

Laura choked on a piece of what might once have been lettuce.

"Actually," continued Ross. "The apologizing I can live with… it's the undignified sobbing I can't stand."

It looked like Laura was actually going to snot hot sauce out of her nose. She was genuinely holding herself up on a convenient lamppost, paroxysms of giggles hampering her breathing. Ross soldiered on in a faltering whimper. "'I'm so sorry… that's never happened before. Honestly. Look… it must be because you turn me on so much. It'll clean off, don't worry. I can try again in a minute.'"

Laura was definitely in danger of collapsing now. Kris was faking a laugh, trying to emulate good humour, but his eyes betrayed his real opinion of Ross's impromptu characterization, a comedy act that Ross was in no mood to break-off; it was a catharsis at the end of a bloody awful day, and a morsel of revenge for Kris driving Mags away.

"'Look… please don't tell anyone. Honestly that's never happened before. I promise. Tell you what… I'll go and get my bicycle pump and a pot of yoghurt… if I warm it up, you'll never know the difference.'"

"Eewwww…" squealed Laura. "Gross!" But she was clearly enjoying Kris's discomfort.

"Aye, very good," Kris conceded. "You can crash on the sofa, but no farting in the living room."

This was Kris's vain attempt at the last word. It fell a bit short of Ross's repartee, and they both knew it, but Ross let it go.

# Chapter 7

Saturday morning, mouth congealed with lager and grease, face stuck to the leatherette sofa by potentially corrosive saliva, the worst of Ross's pain was reserved for his back and legs. Surprisingly, his head didn't feel too bad, his system had probably been cushioned by the kebab he was still savouring, but he definitely knew he'd been drinking. He had that washed out feeling; tired but incapable of satisfying sleep.

No, the worst was spending the night compressed to a loose-Z shape by the two seat sofa. Even at Ross's diminutive height, there was no chance to straighten out. He had briefly experimented with sleeping on the floor, but the unpleasant smell and peeling sound every time he moved his sleeping bag hinted that the last attempt at cleaning had been by the original builders, back in the 18th century.

Not much further back in Scottish history, there had indeed been a form of punishment known as "Little Ease". The convicted individual would be confined to a cage ergonomically designed to prevent standing, sitting or lying down. The muscular torment and sleep deprivation would drive most victims to the very edge of insanity, and beyond. Such barbarism had long been outlawed, but the age of budget airlines has seen a tentative resurgence. The worst of it was knowing that it was your own body inflicting the pain… kind of like a hangover but without the compensation of knowing you'd had a good session to deserve it.

By God, Ross deserved punishment for what he'd put away last night, but he seemed to have escaped with a pretty lenient sentence. Conversational details were a bit hazy, but he was crystal clear on a few points:

He and Kris were heading out to the countryside today; the proposed early start was now a distant fantasy.

He and Kris had probably solved some tricky aspect of their joint project on a beer mat that was now slowly disintegrating in the gutter of Ashton Lane, as permanently lost as whatever brain-cells had been martyred to the cause.

He had tried and failed to chat up some girl, and Kris had screwed it up for him again, although he couldn't quite remember how.

Kris had dragged some poor lass back to his lair.

Ross had quite definitely managed to pee on his own face. The last point was underlined by the vague smell of urine he could just detect at the edge of his senses, but they had been drinking Stella Artois at some point, so there might be a less embarrassing explanation for the aroma. It was probably just Belgian lager spillage, only a bit of fizz away from pee at the best of times.

Ross caterpillared himself, still cocooned in his sleeping bag, to a sitting position and pried the living room door open, just in time to see Laura surreptitiously turning the handle of the front door, shoes in hand. She placed her finger to her lips in the universal language of "I may have lost my self-respect, but at least I found my knickers", winked at Ross and disappeared.

Ross turned to face forwards again and felt the release of blood pressure unleash a heartbeat of pain in his head. If he tensed up, he could delay the ache, but not avoid it forever. Perhaps if he tensed and released very slowly, he could tolerate the individual rations of agony, even if they were collectively going to last longer. He rubbed his eyelids shut and let his hand fall back to the rolled up jeans that had been his makeshift pillow last night. Somehow, Ross drifted back into a shallow sleep, propped up by the arm of the sofa.

"Ross... hoy... Fuck-knuckle... hands off cocks and on with socks!"

Ross was well aware that Kris was leaning over and trying to wake him, but he faked sleep a moment or two longer. Not too long though; it was only a matter of time before he got a slap. He waited till Kris was close enough.

"Boo!" he yelled.

"Jesus Christ! I nearly shat myself... Fucksakes!"

"As ye sow, so shall ye reap."

Kris rocked back.

"Talking of sowing and reaping," Ross made a show of looking round. "Where's the Lovely Laura?"

"Oh, she had to leave early this morning. Saturday job." Kris bluffed without hesitation.

"Fair enough. So what did she write?" Ross would store the truth for later use, should the occasion arise.

"Eh?"

"On your tat... did she fill in any speech bubbles?"

Kris twisted his arm to check. "I'm pretty sure she did... but I can't see anything. Can you check my back?"

He didn't wait for a reply but turned and pulled his T-shirt up and over his head, arms still in the sleeves, to reveal his shoulders. Ross stood up, holding his sleeping bag around his chest. On Kris's right shoulder blade was a cropped close-up of a wide-eyed, redhead femme fatale, mouth open in shock; sure enough, Laura had put words in her lip-sticked mouth: "Hung like a gerbil."

Ross suppressed a snigger, "Aye mate. She's given you 9/10 for style but only 6/10 for effort. 'Must try harder.'"

"Class." Kris preened. "Not a bad write-up, post-piss-up." He grabbed the crotch of his boxers and jiggled the contents. "Another satisfied customer. Right. Cup o' tea... shit, shower and shave... packed and we're off. What time is it?"

57

"Not sure… sometime around 12-ish, I reckon." Ross hazarded, squinting at the slices of sunlight scouring his optic nerve through the venetian blinds.

"Magic. If we get a move on we can be in 'Balaichen in time for 'Who told them they could'. It's Russell Brand tonight."

"For what?"

"Remember those reality TV shows that were all the rage? It's like that but…"

Ross interrupted. "Reality shows? You're kidding? That's bollocks. When I'm First Minister, I'm having that kind of shite banned. I thought you hated it?"

"Naw. This is classic. Remember 'X-Factor' and 'Britain's Next Top Waste Of Space' and all that fanny? They took total no-hopers and turned them into so-called celebrities…"

Ross sighed. "Nope. I worked hard to avoid being subjected to all that crap."

"Well, this is like that but backwards. They take current 'celebrities'", Kris managed to pronounce the inverted commas, "and rip them apart. They challenge them to prove they can do what they say they can. Tonight it's 'Who told Russell Brand he was funny?'"

"I can't stand that twat. He's about as funny as a dose of piles, but without the good looks. And he was shagging that Katy Perry."

"Bastard," Kris offered.

"Bastard," Ross confirmed.

They hung their heads for a moment of silent contemplation at the prospect of climbing up on the ex-Mrs Brand.

"I tell you," confessed Kris. "I'd crawl a mile on my belly to eat the sweet-corn out of her shite."

"Yeah, but I'd be fighting you for the peanuts," Ross added.

"Anyhow," continued Kris. "Tonight, my friend, he heads back to the dole queue. Sling your gear in the car… we're spinning the wheels in 20 minutes."

Two hours into the journey and well outside Glasgow, Ross was drifting in and out of sleep. Conversation with Krister had tailed off, and for once, he was driving with a modicum of consideration for other road users. He was usually of the school of thought whereby his driver's licence and the fact that he paid his road tax (or daddy's firm paid it as a "business expense") meant the road was his private playground; scant regard was paid to other cars, buses, pedestrians, animals, even scenery. There was a good chance he was still over the drink-driving limit from the previous night's excesses and didn't want to draw undue attention to himself; the slab of beer on the back seat, minus the two cans he and Laura had consumed as a night-cap, would be enough to merit a breathalyser.

It was no surprise then, that when his phone played its obnoxiously twee little ring-tone, Kris promoted Ross from "loyal minion" to "secretary". It was another of Kris's effortless statements against society that he had stuck rigidly to his antiquated Nokia. It didn't take photos, it played one game (an unbearably miniaturized version of Tetris), it made phone calls and could just about handle brief text messages as long as there were no attachments.

"Check that for us, eh?" He reached for the open ashtray where Kris usually parked his phone.

"It's a text: From R. 'Just give me another couple of days'."

Ross put the phone back in its makeshift cradle. "Must be some bird you couldn't satisfy, eh?"

"Eh, no… Rob. In Economics. I leant him a ton a couple of weeks back. He's late paying." Kris took the phone without looking and twisted in the seat to let it slip into the pocket of his jeans.

"A hundred quid? What, you? Did he have incriminating pictures of you and some farm animal, or something? What was it? A sheep? Did you dress it up? Were you the shagger or the shaggee?"

"I'm a giver, not a taker…" Kris frowned in tight-lipped concentration.

As the landscape unwound from blighted post-industrial to poetic farmland to unkempt nature, Ross let the upper seatbelt support his head and he curled to doze more comfortably. The car radio had mercifully given up on the uber-cool DJs of Radio Clyde and was now gently cycling between the more soothing and plausible local stations. Cheaply recorded adverts for local businesses, almost every one using Tina Turner's "Simply The Best" to define anything from carpets to curry-houses, tiles to toiletries; alternating snippets of parochial news and memorable songs from years past, probably chosen more on the basis of reduced performance fees than on musical merit; best wishes and dedications.

The first punch jolted Ross awake.

Eyes sealed shut, half with sleep, half with fear. Instinctively he grabbed the back of his head with both hands, tucked his face between his elbows.

A second blow found its mark at his right ear. The impact threatened to weld his jaw permanently shut; he felt the force travel across his cheek and sicken his sinuses with pain. Panicked, Ross tried in vain to get up; realization that he was being held down. There were more than one of them.

Two more clattering thumps to his left side; the first at his ribs almost persuaded him to uncover his head. The second on his raised elbow felt like it would jerk his shoulder from the socket.

A sneering voice: "And this one's for Susan."

A mistimed kick as his head rocked back glanced from his cheek and across his nose. Cartilage was snapped free with an audible click; liquid ran freely down Ross's lip. He opened his mouth to scream "I don't know any Susan", the iron taste of blood mixed with salt mucus swirled over his tongue. He choked back the words. Whatever inescapable pressure had been holding him down was released. He squirmed over and curled tighter into a protective ball. Ross tried to open his eyes. There was no sense in what he saw. Details were focused by the acid panic searing his mind; he was minutely aware of the grain of a carpet a few inches from his nose.

Something metallic whipped into the base of his skull. Vision grey and tunnelled, his hearing no more than a muffled fuzz, Ross felt his consciousness slip away. As he let go, Ross couldn't piece it together. His last memories were of Kris, Laura and himself walking. Had someone mugged them? But why the carpet? Had they been taken somewhere?

Straining to stay aware, listening as though underwater, the last thing Ross knew as he slipped into the beckoning darkness was that someone was laughing. Nothing funny… just the maniacal giggling of someone not firmly grounded in sanity.

The cold damp of the surface beneath Ross's head dribbled consciousness back into his fragmented mind. His cheek, swollen and raw, felt like a heavy weight was being pushed into it. Breathing through his abused nose was impossible. Mouth open, Ross choked on the congealed lumps of blood sliding over his throat as he tried to swallow. He gagged and retched. The coughing awakened the rodent that was chewing its way out through his lungs. Ross carefully forced himself to breathe in the top of his chest; the grating of his lower ribs warned that something was badly wrong down there, maybe cracked or dislodged.

More sniggering. Whoever had administered the beating was still there. The idea that maybe they had waited for Ross to wake up turned his bowels to water. The attackers wanted him to feel the rest of whatever punishment they thought he was due; it would be no fun if he was unconscious.

The name Susan welled up from somewhere in Ross's mind. "I don't know her, honest. You've got the wrong guy."

"Don't know who?" It was Kris. He giggled.

"Kris? What the fuck?"

"Are you OK?"

Ross's eyes were still closed. He didn't want to see the damage he could feel.

"Are you OK? Ross?"

Ross counted a few seconds in his mind.

"What the fuck happened? Who were they?" he asked. His words cracked the fresh skin of blood on his lips.

"Who were who? And who's Susan?"

"That's what I want to know." Ross could feel the breeze across his face now; droplets of cool water were soothing his damaged flesh.

"You were muttering something about Susan. Who the hell is she?"

"I don't know. Kris, are you OK? Who were they?"

"Me… I'm fine. A bit shaken, but I'm OK. I think the car is kind of fucked though."

"What?"

"Mum's going to kill me." Kris giggled again, but with less enthusiasm this time.

"What car?"

"The Fiesta."

"I don't… what? I don't get it." The insistent pounding in Ross's head told him that most of his systems were coming back on line again. His heartbeat pulsated through his body; the fresh swellings around the impact zones hummed in time.

"Look, Ross. You need to back me up. Tell her a sheep jumped out in front of us and I had to swerve to miss it."

"Kris. Where did they go?" Ross finally gave in and opened his eyes, or at least tried; his left was already swelling shut, and trying to open his right painfully creased the skin of his forehead. Squinting at the sky, overcast as it was, burned new pain through his visual cortex, to brand and singe the rest of his brain.

Kris leaned across his friend and looked into the half-available right eye. "Mate, I think you're concussed. Should I try and get you to a hospital? Or I'll try and phone someone."

"No… no… I'm OK. Just… what happened?"

Kris hesitated and sighed. He despised admitting fault in anything. "I spun the car. You were asleep so I got bored."

*Here it comes*, thought Ross, *my fault.*

Kris sat back on the mossy embankment, knees up and hands clasped. "I was trying to see if I could left-foot brake around the corner. I think I overdid it."

Ross ignored the stabbing from his ribs and pushed himself over to look at where Kris was pointing. Sure enough, there was a carving of mud through the lush green of the gentle slope. Ross traced it from the corner of the road down the incline to where the little red car sat facing back up the hill. The paintwork was a mottled, faded pink, like it had been washed at too high a temperature, incongruous against the verdant backdrop of the glen.

"You crashed?" Ross twisted painfully to look at Kris. His hair was standing up like he'd just pulled his fingers from an electric power socket, and he sported a thin smear of blood down his cheek, but otherwise, he seemed undamaged.

"We crashed," Kris confirmed. He stressed that both of them were involved.

Ross considered the car again. "It doesn't look too bad. Is it drivable?"

"Em… I don't know. You should see the passenger side. I think we hit a rock or something. It flipped pretty hard, went on its side and ended up back on its wheels again."

Ross looked the car over again. He could see through to where he had been sitting. The door was twisted but open, the window was missing. Such luggage as was still in the car was blended together, the remnants were laid in a swath from the rock Kris had indicated to just short of where the car sat now.

Ross was struggling to stand. Kris jumped to his feet with uncharacteristic speed and offered his hand. Picking their way gingerly through the heather, Ross holding his ribs, they reluctantly approached the Ford. A disembodied voice from the car told them that Oban Carpet Warehouse was "Simply The Best".

"And this one's for Kenneth McAlpine of Balindore, from his wife Amy. Married for 15 years and still very much in love. 15 years Kenneth? Good effort. No time off for good behaviour, eh?"

The melancholy and desolate beauty of the glen was torn asunder by the terrifying warble of Whitney Houston wailing through "I will always love you."

The pair stared speechless at the damaged car.

"Kris?" Ross asked.

"Yeah, mate?"

Ross paused, never taking his eyes off the tortured vehicle, "Either you turn that shite off, or I'm going to finish the job and torch the car."

"Good call."

# Chapter 8

Kris pulled open the driver's side door and yanked the key from the ignition, silencing the radio. The glen was once again a haven of tranquillity, but just as staring at a bright light leaves an imprint on the retina, so did Miss Houston leave an overlay on the silence; the peace was etched by her aftermath. He walked back to Ross's side and turned to join him in slowly assessing the car.

"Susan." Ross said. "Whoever beat us up said it was for Susan."

"Nobody beat us up," Kris reaffirmed. "Although my mum will give it a good go when she finds out."

Ross concentrated through the pain in his skull. It was subsiding from a steady pounding to a less severe but continuous halo of discomfort. "No. One of them said it was for Susan then put the boot in."

"Ross. Are you sure you're not concussed? There's nobody for miles…. Actually," Kris realized, "That means we're really fucked. I'm pretty sure there's no phone reception out here."

"Then who kicked me?"

"I told you. We flipped the car. I guess you got thrown around pretty hard. Thank God you had your belt on."

Ross looked at his feet. He suddenly sniggered, gingerly, mindful of his ribs. "It was the fucking radio," he realized. "'This one's for Susan'. It was a dedication. Awe, for fuck's sake."

Kris looked to Ross. He looked to the ground. He looked to the car, then the heavens, and started to seriously laugh. It was the release of panic and shock that his previous manic giggling had been building up to. Eventually, through his tears, he calmed down enough to speak. "I tell you what then. If it was that Brian Adams 'Everything I Do I Do For You'... again... it's no wonder I crashed. It was probably a subconscious suicide attempt."

Ross desperately tried to not to join in with the howling Kris. His ribs forbid it, but the harder he tried to suppress the laughter, the more difficult it became. The pain almost added to the humour. "So how come we landed so far from the car?" Ross struggled through his sniggers.

"What? No... we didn't. I dragged you out in case it caught fire."

"Do you think it will?"

"Well, it hasn't so far... so I reckon it's not going to now," Kris mused, rubbing his chin.

"How long was I out for?"

"Ach, only a few minutes. Are you sure you're OK?" This was out of character for Kris. It would never normally cross his mind to ask about another person's well-being unless there was something in it for himself. Ross put it down to shock, or the fact that Kris might cop the blame for something he couldn't talk his way out of.

"Yeah. A bit sore, but it's just a flesh wound. It'll grow back." Ross misquoted Monty Python.

Kris approached the car to assess the situation. He opened the boot. It creaked in protest; the distorted body shell was fighting against the hinges. "Awe, bollocks!" Kris was heartfelt in his horror.

"What? What's up?" Ross edged towards him.

"All the fucking beer cans are all over the place. They'll all be fizzed up to fuck."

66

Ross reached in to retrieve a tin. He gently lifted it like a bomb disposal expert with a potentially lethal grenade. With his free hand, he tentatively explored the bump at the back of his head. "That's the first time this stuff has given me a headache without drinking it first," he pondered. "I reckon that's what clattered me." He winced as his fingertips found the cut where a can had broken the flesh. Dried flakes of blood came away with his hand.

Kris had already headed back to where the car had struck the rock. The moss was peeled back, and a collection of parallel scuffs in the stone marked where some part of the car had impacted. He was gathering their belongings, working his way back to Ross. He put the salvaged items in the boot and forced it closed. It took three attempts for the lock to engage.

"At least that'll keep it dry for the moment."

Ross nodded slowly. "So what now?"

Kris already had his mobile phone in hand, but there was resolutely no signal. "Can you try yours?"

"No point," shrugged Ross. "No credit."

Kris gazed around the scenery, ruggedly beautiful but unforgiving and utterly impenetrable to modern telecommunications. "Well..." he considered. "We've got a few options. The phone won't work, so... we can either wait here till someone comes along."

"Yeah... that could be today, tomorrow or next year."

"Yeah... or we can try and get to the top of a hill and see if we can get some signal."

Ross looked around at the nearby peaks. "I don't think that'll make much difference. We're in the absolute arsehole of nowhere... there won't be any towers anywhere near here."

"Hmm..." Kris conceded. "Fair point. OK... we can walk to the nearest house and ask for help, but that could be miles."

"Or..." Ross offered. "We could sit here and get the rest of the beer down our necks? Make a picnic of it?"

"No, look. I'm serious. We can't stay out here all night." He walked along the most damaged side of the car, running his hand over the misshapen body work. The sill was creased and the front wing was folded against the tyre. "What do you reckon? Do you think it'll start?"

"How would I know? The electric was still working. Maybe it'll run, but I wouldn't guarantee it'll go for long."

Kris looked back at Ross and grinned. "Let's give it a go."

"Wait mate. Before you risk blowing yourself up... 'cause I'll be standing right over there when you turn it on," Ross pointed back to the road. "Check there's no fuel leaking out. Pop the bonnet."

"Any idea how to do that?"

"Nope. It's your car."

"True," Kris acknowledged. "But we have chaps to do that sort of thing for us. No sense in chipping a nail when there's proletariat grateful of the work."

"Just have a look," Ross suggested, exasperated that the real Kris was surfacing again.

A few moments and some muffled swearing later, the bonnet sprung open.

"You lift it, I'll look," said Ross. He didn't feel like listening to his ribs protesting again if he tried to move the engine cover, but he neither trusted Kris's ability with machinery, nor did he trust him to give an honest opinion even if he did spot something amiss.

The engine bay was leak free. There was a residual tang of petrol, but it was likely that the float chamber in the carburettor had pissed itself in fright at the impact. There was no liquid visible. Ross couldn't bend over easily so he directed Kris to check the underside and the fuel tank; all clear.

"OK," said Kris. "Good to go. Here's the key."

"No way. It's your car. You start it."

"No... look... you know more about these things than I do." He prodded the key towards Ross's unwilling hand.

"Uh uh. No chance." Ross pushed Kris's hand back. "It's just starting a car. You do that all the time. Even you can manage that."

"Yeah, but how will I know if..."

"Just start the fucking car, Kris." The expression on Ross's face, combined with the aggressive looking swelling brooked no argument.

Kris looked genuinely chastised and turned towards the battered Ford.

"Anyway," Ross mellowed. "With these ribs, I can't get out quick enough if it does go up. You'll have to do it."

Ross turned and walked what he thought might be a safe distance away. He debated taking cover behind the rock just to wind Kris up some more, but it wasn't worth the pain of bending over.

Kris ensured the door would remain as open as possible and slid backwards into the seat, keeping his feet on the turf outside. With the key in the ignition, he leaned forwards into a semi-sprinter crouch, stared at Ross, breathed out slowly, and twisted the key. The little Fiesta jolted forwards, the driver's side door slammed shut on Kris's shins. "Fuckity fucking fucky fuck fuck!"

"Mate..." Ross spoke in measured tones. "Make sure it's out of gear before you try turning it on."

Kris kicked the door hard open, and caught it with his hands as it rebounded closed again. "D'you reckon? Yeah, thanks for that."

The starter whined, the Fiesta hacked and coughed twice, the exhaust belched white smoke.

"Kris... either you just elected a new pope or it seems to be running." Ross yelled over the revving. "Will it move?"

Mud and shredded turf sprayed the wheel arch as the Fiesta slithered forward, accelerating to a geriatric shuffling speed, lurching drunkenly between trapped and traction. An orchestration of screeching and tortured squealing signalled that all was not as it should be... maybe the fan belt was slipping on its spindle... or perhaps the radio was still forcing Whitney Houston on them. Either way, forward motion had been mercifully achieved. Ross frantically waved Kris on with his free hand, holding his chest with the other.

"Don't stop! Keep going! Get it back on the road!"

Thirty minutes and a mere six miles later, Ross had had enough. "Mate! Will you please stop! I'd rather bloody walk!"

Kris had been clutching the steering wheel, knuckles white, since Ross had eased himself back into the passenger seat. The little car seemed to want to make an ever tightening circle like water spinning down a plug hole, and the effort of keeping the Fiesta pointing down the road was setting fire to the muscles of Kris's chest and arms. His teeth were bared and clenched, the sinews of his neck taut as guitar strings.

The ever-present rhythmic thudding of a fold of metal against the tyre treads was a water-torture to the prisoner of Ross's ears. A gear linkage had twisted or come loose refusing to let Kris select anything above second. Progress was laboured, despite the perpetual 5000 rpm whine of the pitiful 1.2 litre engine. If it made it as far as the cottage, without destroying either itself, the already fragile friendship of the two, or at the very least, their sanity, it would be nothing short of a miracle. Already, at the very edge of hearing, becoming audible between the rubber heartbeats of the tyre, was an ominous ticking; the time-bomb of the valve tappets was counting down.

Kris said nothing. He glared round at Ross, head jiggling nervously, his manic grimace fearful in its intensity, and held his gaze just a fraction too long for comfort. He consoled himself that if they came off the road again at least they weren't going fast enough to cause any more significant damage. The first junction in what seemed like a week announced it was only two miles to Glen Fanaidh Balaichen, from there it could only be another mile at the most to the holiday cottage.

Ross's head was pounding. He would hear the death rattles of the Ford in his dreams, he knew it. The dripping of his nose had long since slowed and stopped, but past the blockage of congealed blood, he thought he could detect an artificially sweet scent, perhaps the loss of some essential life-fluid under the bonnet, being slowly roasted on the pain-wracked motor. He wrinkled his nose, almost enjoying the tension of the clot loosening its grip on the flesh. Maybe the exhaust was cracked and seeping luxurious, lingering, monoxide death into the cabin; that would explain why his headache was getting worse, but at least it held the promise of saving him from sitting tight lipped through Kris's inevitable tirade against the road-builders, car-designers, signposts, his parents, Ross's parents, the Tories, Labour, the Lib-Dem also-rans, the EEC, farmers, butchers, bakers, candlestick makers. Yup, death would be a sweet reprieve from what was surely yet to come.

# Chapter 9

That evening, Kris was in surprisingly good form. Sure enough, the rant against the world had bubbled up, washed over Ross like a sudden downpour, and evaporated. It left a peaceful bonhomie between the two like the sweet smell on a summer's day after a long awaited shower has dampened the dust.

They had sat together on mildewed plastic chairs outside the cottage watching the sun sink behind what was left of the Fiesta. It shone weakly across the windscreen, forcing the boys to squint and shield their eyes. As they cracked their first beers, the only sound was the pink-click-pink of the engine gratefully surrendering its heat to the encroaching chill of the highland evening.

"Well, at least we made it." Kris toasted the car. It would be the first of many times he'd offer up that little mantra this evening.

"Yeah, mate." The beer was a little too warm, but welcome nonetheless.

"My mum really is going to slow-cook my testicles for this, though."

Ross ruminated on the damage to the car, took a long swig from his can and eventually swallowed. "Naw, you're in one piece. She'll be happy about that."

"She couldn't give a crap about me. She'll give me brain damage about the car though."

"It's your car… and it was a bit of a basket case to begin with. Now it's just a little nearer to the grave than it already was." It was the closest Ross could get to offering comfort.

"Technically it's her car. She had it for years. Dad got her a little Toyota sports car thing a couple of years ago, but for some reason she still preferred the Fiesta. She always said she wanted it back after I was finished uni."

Kris actually sounded genuinely worried. The crash itself hadn't fazed him too badly, although nursing the handicapped car round the country roads had nearly finished him. It seemed like the one thing he was mortally scared of was Mummy Bonn.

Ross let the silence linger. The tinkle of the engine cooling was slowing; he could see a puddle of gathering liquid under the nose of the car shimmering in the last rays of the sun. "You know what she calls the Toyota?"

Ross raised an eyebrow to Kris's question and said nothing.

"Her Meno-porsche." Another sip of beer. "She reckons it's dad's last attempt to convince her they're both still young at heart."

A gentle pause…

"So you're telling me, the Toyota is a symbol of her dwindling ability to reproduce? I thought it was only guys did that."

"Maybe that's why she liked the Fiesta so much. It doesn't make any statement except 'I don't give a shit'. I think she liked not having to worry about it getting vandalized."

Kris leaned down to place his rapidly emptied can on the ground. The plastic chair distorted alarmingly, but reassumed its shape as he sat upright. "Yeah… like I said. Dad bought the MR2 for her. I don't think she ever really liked it."

Ross paused to consider this. "So if guys get sports cars as penis substitutes… what's the Toyota a substitute for? Her minge?"

Kris barked a short laugh. "I guess so."

"No way. That can't be right." Ross contradicted.

Kris knew his mate and braced himself.

74

"You can only get two people in a Toyota MR2. I'm sure you're mum's had much more than that up her twat."

"Awe, for fucks sakes, man. Is nothing off limits to you?" But there was a sparkle in Kris's eye. It had been missing all day. Ross pushed on. Kris opened a fresh can one-handed.

"To be honest, though, a wrecked, cheap little runabout that dribbles out its front," Ross waved his can at the puddle under the car, "with a perpetual smell of burning rubber, and it hasn't had a decent servicing in years… now that's more of a metaphor for your mum's undercarriage."

Ross's timing was impeccable. Kris sneezed a fountain of beery foam from his nose and spat what was left in his mouth straight at the Fiesta. The bubbles meandered their way down through the mud and grit unveiling traces of the paintwork beneath.

Kris turned, eyes reddened by the half-inhaled lager, unable to speak for laughter. He weakly raised a thumb to Ross and toasted him with the still overflowing can.

"Seriously, though. What are we going to do about this?" Ross held his friend's gaze and tipped his head towards the car.

Kris stretched back in the garden chair, revelling in the last liquid drops of highland sun. He raised his eyes to the sky and breathed deeply, gorging himself on the peat and heather aroma. The faint reek of the Fiesta's engine couldn't diminish his obvious pleasure. "I really love it here, you know that?" It was a bit of a non-sequitur, even for Kris.

He paused, breathed deeply once more and continued. "It takes me back to my childhood. I mean, I know that wasn't so long ago… but I get tired of the city sometimes." Arms outstretched, he stomach-curled himself forward, retracting his legs like an aircraft landing gear. Turning to face Ross, he explained. "I mean, the city is full of pretentious wankers. Present company excepted, of course."

*Present company especially*, thought Ross, *looking at Kris*.

"My folks only moved back to Glasgow for me to start secondary school. I think dad reckoned he couldn't make enough cash out here cooking the books for the farmers and B-and-Bs, what with having a family and responsibilities."

"Uh huh." It was all Kris could think of.

"So… what's the rush? Do you really need to be back in Glasgow any time soon? Term doesn't start till October…"

"I guess not but…"

"But nothing. I mean, your dad has repossessed your flat… you don't have a job… Miranda left you… what have you got to get back for?"

That wasn't fair. Ross had successfully put Miranda far from his mind. The previous night's drinking, the crash, the unity in adversity between him and his travelling companion, it had all helped; but now, he was suddenly back in the pit. The sweet song of the evening blackbird, the sun gently disappearing behind the soft hills, the slight chill that made him hug himself… it all gave an outline to his maudlin mood. This was a place he would have shared with Miranda.

He shivered.

"Let's get inside, mate." Ross managed to say the word "mate" sarcastically enough to satisfy his own needs, but not so much that Kris would notice. It wasn't worth the hassle. "It's getting cold."

The interior of the cottage smelled of damp carpet, empty cupboards and infrequent use. With each breath, the effect diminished as the long discouraged air began to circulate and the two students became accustomed to their surroundings. Brass light switches, repeatedly painted over, and worn linoleum spoke of a long occupation. Details that would have been apparent to any new resident had faded into the background with the years of familiarity and were duly ignored. Not actual neglect, but a benign acceptance that things were as they needed to be, no more, no less.

The short hallway, more of a demarcation between rooms than a useable space sported a row of iron coat hooks above a slice of telephone table, gilt edged and looking permanently ready to topple over. Filling the limited space of the table top were an antiquated rotary dial phone, drab olive, with a matching number index book also sporting a rotary dial, both consigned to desuetude by the age of modern mobile phones.

Overhanging the edge of the little table, a guest book for comments and suggestions, and a neat stack of monogrammed envelopes with matching writing paper; the former was "Facebooked" into obscurity, the latter done for by emails.

Ross turned the first few pages of the guest book; it was mostly family, probably renting the cottage in return for a bottle of wine or as payback of a favour. It was unlikely to ever have been financially viable, remote as it was, with little in the vicinity except scenery and a one-pub village at least a mile away. Nevertheless, Abbey, Kris's mother, had decided to invest in a headed writing set of the kind she'd first found in a hotel in Stockholm. It would be a classy touch, elevating the little cottage to the status of guest house. Clearly, investing in the paper had taken priority over such banalities as updating the decor or fitting double glazing against the harsh highland winter. Convinced she had made an invaluable contribution, Abbey had relaxed her efforts.

Lifting the pad of writing paper to read the monogram at the head of each page, Ross asked over his shoulder, "Mate, what's Slighe D'Ahla?"

Kris's voice came from a little room at the end of the hall. "It's the house name. It's Gaelic. It means 'Crossroads'".

"OK... but I didn't see a crossroad on the way up... not anywhere nearby, anyway." *Mind you*, he added to himself, *I did have my eyes screwed shut in silent prayer.*

"I don't know. Maybe there used to be."

Ross followed the sound of Kris's voice into a living room, pitifully small by modern standards.

"Maybe it's metaphorical," Kris continued without looking. "Maybe it was a cross roads in their life when they bought the place. Who knows? Maybe they liked the TV show... or the film... fuck-it... it could be the Clapton track for all I know."

Ross was about to remind Kris that 'Crossroads' was written by Robert Johnson, but thought better of igniting a futile argument when he knew he'd end up capitulating anyway.

A small portable TV with a ring antenna gazed out from the corner. It occupied half of a 60's style coffee table; the other half bore nothing but cup marks and a square-edged remote control, lines of tape replacing its missing battery cover.

Kris turned to the fireplace and checked for matches, firelighters and coal. Following his instructions, Ross opened each door in turn to "let the place air a little". It would have made sense to do so when they arrived, but a couple of beers had seemed a higher priority.

Each little room released its own version of the building's scent, as though the house was relinquishing whispered stories of a life lived there weeks, months or years ago. One door remained firmly closed.

"Done. There's one locked though." Ross announced as he sank into a narrow, but surprisingly well-sprung settee, upholstered in a roughly textured floral pattern, faded and smoothed by time. He turned to look along the back at the antimacassars, and stretched an arm out to lift the lace corner.

Kris didn't look up from his task of twisting sheets of newspaper into useable kindling. He paused to appreciate a vintage "page 3" girl, evidently photographed on a cold day, before consigning "Becky from Lancaster" to immolation. "Yeah, that'll be dad's office. I've got a key somewhere. I'll get this lit first."

"No rush…" Ross was still idly and rhythmically toying with the ornate edge of the sofa's doily. He mulled over his recent conversations with Kris. Something nagged at the back of his mind, but it eluded his probing. It was like the kid's game "What's the time, Mr. Wolf". When he turned to look, all motion stopped. If he stopped searching, perhaps it would sneak up close enough behind him to be snatched.

The firelighters weren't doing much more than warming the coal, but Kris declared the fire to be lit and went to wash his hands before searching his pockets. The click of the lock tumblers brought Ross to his feet. He joined his friend just as Kris found the wall switch. The sunken dome lights defined bright disks on the polished wooden floorboards and glinted off the chrome supports of the sumptuous, leather office chair. A frosted glass table boasted matching metal legs and a pair of wide-screen monitors. Although the cabling disappeared discretely into a cavity in the desk, there was no sign of anything as crass as a computer; that was tucked away, underslung, out of sight, out of mind.

The room was utterly incongruous with the rest of the cottage. Ross turned back into the hallway and half expected a special effects shimmer as he stepped from one dimension to the alternative reality. He rotated and crept gingerly onto the soothing burgundy rug in the centre of the polished floorboards. It seemed a violation to desecrate this holy sanctum with his feet.

He began to mouth "Wha…", but Kris cut him off.

"Dad still likes to work here, from time to time. It's kind of creepy, but this is an exact replica of his office in Glasgow."

"It's not creepy… it's just weird… it's like a villain's hidden lair in a Bond film." Ross was turning slowly on the spot to admire the geometrically aligned book shelves, every identically bound volume not a hair's breadth from flush.

"Bond villain… yeah, pretty accurate. Personally, I think it's a tax fiddle. If dad can convince the authorities that this place is a genuine office, he can write the whole lot off as an expense."

Kris edged behind the desk, flopped in the leather seat and dumped his feet on the corner of the desk. "But… on the plus side… this…", he lightly pressed a translucent panel in the desk; it soughed down like the kind of hi-fi system that has had more design work done on the way its apertures open than on the way it sounds. "This… is a serious piece of kit… we can have some intense, and I mean orgasmic, game sessions on this baby…"

"Or we could work on the term project…," Ross suggested, without much hope.

"We could…," Kris rubbed his chin. "Or we could play shoot-em-ups till our eyeballs bleed…"

Kris stroked both hands back across the revealed shelf, teasing the peripherals towards his body like an unhurried lover; a keyboard, mouse, DVD drive, headphone socket… all of the genitalia needed for a human to fornicate with technology; an embarrassingly phallic microphone bobbed erect and aimed at the Kris, vibrating slightly on its spring mounting. He soothed himself into the not-quite-black of the chair as the puffed leather sighed in satisfaction. He slid a slim external hard-drive from his pocket onto the table, rested his elbows on the arms of the chair and slowly opened his hands like a conjuror revealing that he has just laid the card you chose before your eyes.

"I built it… over-spec'd it really… it's got a graphics card in there that would make Da Vinci weep… It's my creation! She's my baby! And then the bastard goes and changes the password on me!" Kris was clearly rehashing an old argument. "He thinks he's clued up, but he doesn't know I cloned the OS." He ducked below the desk to plug the drive into a USB port and re-emerged triumphant. "All we do is fire her up in BIOS, change the boot device and we're away…"

Ross stalked behind Kris to admire the gadgetry. The brushed aluminium surrounding of the keyboard was in perfect harmony with the subtly ghost lettered black keyboard. Kris delicately stroked an almost invisible panel on the left monitor and the keyboard twinkled, a sumptuous wave of blue LED coruscated from top left to bottom right, blissfully illuminating each key in turn before ebbing back the way it had arrived leaving each character as a faint electric outline.

The gentle breaking of an ocean wave, its stereo pan across the room in unblemished synchronisation with the swish of the keyboard lighting, told the boys that they were to be granted an audience with a superior being… the computer had awoken.

Ross looked round for the source of the sound, but there was no sign of any speakers. Nor were there any hints that something so capable of utter sonic perfection was hidden anywhere.

Kris tore his loving gaze from the keyboard to Ross. "Looking for the speakers?"

Ross nodded, reluctant to break the spell; the last whispers of the wave were still swirling across his ears. "Where are they? You can't get that kind of sound out of anything hidden."

Kris pointed. "Look at the light fittings. Each one has a ring of micro-speakers. Get them working together the right way and you can put any sound you want anywhere in the room."

"Really?" He squinted into the light and could just make out the perforations of the speakers. "But what about the bass? And the height? I swear I heard the wave drop from above my head and finish down there." He pointed into the corner of the room.

"It's all interference patterns. You can add the small vibrations of the speakers together to make anything possible."

"I've never seen, I mean heard... seen... anything like that before."

"No... probably not... I set it up and programmed it for him." Kris smiled wistfully and fondled the keyboard once more.

"It takes a bit of processing grunt, but this PC has everything I could ever want..."

Kris laid the side of his head on the desk and stretched out his arms. Ross was astonished. Not only was he seeing the results of Kris actually applying his dangerously agile mind to some work, but he was witnessing a phenomenon he had never thought possible... Kris was unabashedly in love with something other than himself. "Dad calls her Cassandra." His speech was hampered by leaning his cheek on the table. "From mythology. She knew everything, but was cursed that nobody would believe her... but I believe Cassandra." He drew out the "ss", savouring the taste of the name on his tongue.

"Nah, she could predict the future... I'm sure. Was it Roman or Greek?"

"How the fuck should I know?" snapped Kris, suddenly standing up. "Greek, Roman, Turkish... some sun-drenched, EU-parasitic, olive-muncher anyway." He stomped to the door and waited for Ross to leave the room before following and locking up; the key disappeared into the pocket of his jeans.

# Chapter 10

"Did you hear?" Kris gave the end of the joint a final twist and sighted along its length, like a novice buyer at a gun festival. "The Referendum... apparently they were telling migrants that if they voted for Scottish Independence to leave the UK, they'd have to leave..."

Ross shook his head. "Bastards... I heard they told the old folk they'd lose their pensions..."

"I know. We had the friggin' chance and blew it. They said if we left the UK, we lose the EU... now we're losing it anyway." Kris shook out the match. He drew deep on the joint and held it between his second and third fingers. It was a curiously feminine way of holding a smoke, made more so by his gesticulations as he emphasized his point. He continued. "So when are us Scots going to get off our arses and do something about it?"

"Mate... you're half Scandiwegian... your dad is from Malmo... that makes your mum a Swede-o-phile..."

"Aye, very good. OK. When are us Scots and Scottish-Viking-Hybrids going to rise up and be a nation again? The result... broke my heart."

"We'd better do it quick before the oil completely runs out. After that, what have we got? Hydro-electric and wind-power? And a couple of dodgy nuclear reactors in the arsehole of nowhere?"

"I know. But what I want to know is how come we're stuck with it? We should get independence."

Ross half-passed the half-smoked joint to Kris, who fully grabbed it, and immediately started to construct another. He laid out five papers for a double-length number... it was an ambitious move, but he was well and truly on a mission now.

"Kris," lick of the paper, "Independence won't do us any good and you know it."

In common with all converts and adoptive nationalists, Kris was adamant. "How come? It's that defeatist attitude that's cost us the vote."

"No... I mean... right now, we get a public holiday on the Queen's birthday. I'm not giving that up."

Kris spat a short laugh of derision. "So, we get Independence Day like the States."

"I'm not having that." Ross was suddenly swept along by Kris's nationalistic fervour. "Independence Day means we were once dependent. We were only held in subjugation 'cause we lost all our jobs and stuff and... and... shit..."

Ross brow twisted in concentration as he sprinkled grass into the crease of his origami magnum opus. "A little half-and-half?" He leant to reach the block of resin and cooked the edge with the lighter.

"No... how about this," he continued. "Every year, during the Hogmanay party, some computer somewhere randomly picks a Scottish citizen, and that year, the whole country celebrates their birthday. The winner gets announced as the bells ring."

Kris snapped his fingers. The retort was surprisingly loud in the tranquillity of the little cottage. "Brilliant! But what if it's a weekend? That'd be a waste of a holiday..."

Ross tried to answer, but Kris beat him to it. "Easy. Keep picking till we get one on a Monday. Long weekend... ya dancer!"

Ross fluidly picked up where his friend left off. "And we could get paper plates printed, bunting, news coverage, street parties... the lot."

Kris athletically leapt aboard the train of thought: "It'd be a symbol for the People's Free Republic of Scotland! Egalitarian! Open! Some wee ned from Maryhill has as much chance as a Morningside lawyer! It's a winner!"

The burst of excited chat was giving Ross a vague headache behind his eyes, like an increase in air pressure or the onset of a summer cold; his head was stuffed with warm cotton wool. Deflated, he paused in tucking in the frayed end of the joint. "Aye, nice idea. But we'll never get there. There's too much vested interest in the money men to stay part of the UK."

"Sad but true, my friend, sad but true. But it's not fair is it... I mean, any time some tin-pot little dictatorship in the Gulf somewhere needs a change, all they do is get a bit shirty, and Uncle Sam comes steaming in, all guns blazing... a few months later..."

"Years" Ross interrupted.

"Or years..." Kris raised and turned his hand, acknowledging the veracity of Ross's point, "... years... later... new tin-pot dictator... regime change... Hollywood gets the film rights..."

"Exxon get the oil rights," Ross finished.

"That's the key to it. The good old boys across the pond there," he waved in what he thought was the direction of the Atlantic; he was only wrong by 90 degrees. "They're only ready to help if there's oil in it for them."

They both gazed, transfixed, into the candle sputtering feeble light around the room. The shadows jumped restlessly around their faces, their docile features given unnatural life by the erratic glow. Ross turned his head sideways to ignite his latest creation in the flame. He inhaled, eyes closed, and breathed a thick pall of smoke out past the joint hanging from his lips. "Fufufufufuck... I am wasted, man."

"Fufufufufuck... we have oil."

"True... but..."

"But nothing..."

"But, those ignorant wankers in 'Murica think Scotland is a trademark. As far as they're concerned we manufacture Whiskey and golf clubs… that's it."

"Then they shall have the error of their ways pointed out to them."

# Chapter 11

"Naw… say Dear Mr. President USA," Kris was trying to sound serious for a moment, but his eyes were streaming from the combined effects of a giggle fit and the thick, sweet fug of purple smoke that filled the compact little kitchen. "That'll sound more foreign." He bowed his head to align yet more rolling papers on the Formica topped table.

"Yeah, yeah… then what? How about 'Please help. We are small country with aggressive neighbour.'"

Kris was watching Ross writing upside down. "Yeah… but write 'neighbour' as with 'bor'… that's more international."

Ross thickened the 'o' and the 'r' to mask the 'u'. "OK… 'Please help us defend our democratic rights. Our oil reserves are being stolen by neighbor country.' That'll bring them running."

"Deffo…." Kris slithered his tongue with amphibian precision under the loose edge of one of the cigarette papers to seal his latest joint, twisted the end and lit up.

Ross vaguely suspected that it was his fault, but he wasn't sure. He had simply wondered whatever happened to democracy. Kris had added that Scotland, for years, had been ruled by a government for which it had never voted. In Iraq, good old Uncle Sam had waded in, probably uninvited, and toppled the dictator. In Afghanistan, somebody was getting a bloody good hiding, although neither of the boys could quite figure out who or why. But Scotland was left to its own devices; dragged out of the EU, lied to, pillaged, broken, denied a democratic voice in an increasingly globalised world...

It had seemed like a hell of a funny idea at the time, but, as usual, Kris was taking the joke too far. He decided they should write to the president and make him aware. Realistically, the letter would remain unsent, but it was giving them both a good giggle imagining what the White House would make of it.

"Shit man... I've got major munchies." Ross dug his fingers into his stomach to emphasize the point. "Is that curry not ready yet? I could eat the rectum out of a rotting rhino."

He slowly got to his feet, a little unsteady, but vaguely aiming for the pot bubbling on the stovetop. He wordlessly plucked the fresh spliff from Kris's fingers and inhaled heavily. He felt his vision tunnel, his hearing muffle. He flopped back into his seat, hot rocks of burning cannabis falling from the end of the joint to the table top.

"Fucks sakes, man! Watch it! You're burning the letter that's going to save Scotland!" Kris exclaimed in mock patriotic fury. He beat his fist to his chest and gazed heroically into a distant, Utopian future. Tiny, sparkling embers were singeing the paper, leaving brown edged holes next to the last hand-written words, "Our identity must remain secret."

Ross's head wobbled as he tried to focus his gaze downwards. He slid the paper unsteadily to the edge of the table and held it up to the light, before slowly and deliberately pushing the burning end of the joint through the sheet. "Mr. President, sir," he drawled in a painful attempt at an American accent. "We believe there is a justifiable certainty, sir, that this manuscript, sir, has evidentially sustained shrapnel and/or small arms fire damage, sir." He grinned inanely at Kris, took another ill-advised deep draw on the spliff, and once again tried to make it as far as the aromatic pot of chicken madras about a hundred miles away on the stove top.

Their conversation had slithered from the giggling excitement of a mild toke to the fluffy-headed incompetence of a major session. Both boys had points they tried to make, epic deal-clinchers that would change the world, but somehow couldn't quite manage to enunciate the razor sharp logic that would be so evident to any right-thinking individual, if only it could just be explained.

Ideas and dialogue ebbed and flowed... waves combining and cancelling, reinforcing and annulling, agreeing and negating, constructive and destructive interference. Layers of conscious and subconscious thought surfaced and submerged, riding the roundabout of the spoken words, occasionally falling off, running alongside, catching up, jumping on for one more spin.

Ross: "If you're so against smoking..."

Kris wearily raised his head to the challenge.

"How come you're such a dope fiend?"

Kris: "'Cause tobacco is pointless... and it puts money in the tax man's pocket." It was another postured stance. He was stronger than the nicotine, stronger than the tobacco companies, stronger than the government. His body was subservient to his will and his will alone.

Ross: "Yeah, at least spliff makes you feel good. And it puts money in the dealer's pocket."

Kris: "Exactly. Keep it in circulation... no tax... no middle man... no... no... em...."

Ross: "No... no... no wanky adverts telling us we're making a discerning choice... or 'cause we're worth it...'". Kris: "Or... that it's got a new recipe" Ross: "Or that it'll help me lose weight..." "Definitely not in your case... you chew through the munchies when you're wasted..." "But that's not a waste either" "Ether... have you ever tried that?" "Tried what?"

"Ether"

"Not intentionally."

"What does it do?" "It's a sleepy thing..."

"That's no fun." *Who wants to sleep? We get stoned, giggle, pass out... it's the natural way of things.*

"I know. I tried speed once… had to get stoned again to stop it." *I'll roll another.*

"Go on… wrap up another."

*If I roll another, this has to be the last.* "Definitely. In till the finish." *I am ready to white-out.*

"Till death do us part."

"Till death do us party."

The conversation waned into disjointed incoherence and further into vacuous silence.

Ross slowly slumped low in his chair, his forehead banged the table reawakening the wound in his nose; a thinly diluted trickle of blood seeped from the corner of his nostril and onto the table as his head rocked gently to the side between his outstretched arms. A greasy sheen of sweat sparkled on his pallid flesh in the dying light of the candle. He vomited kaleidoscopically, without any apparent effort, without even moving his lips; it just emerged without ceremony from his mouth. A mixture of madras sauce and cheap lager slopped heavily from the raised lip of the table to edge of the seat and thence onto the kitchen floor.

Kris watched in silence; his friend's predicament reminded him one of those office toys that drips liquid over a complex architecture of steps; turn it over and the liquid runs home, although probably not in this case. Arrhythmic glutinous splats launched tiny globules of bile and rancid stomach contents onto the frayed hem of Ross's jeans. He was too far gone to notice.

With surprising delicacy of touch, Kris slid the singed and curry-stained letter to the self-proclaimed 'Leader of the Free World' from under Ross's unfeeling hand, across the contaminated table and into the back pocket of his jeans, leaving the unconscious boy to sleep it off where he lay.

The evening was over.

Sorting out the mess was a problem for tomorrow.

90

# Chapter 12

"You have mail."

The chirpy Mid-West singsong grated across what was left of Kurt's mind. Never tolerant of automated niceness at the best of times, the edge of his hangover was honed to a new sharpness on the whetstone of the email notification.

He had tried, God knows he had tried, to permanently silence his laptop but department policy dictated that audible notifications be enabled to ensure prompt response and thereby heighten customer satisfaction. This was the military. The American military, no less! Why in the name of Satan's sphincter would they care about customer satisfaction? Surely the customer was the enemy! Shouldn't satisfaction be the lowest priority?

And yet, here he was; victim of yet another reorganization. Kurt's new department manager (he didn't even have a superior officer any more), trying to effect change for the sake of change, ensuring he had a bullet point for his next performance appraisal.

As close as he was to retirement, Kurt still felt he had a duty to at least find out what he was about to ignore; probably another "User Engagement" survey from the I.T. department. He'd answered the last with one comment, "You can't spell SHIT without I.T." and the petty bastards seemed to have taken it to heart. He was regularly singled out for I.P. traffic content audits, speed of response audits, server utilization audits, audit audits… you name it. When the broad-shouldered, shiny-faced, straight-from-the-wrapper Private Kurt Weissmuller had reported to his first posting, full of bustling and helpful efficiency, he'd been prepared for a "freshman beasting". There was no way he expected to again be the victim of ritual abuse more than twenty years later.

He nudged the mouse to rejuvenate the PC screen. No movement. He pushed the device harder with the heel of his palm and felt it break free of whatever adhesive held it to the desk. At first he suspected one of the juniors was playing yet another side-splitting practical joke on the old guy, but it was just as likely to be a glutinous cocktail of spilled cola, mayonnaise and dandruff; the detritus of too many lunches eaten al-desko and his reluctant approach to personal hygiene.

Inbox (1).

He did at least keep tidy mail folders. On rapid rundown to duration-recognition-smart-sizing (formerly known as 'retirement'), little of importance ever arrived that couldn't be procrastinated until it was auto-delegated to one of his fellow inmates. Unless it was a post notification; they had to be dealt with by the recipient.

"Attention: Sergeant Weissmuller, K."

"Hard copy mail awaiting collection at Postal Receiving."

"Damn," Kurt whispered aloud.

"Please acknowledge receipt of this email."

Yeah, right. Like hell he would. If he collected the post before ACK-ing the email, it would create a little Mobius band of work for someone to unravel. It wasn't following procedure, but Kurt felt he deserved one little victory for the day, trivial though it may be.

Levering his rear out of the chair, he tried to ignore the tortured complaints of the arms springing back to vertical when he released the load that he daily inflicted upon them. It wasn't enough that his wife constantly nagged him about his increasing girth, the office furniture was moaning at him too. The pneumatics of the chair's central support gasped with relief as Kurt gained his feet and headed for Postal Receiving… maybe a little detour via the vending machine to garner his strength was in order.

Twenty minutes, two Hershey-bars and another Coke (Diet… it was a token gesture), Kurt stepped from the elevator on flattened feet.

During the two floor journey, he'd again questioned what was wrong with this picture. Eighteen months previously, a site-wide edict had proclaimed a strategic landmark in the omnipresent quest for efficiency. Personnel would be required to collect post rather than have it delivered, thus saving the salary cost of a dedicated mailperson, freeing budget to invest elsewhere.

The latest missive, not yet implemented, had, of course, reversed this decision when some aspiring thinker remembered that the Pentagon housed upwards of 25000 people. The one staff member remaining who could still do arithmetic pointed out that the productivity loss caused by desks being abandoned for mail collection ran into thousands of person-hours annually.

Salary cost saved by "downsizing" = $35000 p.a.

Severance pay = $250 per year of service = $5000

Cost-saving "performance" bonus for manager = $2000

Estimated cost of lost productivity due to postal collection = $120000 p.a.

Consultancy fee for time-and-motion study to identify cause of shortfall in key performance metrics = $45000

Cost of working group, tiger-team and focus liaison meetings = $28000

Advertising to hire new internal postman = $450

Security processing for new hire = $12000

Human Resources overhead for recruitment and new hire induction = $8000

Net cost to U.S. Taxpayer = $227950.

This kind of thing happens all the time.

"Jessica… light of my life. How is your radiant self today?"

Kurt flirted with Jess, but with no inherent desire; it was just a habit. She had 2 years on him, a residual smell of naphthalene, and a fatuously optimistic and over-liberal approach to cosmetics. Kurt often thought that if she turned her head too quickly, the layers of make-up would slide round her face. He wondered if her lipstick would wobble back to position like the dangling wattle that hung in folds beneath her jaw.

"Uh-huh." Not so much a reply as a recognition of Kurt's presence.

"Tell me, my angel. Why do I need to leave my post to collect my post? Why can't you grace our humble workplace and hand-deliver?"

"Uh-huh."

"I mean… while I'm whispering sweetnesses to you, down here in your boudoir, national security is at stake. At this very moment, the Axis Of Evil is most likely plotting it's subversion of our way of life."

"Sergeant Weissmuller…"

"Please… call me Kurt." He leaned forward, resting his ample bosom on the chest high counter.

Jess recoiled from the reek of last night's beer that Kurt was still sweating out. She pursed lips that were already puckered by a long and happy affair with Marlboro filters and made a show of checking Kurt's ID badge. "Sergeant Weissmuller. You file reports. Your contribution to keeping our borders secure is to stack paper."

"Ah, desire of my desires… but what paper? Perhaps intelligence? Perhaps Ahmed has discovered a way to turn camel turds into plutonium? Maybe our Brothers of the Sands are massing at the Port of Anzali as we speak, raising their towelled heads to howl their banshee war cries, ready to ravish our womenfolk…" He raised an eyebrow, tipped his doughy face to the side. "Ready to burn our…"

"Sergeant." She stopped his oratory. "You work in language and foreign media. You analyse documents and file reports. Period. Here's your mail." She placed an internal mail pouch on the counter rather than hand it to him and leaned back against her desk, arms folded.

Kurt stepped back and clasped his hands to his chest in mock appreciation. "For me? Oh, you shouldn't have." He swept up the bag as a lover might pick a carnation for his buttonhole, and flourished it beneath his strawberry nose. "Ah… such a delicate scent. Does the lady wear Eau de Chanel? Guy Laroche? Or is it a mélange of desire and of silent longing? A bientot, ma Cherie. Auf Wiedersehen, meine Liebling. Saida Habibity."

Kurt backed gracefully from Postal Receiving, gently bowed at the waist, his head lowered, gazing from beneath his eyelashes at Jessica. As he disappeared from view, Jess permitted the hint of a smile to crack her makeup. Despite herself, she couldn't help liking Sergeant Weissmuller… Kurt... She just didn't want him to know that.

Padding the corridors back to his desk, Kurt slipped the pouch into a breast pocket notably unobstructed by medal ribbons. It was an auditable breach to open the pouch anywhere but within a secure area, but Kurt actually relished this particular constraint; it gave him an opportunity to show off that he was still in the loop, still relevant.

Kurt touched his badge to the electronic reader at the main door to his section. The lock buzzed and he fended the door open, barely breaking stride. His timing perfected by years in the same area, same role, often differing job titles, but effectively always doing the self-same thing.

He walked lightly for such a big man, quietly. Fallen arches and a sympathetic chiropodist had excused Kurt from his army issue boots. He used to like to lean back in his chair and prop his feet on the desk. It reminded the young guns of his footwear privileges, as if anybody paid any attention. It was a few years since he'd managed that particular trick.

There were not enough eyes around to see him open the pouch. He'd wait till he had a bigger audience. The ritual show of opening the bag, a loud tut, exasperated sigh, slight shake of the head as if to question the sanity of the world. He would do this whether it was a warning of imminent chemical warfare or a circular for Reader's Digest, but it was only worth it if there was someone to impress. Kurt ached for the responsibility that had so far eluded his career.

Finally, he deemed there to be a sufficient throng deserving of a command performance and he tugged the letter from the pouch. He sighed as he slipped his small glasses onto the bridge of his nose, then pointlessly looked over the top of the lenses. He loudly snapped the case shut with his left hand; a habit that ground the teeth of the girls at the nearby desk, and earned him a higher spot than he would have liked on the hit-list of the psychotic underachieving loner two rows behind his.

"Dear Mr. President USA," he read.

The media assessment form, already open on his PC desktop, he clicked in the first 'Observation' field. "Lack of possessive pronoun," he typed, two fingered. Tab to the 'Conclusion' box.

Conclusion: "Possible Indo-Chinese. Arabic.... Russian," he hazarded. The great thing about being an analyst in such an all pervasive yet vague field was he could add any amount of wild-card guesses he liked and all it would do was improve his chances of a hit. Nobody would read this nonsense anyway. He could bet the house on 'Klingon' for all it mattered.

Tab.

Next 'Observation'.

"Address line: none. Headed paper- Slighe D'Ahla, Fanaidh Balaichen, Alba".

Kurt lavishly entertained the notion that he could still outsmart the might of Google, but his heart wasn't in it today. He selected the 'Lingual Match' option. The 'Conclusion' field was auto-completed as "Latvian".

Kurt returned to his first input and changed the conclusion to be "Probable Baltic-state, or Russian/Polish. Arabic." It didn't hurt his ego one bit, as long as nobody else found out.

The letter was hand-written; unsteady penmanship. The paper could have once been an expensive brand but had clearly been damp for some time. Through the clear plastic envelope, Kurt could see other marks and flecks of something dark brown; perhaps a dried liquid. Four neatly clipped out sections, approximately one square centimetre each, announced that Forensics had already taken their

96

samples. Holding the bag to the light, Kurt could make out a few areas where the fibres were disturbed, probably scraped with a scalpel to release whatever had been adhering to the paper. Light black dust confirmed that the finger-printer had got there before him. Kurt raised the zip-lock edge of the bag to his nose and inhaled deeply. He wouldn't be able to detect the smell of Luminal, especially not with the bag sealed, but it was a fair bet that the blood-splatter guy had already got his turn too.

Kurt rankled that he was always last, lowest in the pecking order, lower even than the chemicals that only offered an opinion in deference to the mindless interaction of their molecules with whatever other molecules they happened to contact. If Kurt's disenchantment had allowed him to think dispassionately, he would have realized there were solid technical reasons why he was last on the distribution list. Lab results took time. Chemical analysis of samples could be performed during the linguistic analysis. Sample contamination was a perennial problem. The less individuals handling a sample before forensics, even bagged and sealed, the better.

No. All Kurt could see was that he was bottom of the heap. He stabbed the keyboard angrily.

Tab.

Observation: "Aggressive neighbor."

Tab.

Kurt left the conclusion blank. He could leave explanations of the blindingly obvious to his manager.

Tab.

Observation: "Oil."

Tab.

Conclusion: "Knowledge of USA. Not likely censored media."

At this point, Kurt really felt like he couldn't care less. A job he had once felt was a valued contribution was reduced to no more than that of a glorified typist. However, the spilling of those three simple characters, 'oil', into Kurt's keyboard was giving birth to almost imperceptibly tiny ripples; ripples which would combine and reinforce until they became waves, waves with the destructive power of a tsunami.

Three characters expanded out to become 24 bits of ASCII.

24 bits of ASCII coalesced and flowed into a reservoir of similar data.

The reservoir would be filtered and distilled until a single pure droplet of resultant action would glisten into being.

Deep in the omniscient software systems of the Pentagon, a significant bit had changed from 0 to 1.

0 to 1.

0 into 1.

0 is 1.

0i1.

Oil.

The leviathan that was the American Military-Commercial Intelligence Division, Sub-sector Mineral Resource, shook itself from its dormancy and lumbered to its feet.

# Chapter 13

Kurt was blissfully ignorant of the machine he had set in motion. He gazed at the missive, protected by plastic, a hair's breadth from his fingers but utterly out of reach. He longed to tug the paper from its protective pouch, to feel the weft and weave of the sheet beneath his sensitive fingers. Somehow, if he could touch what was written, perhaps he could touch the writer? Feel whatever fear was hidden behind their obviously laboured scripting. Were they writing under duress? Was there a knife to their throat? Were they even still alive? Perhaps, having performed their forced transcription, their fetid corpse was already dumped like yesterday's rubbish.

But, he'd tried that once before and had received a humiliating dressing-down for breaching procedure. The fact that his insights had helped track down the author of that particular poison pen-letter hadn't worked one bit in his defence. Added to which, that it had originated from the desk of the husband of the Secretary of State had buried Kurt that little bit deeper.

Apparently the husband in question found himself side lined by his wife's success and late office hours; somehow his tortured logic figured out that he'd steal back his lost spouse by being supportive and strong if she felt threatened. If he had to make that threat himself, so be it.

Kurt had indulged in a little misplaced psychotherapy and voiced his theory to the lady Secretary. She had damn near put him over her knee and paddled his broad-beamed ass.

Kurt lifted the clear plastic bag and tapped the edge to tempt the paper out from under the sticky label. The evidence number, PL-3942-7-10, had previously been obscuring the corner of the note. There was definitely another stain of some description. Following procedure, he should really point it out to those smug, elitist bastards in the forensics clique. In all likelihood, they had already spotted it and analysis was already underway, but, process was process; and lo, it was commanded thus: it is the duty of a "second pair of eyes", on finding any kind of anomaly, to ensure notification of the appropriate head of department.

However, such a notification would doubtless be met with a disdainful response, and Kurt would be made to feel like a dumb little pre-school kid pointing out that the sky was blue. He hit the "SAVE" option, leaned back in his seat and closed his eyes in contemplation.

The subdivision of departments within the Pentagon was yet another misdirected cost-cutting scheme. The only area any money was being saved was in the bank accounts of the consultants brought in to steer the latest fad in management techniques from fevered imagination to reality; and if not reality, then at least to a collection of glittering Power-point slides, replete with dynamic colour schemes, excellent font choice, and utterly bereft of technical content or merit.

Forensics. It wasn't anything Kurt couldn't do himself; he'd watched every episode of "Crime Scene Investigation" at least twice. It was all about drawing conclusions based on the most marginal information. According to his wife, he did exactly that on a daily basis.

Forensic pantywastes! They'd gather at the water fountain, drink their forensic water, and smirk their forensic smirks at each other. If Kurt dared to eavesdrop, never mind show any kind of reaction to their forensic in-jokes, they'd stare tight-lipped at the interloper until he padded away, neck burning under their fucking forensically microscopic gaze.

Truth be told, they actually held Kurt in some kind of professional awe. He was self-driven decision maker; he could make his case without the quantitative pedantry of court-approved evidence. They envied Kurt his freedom… he envied their analytical focus. Neither dared talk to each other, a state of affairs that had gone on far too long to ever change.

# Chapter 14

"You have mail."

If there was a hell, whichever "dubbing artist" had given saw-toothed voice to Kurt's nemesis was undoubtedly roasting on a spit already. Twice in less than an hour. This "job" was beginning to look suspiciously like work. Kurt disengaged himself from the embrace of his chair, leaned forward and placed his hands on the desk before reluctantly opening his eyes.

Inbox(1).

"Subject: Intelligence Appraisal - PL

From: Brigadier General Kirk, A

Required: De-Giovanni, E; Hessellmann, R; Weissmuller, K; Rosso, C; Harding, C; McPherson, S

Optional: Chambers, D; Harris, R.

Location: Meeting Room 2-4-88

When: Thursday, July 11 15:00-16:00

Agenda:

Introduction & Round-table

Actions arising from previous meeting

Assessment of intelligence: PL-3999-7-9, PL-3942-7-10, PL-3950-7-10

Forensics report
Linguistics report
Media report
Technical report
Correlation report
Weighting
Risk assessment
Conclusions
Project planning
AOB

Participants are required to prepare one slide per discipline per assigned intelligence item."

God damn it. Kurt's plan for an afternoon nap in the defunct microfiche room had just evaporated. Still... he hadn't attended the last such briefing so no actions pending. He was only involved in one of the three "squeals", as they called them... and of that, he had only logged a single linguistics report. There wasn't any media or correlation work as far as he knew. A quick internet search would verify that... one Power-point slide... all style, no content... shouldn't take him more than 5 minutes. No panic.

Kurt scanned the list of attendees for allies or eye-candy, but none of the names meant anything to him. He dragged a few text blocks around the Power-Point slide in a desultory fashion, contemplated adding some animations and transitions, but thought better of it; once you start masking a lack of value with that kind of graphic in your presentation, it's time to hang up the mouse... you've nothing left to say.

One thing that was important... add some colours for the management; it helps them think they understand. He randomly selected an insipid pale green for his bullet points... as an afterthought, he pasted his name, rank, department number and date into the bottom right corner. It was all done pretty much on automatic pilot.

Meeting at 1500, he mused. OK. It's 1430 now... one hour meeting... probably run over... say... 2 hours... out of here by 5 pm... best get moving... can't be late... but, Jesus, I've got the sweats... and the shakes... time for another 'black Tylenol'.

Kurt waited in line at the drinks machine to get his medicinal Coke... not unleaded this time. He needed the sugar of "The Real Thing" if he was to stay awake for two hours. The can was already glistening with droplets of water, condensed out of the humid air by the near freezing temperature of the metal. If Kurt had thought logically, he would have realized the moisture was the exhaled breath and distilled perspiration of his co-workers. However, his addled brain was in no state to get anywhere close to such a conclusion, so he ran the can around his forehead and the back of his neck before popping the ring-pull with a well-practiced single-handed action.

Second wing, floor 4, room number 88. The door was already closed, muffled discussion sneaking out. Kurt checked his antiquated Casio diver's watch, the bezel now mounted in a cheap replacement leather strap. He was nowhere near late; if anything he was 5 minutes early. He shuffled from foot to foot in an agony of indecision. Should he knock and disturb a previous meeting which was clearly overrunning? Or confidently tap the door and stride in?

"Weissmuller? Who are you dancing with out there? Get in here!" Problem solved.

A little unnerved at the omniscience of whoever had yelled at him, he eased the door open and slipped into the undersized meeting room. He employed the short-stepped, slightly rolling shuffle of someone trying not to be noticed, childlike, projecting total innocence and a desire to please. Kurt scanned the room, hauled himself upright and fumbled an approximate salute at the oldest man in the room; it was the safest bet.

The gentleman, not unkindly, gave an almost imperceptible shake of his head, and raised his forefinger slightly from its grip on his jacket lapel to indicate a younger man standing in the corner of the room by the whiteboard. Kurt rotated on the spot and snapped his arm back to his side. His waistline prevented his arm achieving the regulation vertical resting position, but it was the best he could do.

Brigadier General Kirk received the salute with a nod. "Please, be seated everyone."

There was a scraping of chairs as the participants took their places, leaving only two options for Kurt. He could sit plum next to the Brigadier, which might look a little too keen, but worse still, ran the risk of the highest ranking officer in the room becoming acutely aware of just how rank Kurt was; Kurt was painfully conscious of the fug of stale alcohol orbiting his far from heavenly body. That left only one seat, immediately to the right of the only woman in the room. Kurt flicked his eyes between the two empty chairs and opted for female company. It wasn't such an easy choice; he didn't want to be seen as the kind of guy who would slither up next to any woman around. It was too sexually aggressive to sit easily on his normally courteous and considerate demeanour.

As Kurt eased himself between the wall and her back, he sucked his ample stomach in to avoid nudging the back of her head, aware that he was one dirty thought from tickling her neck with his genitals. She very deliberately pulled her seat in to the table, and then meaningfully away from Kurt's intended place.

Brigadier General Kirk tapped the table twice to indicate the meeting proper was to begin. His skin seemed at least one size too small for his face, stretched to the point of translucency over this framework of his skull; a suggestion of narrow lips served only to mark where his teeth ended and his flesh began. There was no expression other than a permanent, undirected mild aversion to the world around him. "A quick round table. You begin." He stabbed a cadaverous finger at the elderly gentleman opposite his position.

"De-Giovanni. Correlation and weighting." He glanced round at the other participants, eager to make eye contact. "'Waiting' for the results of your analysis." His eyes sparkled, and he forced a smile as he waited for a response to a joke he'd never tired of trying out, no matter how many times if fell flat.

"Next." Kirk announced. De-Giovanni's smile faded from his eyes first, his mouth surrendered last.

"My name's Captain Sean Hessellmann." Kurt guessed at technical. The way the guy had lined his collection of pens and his notepad up to the grain of the artificial wood of the table was a dead give-away. He was definitely an engineer.

"Risk assessment," Sean continued.

*OK*, thought Kurt. *For sure that has to be Harding, then. He's the techie. Civilian. Excellent at his job; it's the only reason he gets away with an un-ironed shirt and no tie.*

"Harding," said the next man. "Technical. It's up to me to determine technical feasibility of any hypothesis. I specialize in mineral and extraction tech. But, I've been known to dally in aerospace. Actually, a few years ago I was trying to figure out if Sadaam's radar system had the coverage we suspected but when we started…"

"OK." Kirk raised a hand. "If you want to get your CV out there, it's because you're looking for another job. Is that the case?"

"No, sir." Harding stared hard at the agenda projected on the white-board, signalling he'd got the message and was ready for business.

Working anticlockwise (or counter-clockwise in Kurt's American mind), there was one further empty seat before the room's only woman.

"Christina Rosso. Forensics. In particular, fluid and residue analysis. My colleague Doctor Harris sends his apologies; he's giving court evidence. He will join us as soon as practical."

Christina was staring fixedly forwards to a point in empty space during her introduction. Kurt watched her in profile, all the while valiantly, and largely unsuccessfully, trying not to stare at the gap between the buttons of her silk top. A gap through which he could just make out a map of lace giving definition to the contour of her breast… yes, very much a contour. Yes… very much a breast. Six million years of evolution, and a set of XY chromosomes overcame his limited willpower. Kurt found his eyes repeatedly dragged back to that tantalizing chink in her armour, somehow far more enticing and alluring for its forbidden nature than any overt display at a lap-dancing club. She sported an ample paunch; seated, it buttressed the equally ample weight of her chest and caused her blouse to bulge outwards, affording the view into its contents. Christina was as much over her fighting weight as Kurt was, although the excess was not distributed as uniformly.

As a woman in a predominantly male environment, she had at first relished the abundant attention previously denied her at high school, and later through college. While those classmates with trim figures, clear skin and voices like a cat being stretched over a barbecue were fluttering their bovine eyelids at the testosterone-fuelled gym-junkies that seemed to sprout from the very soil of the campus, she had hit the books hard. Under no illusions as to her chances, Christina had been determined to make it on her own terms; study hard, work hard, depend on no man for anything.

Suddenly, her first professional posting had deposited her as a very round peg in a square shouldered hole, and her male colleagues had flocked to romance the only assuredly single female for miles around. Yes, she had enjoyed it, even been flattered at first, but she rapidly came to resent the implication that her self-reliance was of no consequence in the workplace; as "coyote ugly, but got a nice personality", she loathed that the almost exclusively married men in the office didn't seem to care what she looked like or how her brain worked. She was, to them, what should have been an easy lay, just another receptacle.

Somehow, it would have been easier if she'd had a better self-image. At least then, she could have believed that they really wanted her. But, honestly, she knew she was just a target of opportunity. Something to break the physical monotony of a dwindling marriage, something to spur a little guilt trip in the unfaithful partner, maybe unknowingly she'd actually even saved a marriage or two. That was before she decided that she could do without the "nice personality" bit as well. In rejecting one amorous advance after another, her reputation mutated from playing-hard-to-get, to a-bit-feisty, to prude, to ball-buster, to definitely-a-lesbian; finally, she was able to get on with her career.

Kurt was just summing up his assessment of both Christina's physical and psychological make-up when he became suddenly and embarrassingly aware the room was once more waiting for him.

"Sergeant Weissmuller. I do the linguistics and foreign media analysis."

Kirk leaned forward. "Thank you, lady and gentlemen." He raised an eyebrow. Kurt felt it was arched towards him; it meant he fell into neither camp.

"I am Brigadier General Kirk. My task here is as facilitator, mediator and director of analysis into intelligence evidence and releases." The acid taste of the words he'd just uttered was etched into his face. He physically recoiled from what he was saying. A soldier of some 20 years' service, he had climbed the promotion ladder steadily and without ceremony to the rank of captain. The constant reminders that he was now "Captain Kirk", the barely suppressed sniggers, and the Star Trek derived wit scrawled on the restroom walls had spurred him on to greater things; he had doubled his efforts to achieve rapid further advancement away from the hated jokes about Klingons, changing the laws of physics, and Ohura.

"OK. First squeal." He leaned farther forward to tap a button on the remote control without picking the unit up.

"As you can see, the Chinese are opening a new copper mine in Sichuan Province." Kurt winced at the pronunciation. "In itself, this is of no consequence. We are not in the market for selling copper to China, nor are we in competition. However, our head-tail analysis points to an indirect effect on our military presence in the Asia-Pacific region."

He clicked the remote again causing a map to take over the screen with the south east corner highlighted for those unsure of the planet to which he was referring. "Australia currently mines and sells copper at a decent profit, almost exclusively to China. China, therefore, was seen as a threat by Australia who feared, quite rightly, that China might decide to cut their costs and take Australian copper without going to the trouble of paying for it first. Risk?"

Hessellmann turned both hands palms up. "Non-trivial." It looked like he was going to mime a pair of scales hinting that the assessment was subjective at best, but he decided against it.

*He gets paid for that?* Kurt pondered.

"OK," continued the senior officer. "So, how does that affect us?"

He used the remote to flash up the next slide. It was a flow chart. The usual ploy of any presenter trying to justify an utterly implausible conclusion was to use abstract flow charts; the visual context of a logic diagram gave veracity to the flimsiest of thought process. Each time he saw someone pull this stunt, Kurt lost just a little bit more faith in humanity.

"It affects us because Australia currently hosts two US regiments in Darwin. That's the North of Australia, in case you didn't know… i.e. the largest mainland port we can base in, closest to China."

He used the integral laser pointer of the projector remote to highlight Darwin, and tagged Kakadu National Park instead. Kurt thought better of pointing out the difference. "So. Till now, the Australians think China is a threat so they're happy for us to have a toehold in their country to act as a deterrent. As soon as the threat is gone, we're gone. We've burned our bridges and outstayed our welcome in most of the other nations round that area."

The Brigadier-General was getting trigger happy with the laser flashing it liberally around the map. Maybe there was still a bit of the Captain Kirk left in him. "However, the main problem is this. We're not directly interested in China yet, but we're keeping a weather eye on the South China Sea topic, and obviously North Korea. The president is rightly concerned regarding the land reclamation projects which will offer strategic advantage for airborne operations. Even if that problem dies away, we need a large landmass and port from which we can reach Korea." He erringly lasered Japan's Hokkaido Island instead.

Secretly, he felt the Commander In Chief was way out of his depth as far as China was concerned, and would like to have slapped his pinched face from here to Hawaii for throwing this presidential hissy fit, and rattling a fairly blunt sabre, but he had to spout the party line.

In all likelihood, the stance against North Korea was just a bit of impotent posturing, as a reaction to the plain fact that if the USA went up against China, they'd be licking their wounds long after the ensuing congressional hearing had sacrificed a general or two to the media.

"Additionally, Australia has vast reserves of uranium. We need to have dibs on that. If we're already on site, providing much needed protection, we get a bit of a moral claim… at least, we can stop the Ozzies selling it to anybody else with cash."

"Sir," Hessellmann put in. "Surely the Australians limit who can buy their resources, in accordance with the bilateral agreement between our two nations?"

"So far, that's not clear. They have a track record of digging it out of the ground as fast as they can, and shipping it out to the highest bidder. Until now, that has not included uranium… just copper, coal, iron ore… manufacturing materials. However, their government has made a huge political capital out of avoiding the Global Financial Crisis." He turned to Kurt, silently looking for an expected media opinion.

Nothing.

Kirk continued. "They achieved this 'economic miracle' by selling the family jewels to whoever was buying, mostly the Chinese. But, it's only going to last so long. The resources are drying up, the Chinese economic growth has slowed… Down Under is in danger of going down and going under."

Kirk tried to smile, hinting he had made a joke, but his face just wasn't capable. "So. What happens next? They hold an election every few years." He looked to Kurt again, who nodded sagely. It wasn't a nod of agreement, it was the precursor to drifting into a gentle sleep. Kirk took it as confirmation. "Their prime minister, whoever that is this week, wants to win that election, and will only do so on strong economic grounds. The Ozzies vote based on how much their mortgage costs and what they'll pay for a keg of beer. That's the sum of it."

That was the last Kurt was aware of. He slipped into a peaceful doze, vaguely aware of the voices around him discussing a subject he couldn't care less about. One benefit of his multiple chins and the girth of his neck, restrained by a collar size he staunchly claimed still fit him, was that his head remained largely upright despite his lack of consciousness.

He dreamed of guys in Coolie hats digging their way out of a tunnel to emerge, bowing and smiling at his feet.

He dreamed of a place with no water and emaciated children, oblivious to the flies crawling across their parched lips, offering him cupped hands full of diamonds and rubies just to sip at his can of Coke.

He dreamed of lounging, laughing, on a deck-chair, shooing the bothersome children away, a beautiful woman, languorously stroking his hand, whispering his name, over and over. "Sergeant Weissmuller... Weissmuller. Sergeant."

Kurt snorted awake and turned to Ms. Rosso. She arched her eyebrows over her glasses. "And your opinion is?"

Panicked into full wakefulness, Kurt glanced at the images projected on the whiteboard. The Chinese question had been wrapped up. They were onto the Latvian dictatorship, package PL-3942-7-10. Kurt was no stranger to thinking on his feet, metaphorically at least. In fact, he did precious little on his feet if he could at all help it. He hazarded something noncommittal, stalling for thinking time.

"The linguistics traces are, while not conclusive, at least indicative of particular geographical regions." He desperately tried to remember what he'd tagged on the intranet form; he glanced back at the board. Mercifully, Brig-Gen Kirk had opened the automated summary page of Kurt's analysis.

"The general form of the letter was Arabic or Slavic, as evidenced by the lack of possessive pronouns. It was short, and the penmanship was unsteady, indicating it was either written in a hurry, potentially by someone under duress, or by someone not greatly accustomed to writing."

"Leave that to forensics, Sergeant."

"Of course, sir. However, it has a bearing on the interpretation of the content." Kurt was winging it, but sounded plausible to himself. He might get away with it yet.

"The headed paper states 'Slighe D'Ahla'. That's Latvian for 'The Slight of Ahla'. Given the cross-pollination of religions and ethnic backgrounds across that part of the European continent, and the current backlash against governments in the light of the GFC, corona pandemic, the refugee crisis, the Russia-Ukraine problem and the Russian recession, it's possible that this is a radicalized cell, perhaps a breakaway unit from a larger group, feeling disenfranchised by a change in stance or direction of their parent movement."

So far, so good. Kurt had spoken a lot without saying anything that could either be proved or disproved.

"In my opinion, 'The Slight Of Ahla' refers to an act or statement contrary to the Islamic beliefs, either real or perceived. A slight, being a thinly veiled insult, and D'Ahla, is likely an antiquated spelling of D'Allah, that is to say, 'of Allah'. Or potentially an old French colony, so they've assumed elements of French grammar."

"Antiquated?" asked De-Giovanni.

"Yes. Sometimes these extreme breakaway groups hark back to their 'Golden Age', when their laws and traditions were sacrosanct. It's a way of implicitly justifying their stance. Face facts, our Christian fundamentalists do exactly the same thing. They read from the James Bible, i.e. in old English, instead of more modern interpretations. It adds the weight of years to their voice and renders the sentiment incontrovertible. It's like they're saying 'it was true for the last two millennia, so don't argue with it now'."

"And?" De-Giovanni continued. "Even the Republicans are starting to cosy up to the Muslims these days... ferment some kind of backlash against ISIS. Is that what..." He was interrupted.

"Exactly. They're asking for help. If they are a breakaway movement, it may be that they are rebelling against the small minority of more violent upstarts, maybe a younger faction taking control by whatever means necessary."

De-Giovanni nodded. It all sounded pretty plausible. Given that someone was asking for help from the Good Old US of A, he was all for it. His grandfather had fought in WW2, his father in Vietnam, Captain De-Giovanni longed for the chance to stomp up and down, chewing a fat cigar, and cursing a blue streak at any subordinates who were in the wrong place at the wrong time. He'd memorized the best lines from the movie "Platoon" and adapted a few of his own… God, how he longed to give them a try.

"Carry on, Sergeant. The content?" prompted Kirk.

"Yes. As I said, the penmanship is shaky and uneven. They mention oil and a larger, aggressive neighbour. It suggests to me that they are aware of our interests in said oil, and, if they're asking for help, they would be willing to pay for that help."

"In oil," chipped in Harding.

"Well, that's the usual fee, isn't it?" snipped Ms. Rosso, her body tensing.

After college, both the forensics lab and her regular Pentagon trips for meetings like this, anything even vaguely masculine (oil = gas = cars = macho) grated on her nerves. Perhaps it was more that she was weary of scraping body fluids and hair off a range of evidence, every test-tube and petri-dish reminding her of the fragility of human life. And yet, here were these posturing idiots blithely heading towards sending another troop of cannon fodder into a conflict for which there could never be a positive outcome.

Sure, the USA consumed vast amounts of oil, and needed more, but when such a chunk of it was used to fly planes, drive tanks and trucks, run generators to power the air-conditioning units any time the Army felt like flexing its muscles, and therefore justifying its existence, where was the sense in it?

The military research and development budget could probably have solved cold-fusion and given everybody eco-friendly electric transport by now, but where was the fun in that? These macho pricks needed to strut their stuff now and then just to feel like men.

Kirk recognized he had to redirect the lady's ire to a more productive outcome. "Ms. Rosso. Can you provide some forensic information?"

"Case PL-3942-7-10 yielded a sealed envelope containing a handwritten letter." She pointed to a file on the server and asked Kirk to open it; high quality photographs of the letter under different lighting conditions lined up side-by-side on the projector screen.

Christina Rosso stood. The whisper of her stockings as she uncrossed her legs and waddled to screen, thighs rasping, sent delicious shivers across the synapses of the men in the room, even Captain Harding who had been in a fully committed, genuinely loving relationship with a restaurant chef called Peter for the last 5 years felt the breath in his chest grow short. First, he pictured Peter in slithery nylons, then himself rolling them down his muscular legs... then Peter tying his hands behind his back with the stockings, not too tight, but tight enough to make escape impossible... then Pete could help him release some...

"...fluid... And then pressure... Here... and here..." Christina broke Harding's concentration and pointed to two shadows on the second photograph. "These indentations become apparent under oblique lighting. It shows that, at some point, someone has written on something resting on this piece of paper. It was probably one of a larger pad of paper."

"Any idea what it said?" Kirk asked the obvious question.

"Not yet. It is probably a set of acronyms, but nothing we recognize yet. '2 IRN BRU, PKT Ddgrs, S&Vs, CRPWRP'. Some of the characters are conjecture."

"Is the handwriting the same as our letter?" Weissmuller surprised himself by asking a pertinent question.

"Definitely not," Rosso answered. "This is far more assertive, steadier."

Harding interrupted. "Sorry to interrupt." He wasn't. "I've done a bit of aero work. I.R.N. could refer to Inertial Reference Navigation, B.R.U. may be Boresight Reticle Unit. The '2' would suggest dual piloting. They're both avionics terms... more military than civilian...

at least, most civilian fixed and rotary wing aircraft have inertial reference systems. Boresight Reticule Units... that's more military. They're related to head-up helmet mounted displays... the operator can use that to calibrate their point of..."

"Harding. Thank-you." Kirk said firmly. "And the rest? Any clue?"

"Well... " he left his seat, loving every moment in the limelight. "Ms. Rosso said some of the characters are conjecture, I guess because they're not very clear. 'PKT' could be 'RKT', short for rocket. Ddgrs, could be short for dodgers. There are some fly-by-wire systems that are so unstable, they're hard for anti-rocket fire to take out. The SCUD missiles were like that. They were shortened from their original design, but the AFCS (auto-flight control system)," he smiled, unreciprocated, at Rosso again, "was never updated... they became unstable in flight, making them very hard to shoot down. An accidental success. Perhaps Rocket Dodgers is slang for SCUDs?"

The Brigadier looked to Kurt, "Does that make sense from a linguistic standpoint?"

Kurt was engrossed in the play of the projector's light across Christina's semi-see through blouse, especially as she turned bringing further shadows and gossamer detail into play; even the straining hawsers of the bra-straps teased his libido, albeit sparking a certain degree of self-loathing. He suddenly became uncomfortably aware that the focus of the room was on him. "Ah, yes sir. That is a possibility." He hazarded. It was non-specific, non-threatening.

"Harding. Thank-you." Kirk said even more firmly. "Now, briefly, any clue about S&V and CRPWRP?"

"Just a guess, sir. But S&V could be Surveillance and Verification? CRPWRP... Combat Ready Position Weapons Ready Position? It may be a reference to what we would call 'lock-and-load'." He returned to his seat and leant to whisper to Hessellmann. "I do a lot of crosswords," he confided.

"Something else you would like to add, Captain?" Kirk asked, thin reserves of patience already almost exhausted.

"Nothing, sir. Sorry, sir."

"So… what is it?"

"Best guess, sir," offered De-Giovanni, "from a correlation standpoint, at least, is that it's a checklist. Something like a pre-op briefing. It would tie in with the theory that this was written under fire."

Nobody had mentioned anything about 'under-fire', Kurt was certain. However, he wasn't sure enough of his status in this company to challenge it.

"OK." The Brigadier leaned sideways to see the projected image in its entirety. "Something bothers me. Why the headed paper?"

De-Giovanni stepped up again. "Sir, it's possible that if this is a breakaway movement, as we agreed…"

*Agreed*, thought Kurt. *Did we?*

"If so, then perhaps they're trying to show commitment, as much to each other as anything else. Perhaps someone has 'struck the first blow for the new brotherhood' by valiantly getting some printing done?"

A smattering of giggles broke the tension.

"And?" Kirk turned, a little irritated by the levity, once more to Christina, standing forgotten by the projector screen.

"The Luminal photo here," she tapped the board on the third image, "This clearly indicates blood and other body fluids. Doctor Harris will have the type results by tomorrow, DNA if required by next week. However, we're working on the assumption these are human."

"And these other marks?" Kirk used the laser pointer to indicate an area at the bottom of the letter. As he took aim, the laser briefly danced across Christina's bosom. Kurt, who was giving her cleavage something of a forensic examination himself, was shocked to see the laser dot of his aim being tracked so visibly. He looked hurriedly downwards, fearful that anybody else had noticed where he was staring.

"These are burn marks. Several extremely small, and one larger. They're consistent with the slag given off by a phosphor stick. I think we can assume this was written under cover, at night. A lack of electricity or other light source would have necessitated the glow-worm." Kurt recognized the police slang; perhaps Ms. Rosso had seen active service before jumping ship to forensics, or maybe she just watched as much TV as Kurt.

"There are some other latent marks visible under the oblique writing. They look like numbers but could be anything. There's no discernible pattern. We could spend a bit longer checking them through and matching permutations, but the work-package hours for this project are already spent."

She was professional enough to explain only the inferences and definite conclusions, distinguishing between the two. There was no unnecessary explanation of the methodology used to identify the characteristics of the letter. Christina was clearly a veteran of this kind of meeting and did not want to mire the discussion in unnecessary science. If one of the men wanted to know, she could explain, but so no need to prove herself to them, and no reason to offer them more information than she had to.

"And the envelope itself?" Kirk asked. "Anything to report?"

"Forensically, nothing interesting. Finger prints, several sets... but that's normal. The handwriting on the envelope does not match the letter... But, the overlaid pad probably does... although it's a bit steadier, more even. Most likely the individual who wrote the letter did not address the envelope."

Kirk turned, shoulders and head together, to Kurt. "Weissmuller?"

"Sir, there was no stamp, but an office frank. An image of an animal, potentially a heraldic lion on its rear legs. That ties in with Latvia... it's on their crest. There was a motto... hard to read... may be Latin: Libertatem Manuque... that would be 'The Hand Of Freedom'", he ended confidently, but incorrectly. 'Freedom Beckons' would have been more accurate.

The technical, linguistics and correlation reports drew to a close.

The Brigadier-General leaned back in his chair, steepling his fingers beneath the tip of his nose, and touched his thumbs to his sparse lips. He paused, the very picture of a man with immense responsibility weighing heavily on his shoulders, deep in contemplation. In reality, he'd resolved his decision the instant he saw the images of the letter, but preferred to give the impression of someone who dealt only in facts, and not in gut feelings.

"I don't buy it. No way some radical bunch of rag-heads would get their own stationary printed."

"I wasn't being serious, sir." De-Giovanni admitted, quietly.

Kirk ignored him. "And another thing I don't buy is that this 'Slightly Allah' is a breakaway movement."

Kurt felt his neck redden. He'd started this with his lackadaisical word-work. He'd need to distance himself from the conclusions without hanging himself in the process.

"No," Kirk forced. "That's the main group, right there." He flashed the laser pointer at the printed paper heading.

"This," he jerked the red-dot to the last line of the text, "This is somebody who's snatched a chance to send a plea for help, or maybe they don't like what's happening and want to let the world know." America being the world, in Kirk's eyes.

"So... somebody grabbed some paper, scribbled a note, nothing too committal for fear of interception, no identification... and then had the balls to get their office mail system to pay for postage. I like them already."

He pointed both hands, fingers still intertwined, at the board. "Either way, game on, people."

Kurt felt his shoulders relax, the blood flowed out of his cheeks and back into his neck. His ears still burned, but nobody was looking at him; Kirk was centre-stage.

"So," Kirk paused, looking round. "Weighting?"

De-Giovanni licked his dry lips and smiled at Rosso. She looked quickly away and pulled her head back as though recognizing an unpleasant smell.

"As you are aware, any missive including certain keywords has to be given a high priority, in accordance with the dispatch directive PG-H-434."

Harding rolled his eyes; Kurt caught the look and suppressed a grin.

119

"Here we have 'oil', 'Allah', 'defend', 'rights'. We have the trigger words, and we have the 'humanitarian excuse'. If we're asked to defend human rights, we can bypass some of the usual channels and step right in."

Kurt glanced again at the screen. There was no mention of human rights, but the committee were reading into it whatever they felt could justify their individual agendas.

De-Giovanni lifted his watch from the table and clipped it back around his wrist. His position was settled. "The weighting on this one is 90%. Anything above 75% is good enough for immediate response."

"OK", announced Kirk. "Weissmuller. You have the action. I want two operatives chasing this down. We don't need to outsource this one. As stated, anything above 75%... that's fine. So, get Travel to print out two permissions. I want two staff airborne on their way to wherever the hell that is," he pointed at the header of the letter still projected on the white-board, "within 24 hours."

"Sir, yes sir." That tiny, almost cold ember of professional pride deep in his soul had a little air breathed on it; it glowed into trembling life and started to smoulder.

"Now... next squeal. Number...." Kirk consulted the screen of his laptop. "Number PL-3950-7-10. And people..." He looked meaningfully over the top of his glasses. "I want this done and dusted in half an hour. Nothing off-topic."

He clicked again on the combined laser pointer and mouse. A map of Europe, with Greece highlighted, lit the screen: overlarge arrows hinted at the movement of Euros away from the country, and migrants towards its coast. "This, lady and gentlemen... is moving too fast. Gotten outta control. It's gathering steam, and we need to know where the brake lever is. The EU needs a shake down, but we don't want it broken."

Most heads around the table nodded sagely; a couple became suddenly and overwhelmingly interested in the nibs of biro pens and imaginary dirt on fingernails.

The Brigadier-General stared into each face in turn, coming to rest on Sergeant Weissmuller. Kurt seized his opportunity to escape the communal embarrassment. As he took a tentative breath to speak, Kirk raised an eyebrow.

"Sir," he chanced, "If I may be excused. I doubt if I can be of further value at present. With your permission, I will start the travel procedure for the last item immediately. I will have the forms back ready for your signature by the C. O. B. today."

"Very good, Sergeant. Dismissed."

*Damn*, thought Kurt. *I never got to use my presentation. After I spent a whole 3 minutes lovingly crafting it, too.* He smiled to himself as he waddled away down the corridor.

# Chapter 15

"Mate," Ross shouted towards Kris's room. "I'm doing some washing. Do you want me to chuck anything in with it?"

"Lights or colours?"

"Colours… my jeans could walk to the pub on their own. They're fuckin' rank."

The first couple of days in the cottage together had been just the release Ross needed. Drinks, spliff, violent computer games, curry, the occasional bout of fresh air and exercise when it couldn't be avoided. The rot had set in when Ross realized he didn't actually have that much in common with Kris and had started to find his company a bit abrasive in such relentless close-quarters, although not actually unpleasant. Following closely on the heels of that, there had been a fragile overly friendly cooperation. He strove to offer assistance and help Kris whenever he could, perhaps as a subconscious thank-you for the break in the country, but maybe as an unspoken apology for feeling some kind of antipathy towards his friend, even if he had kept it hidden.

"No, mate. I'm good." Kris spoke loudly, knowing the heavy wooden door of his room would deaden most sounds.

Ross stood in his boxer shorts and rummaged through the pockets of his jeans prior to stuffing them into the 70's vintage top-loader washing machine. "A tenner!" he said out loud. "Result." A few coins, a condom, still in its wrapper, mocking him. A piece of paper with the phone number from a girl they'd met in the village pub… never to be used… he could remember nothing about her.

Another tenner! He spread out the crumpled note, mentally already spent. Disappointment. It was the shopping list from last week; he'd lost a round of "Unreal Tournament" to Kris and, as a forfeit, had to do the munchies run to the general-store-cum-Post-Office-cum-DVD-rental-outlet-cum-tourist-information-centre. The two mile walk round-trip wiped out his buzz and meant that by the time he got back, Kris had polished off the last two beers and skinned up at least 3 more spliffs.

He flattened the paper: 2 IRN BRU, PKT Ddgrs, S&Vs, CRPWRP.

Two cans Irn Bru (definitely not diet); that was a given. Whenever Kris got pissed, he demanded to have a couple of cans of something cold and fizzy on standby in case of a hangover. Nothing packed quite so much caffeine and sugar in one hit as "Scotland's Other National Drink". One packet of Jammy Dodgers, as many bags of Salt & Vinegar crisps as he could carry… that was definitely stoner-food… and a couple of rolls of crap wrap. After three days eating nothing but curry and drinking Guinness in the local, they'd chewed through all four rolls of toilet paper they'd brought from Kris's flat.

"Mate… " Kris emerged from the pit of his bedroom into the tiny kitchenette. "How about a little wake-and-bake-shake-the-snake?" He was carrying 6 deeply soiled coffee mugs, the entire supply for the cottage. One of them even sported a greenish beard of mould.

"Huh?"

"A little morning toke and a fuck-flick? I'll fire up Cassandra, you wrap up a number. If I'm the son of my father, chances are, he's got a stash of skin flicks hidden in a vault somewhere as well."

Ross pushed the top of the washing machine closed, turned and leant against it. He was about to protest, but realized it was futile.

The Oedipal question of Kris finding common ground in his father's pornography tastes, given that his father had, at least once upon a time, found Kris's mother highly fuckable, tangled a knot of unsavoury questions in Ross's head. It was far too complex to unravel. From his 'skinning-up-seat' at the table, Ross heard the acoustic signature, the waves crashing, as the PC came on line. He sighed as he licked the open edge of the rolling papers, the joint bridged across his forefingers. The uni assignment was never going to happen.

"Roscoe! C'mere and see this!"

Ross lifted the glowing joint and the ashtray with one hand.

A salacious grin on his face, Kris was hunched over the desk. "The story so far... our comely damsel in distress here, she just called a plumber to sort out the leaky tap in the kitchen. I'm guessing that she's had to turn the water off and has been unable to do any laundry, hence, she's waiting by the door wearing nothing but the slinky little outfit you see here. Honestly, the story line... the angst ridden exposé of the human condition... the acting... I can't believe the Academy overlooked this for the Oscars."

Both boys angled their heads in synchronization with movement on the screen.

"Jesus. She'll catch her death of cold in that. That's not going to keep out the chill."

The pair of them lapsed into silence as they concentrated on the scene. The joint sat smouldering unnoticed in the ashtray.

"Why..." asked Ross, slowly. "Do women look so much better in stockings and suspenders and that than they do naked?"

"I think it's so we can compartmentalize their bodies... you know, divide them up into the subsections that we can cope with separately." Kris paused the playback. He used the mouse to circle the various areas of interest.

"I don't follow, old chap." Ross was Watson to Kris's Sherlock.

"I mean… listen to guys speak about chicks. It's all 'nice butt', 'great legs', 'check out the tits on her'… it's all component parts… not the sum total."

"OK." Ross considered. "And the high heels? I mean, I'm a short-arse, and I still like that."

"That's to give us hope, mate. There's no way she'd be able to outrun even you in 4 inch heels, so you have at least half a chance of catching her."

"True… true."

"Right enough, you'd need to stand on a box when you do catch her… "

"Aye. Funny." Ross was getting a mite tired of the height jokes.

A three-beat knock at the front door broke their intense conversation. Ross reluctantly left his post at the PC screen and edged towards the hallway, eyes still fixed on the screen.

"Oi! Numbnuts! It's on the film."

Cassandra's immaculate sound reproduction had fooled Ross… again.

"Ah… enter stage left… the plumber arrives. And brought only one tool with him, I see."

"Aye… Is that a sink plunger or a monkey wrench in his pocket? Who said you can't get good help these days?"

Both lads recoiled in fear, their heads shot backwards.

"Holy crap! Unleash the beast!"

"What the hell does he feed that on to get it to that size?"

"I think we're about to find out… she's going to get a shock though. All bent over the sink like that, she won't see it coming."

"Fuck! It's seeking her out! It's like a fucking bloodhound!"

Sure enough, the actor's weapon of choice swung heavily from side to side as he advanced on his victim. It seemed to be sniffing the air and homing in on the target zone.

"Definitely! Colour, length, girth… it's only missing the four paws and floppy ears!"

"It's even got a wet, shiny nose!" laughed Ross.

126

A sinister cello sound track would have been more appropriate to the impending carnage than the stereotypical saxophone piece.

"Brace yourself, darling." Ross advised the girl. "It's behind you!" he sang, pantomime style.

"Stay on target! Stay on target!" Kris joined in, his voice rising in pitch with each syllable.

Ross shouted a warning to the human tripod as he grabbed the girl's hips. "Shit, buddy! No way that's going to fit. You'll never get that in there!"

# Chapter 16

"Shit, buddy. No way that's going to fit. You'll never get that in there!"

"If people would stick to the regulation carry-on luggage size, we'd all be able to get our bags in."

Johnson glared round as he struggled with the overhead locker. A few fellow passengers looked sheepishly away and suddenly became fascinated by the in-flight magazine and emergency drill cards.

Overcome by frustration, he rammed his holdall into a narrow gap in the wall of backpacks and duty-free bags. He felt a small nugget of satisfaction when he heard something crack in a definitely-too-large rucksack that was occupying most of the locker space. Johnson's height, coupled with the fact that he invested most of his spare time in the gym back at his unit's base in Maryland, gave him the ability to punch his holdall into place, and the assurance that nobody would dare do anything about it. In fact, if the cramped cabin of the Airbus A340 had offered enough space for a decent backswing, he could probably have punched a hole in the fuselage.

He dropped himself heavily into the narrow seat, his hips already pinched by the arms of the chair. He quite definitely, and without remorse, invaded the personal space of the timid little man in seat B as he rummaged around for the missing end of his seat-belt. Secured, he leaned back and forced his elbows outwards.

Mr. Seat B was going to have a hell of a journey, sandwiched as he was between the muscular Johnson in the aisle seat, and the rotund, mouth-breathing Rafferty blocking the view to the window and beyond. Seven and a half hours to Paris. Seven and a half hours of trying to escape Rafferty's halitosis as he leaned unnecessarily to talk to his colleague Johnson. Johnson's rock-hard physique, his de-facto ownership of the chair arms and, truth be told, a good percentage of the middle seat too, meant the poor guy had nowhere to go.

As Rafferty spoke, wafts of fetid breath invaded Mr. Seat B's nose, and clawed at his lips to gain entry to his mouth. He turned his head and placed his fingers to his nostrils feigning thoughtful contemplation of the book he'd hoped to finish on the flight; a vain attempt to at least reduce the olfactory insult of whatever Rafferty had eaten since he last brushed his teeth... by the smell of it, sometime during the Reagan administration. "Why'd you bring a holdall that size, anyway?" Mr. Seat B flinched at the assault of the aspirated 'h' in 'holdall'.

"Man, the check-in allowance is lousy... and I don't trust them Frenchie ground-crew not to go through my case. Typical cost cutting. We fly economy to save a few bucks... arrive at the other end... totally fucked. Two unproductive days to recover from these kiddie seats they wedge us into... I ask you. Where's the saving?"

"Ha. How true... how true. Hopefully, but I honestly don't hold out much hope...". Seat B glanced around for the sick bag. Every 'h' brought a fresh, to use the term 'fresh' quite wrongly, gag-inducing stench to his throat. He held his breath, his hand now blatantly covering his mouth and nose, and still the chemical weapon that was Rafferty's breath insinuated its way in.

"Some day..." Rafferty continued. "They'll actually have a look at the whole picture, not just the accountable amounts." Seat B felt himself flinch in time with "have" and "whole".

"Yeah, maybe." Johnson tailed off quietly. He didn't particularly want to chat. With any luck, there'd be a halfway decent film on...

something thoughtless and violent to match his mood, dark and short on dialogue to match his personality. He unfolded the airline issue headphones and twisted awkwardly to get them plugged in. None of the in-flight entertainment had begun yet, but he wanted to make a point; headphones are the modern-day equivalent of crossing your arms and scowling... they tend to discourage conversation. Rafferty leaned back and smiled at the irony of his partner's griping.

Ten hours previously they'd been called into Captain Saunders' office as 'volunteers' for an assignment; purely intelligence gathering, of course, but with the prospect of a little recreational violence to keep Johnson happy.

Rafferty was on-board, probably his last foreign assignment before being anchored to a desk, as a minerals, geology and geography expert. He'd gained a working knowledge of the stock-market through a previous posting handling the Greek financial meltdown; nothing approaching Warren Buffet standards, but he was savvy enough to be improving his retirement prospects with a little share trading.

Johnson was also there as a consultant of sorts, bringing his own additional skills to the party. A Latvian mother gave him a grounding in the language, computer hacking was a bonus, but an enthusiastic penchant for unwarranted unpleasantness was his trump card.

Both men had the swarthy dark-skinned look of middle-Europeans. Shadowed eyes, thick dark hair to match, Florida tans; they'd blend in pretty easily.

About half way through the briefing, Rafferty had first to stop himself grinning, and then had to stand on Johnson's foot as a precaution when the big guy started to open his mouth. "So..." Saunders announced, standing up with his hands behind his back. "You pair just need to get over there... get cosy in this Alba place... ask around... get a few photos... come home in one piece... you know the drill. If you can grab some material evidence, so much the better." He walked out from behind his desk. "If you can communicate without raising suspicion, we'd like a daily report... but don't put your necks on the line to do it. No phone... encrypted email is OK. Your cell phones should work over there… tri-band... but only for emergencies, huh?"

Saunders desperately wanted to be a 'people-person', loved and respected by his guys for being scrupulously even-handed and 'one of the boys'. "You're travelling as civilians. IDs are registered, BG Kirk has signed the travel slips. It's all waiting for you downstairs. Good luck, men."

Willis Rafferty cringed at the sentiment but shook the captain's hand. Johnson nearly turned his bones to marmalade with the strength of his grip.

Outside in the corridor, Johnson spun Rafferty round by his shoulder. The force of the move and Rafferty's impressive inertia spun him past Johnson. The big man had to wait for Rafferty to regain his balance.

"What the fuck? You'd better have a good reason for stepping on my new loafers, man?"

"Because…", he grinned lopsidedly, conspiratorial. "Don't you get it? We've just been handed an all expenses vacation… and I didn't want you fucking it up for me."

"What? This ain't no vacation. We got a job to do."

"Listen… I can't stand that fucker Saunders. Give me Captain Freeman any day."

"Yeah, at least you knew where you stood with 'Screamin' Freeman'." Johnson gazed wistfully at the tiled floor.

"Yup…" agreed Rafferty as they strolled unhurriedly down the corridor… "You normally stood about 10 feet away where you wouldn't get spit on… but at least you knew where he was coming from. That brown-nosed suck-up in there… anyone trying to be that 'nicey-nicey' in this place is up to something. I don't trust him."

"Nope… me neither."

"But, tell me, my large-slow-on-the-uptake-friend… What's your handicap?"

"Whaddya mean? Are you calling me a retard or something?" Johnson's stopped dead in his tracks, fists automatically clenched.

The smaller man turned and raised his hands in supplication. "No... no... I mean... Santy Claus in there has just handed us a gift-wrapped golf tour." He gripped Johnson's arm to turn him to walk away from the briefing room. However, Johnson didn't move till Johnson wanted to. Rafferty might as well have tried to take a tree for a stroll. "Come on, buddy. Permit me to enlighten you."

The motion sensitive lights of the corridor winked out behind the pair as they walked on.

"Look. I don't know what they've been smoking upstairs... but this ain't Latvia... it ain't Where-the-fuckistan... and it ain't no break away bunch of towel heads..."

Johnson twisted his permanent scowl of anabolic-steroid-induced anger into a frown of confusion. "So what the fuck are we doin'?"

"We, my friend, are taking a well-deserved break. Alba is Scotland. Home of golf, whisky... and... em.... And more whisky. My Grandpappy Rafferty was from Campbelltown. He was always banging on about how quaint it is there... and how the Scotch invented everything."

"Well, shouldn't we tell someone?"

Rafferty resisted the urge to slap Johnson's forehead. Even if he could reach, it would have been a terminally ill-advised move. "Are you shitting me? First... if we make someone look like a dipshit, we'll be the ones that get dipped in shit. Remember, shit only flows downhill... and we're sure as shit near the bottom." He raised a second finger, chubby as a hotdog, the knuckles obscured by fat. "Second... if someone wants us to investigate this little case, no matter how ill-advised, who are we to question the will of the Pentagon? It's our patriotic duty."

Johnson injected a note of caution. "OK. But, like you said, we're supposed to be gathering intelligence. We gotta deliver something."

"Do you really think they'll even read it? Nah... we spend 2 weeks max... file a couple of false reports... take some tourist snaps of a pile of rocks somewhere.... Then tell them it was a wild goose chase. Nothing to follow up on."

Johnson was starting to catch on. He grinned and straightened from the stoop he adopted to talk to Willis.

"Meanwhile, " he continued, "You and I will be working on our long game and throwing back single malt whiskies like prohibition is coming back."

The big man paused for thought... it was quite a long pause. "But Latvia's nowhere near Scotland. What do we do? Jump ship?"

"Chances are, Troy my boy, they've just signed the travel slips. That means we're supposed to find the flights and fill in the details... back in the good old days, they'd have done that for us, but it's 'cheaper' to get highly paid operatives like us pair of jokers to do it... rather than some cutesy little secretary in a short skirt and pantyhose. "

Willis glanced at his partner to see if anything was sinking in. He sighed and continued slowly in a singsong voice, waiting for Johnson to join in when he knew the words. "So... we pick the flight numbers, AMEX buy the tickets... and..."

The penny dropped. Troy Johnson clapped his shovel hands together. The gunshot report ricocheted up and down the corridor, causing a few heads to cautiously prairie-dog from their offices. "And we try not to spend the whole cash advance in the first bar!"

"Exactly!"

"Let's go to it!" He snapped one of those irritating American-issue salutes. "Our country needs us!"

# Chapter 17

Ross was getting increasingly frustrated. He had no phone credit and no signal anyway. Even if Miranda had been trying to contact him that way, he wouldn't have known it. There was nothing of interest in his emails; just the usual offers… tablets to make his penis bigger because that's what women want, sprays to make it last longer because that's what women want, links to websites full of women 'in your area' who apparently want it whatever it is. He was buggered if he was going to write to her, though. He didn't want to look like a desperate loser, even though he was sure that's exactly what he was. Far better to play it cool and wait to hear from Miranda.

On the plus side, there was nothing from his dad… and nothing from the building supervisor saying the place had been burned down or broken into. In any case, Kris seemed a bit reluctant to let Ross hook up to the internet. It would slow down Cassandra's connection, or it wasn't a flat-rate cost, or they were close to the download limit, whatever.

He logged off his email account and opened the software development environment. The list of files was depressingly short, and each was tagged as 'Last modified by McDade, R'. Having said that, the working folder was pretty well stocked; oddly, almost everything was tagged as 'Created by Bonn, K'. Maybe the lazy bastard was at least making an effort.

So far, he'd managed to debug the initial frequency analysis program. It could now read in stock market data from a text stream, albeit one type of share at a time, and it could map price movement up to a 10 year period as a summation of sine-waves. The idea being that if you could isolate the sine-waves and their rate of propagation, you could see where the share was going to move next. The test cases run over a 5 year period had shown that at least until the GFC kicked off, it wasn't too bad. It could at sort of predict turning points in the share price, if not the magnitude of the change. But then again, occasionally, it got it wildly wrong. And from that point, all subsequent predictions would be skewed off by the inconsistency.

OK, the purpose of the exercise was a university assignment; he (and actually Kris as well, worse luck) would be measured not on the successful predictions of their software, but on the methodology he (Ross, not Kris so much) had used to arrive at the result. Nevertheless, he wanted it to work. He knew it could work. Damn it... it should work.

He opened his headphones, flicked the power-switch and slipped them over his ears. A little classical music often eased his mind through these kinds of problems; nothing too overpowering, no Mussorgsky. Nothing too prancing, no Vivaldi. Maybe a little Handel... Water Music, or perhaps Holz, Venus?

The automated voice twittered "Krister's Laptop" in his ears as the Bluetooth connection was made. The pop-up in the bottom right corner announced "Bluetooth: Audio device connected", hovered for five seconds or so before retracting back into the tool bar. He found the drive assigned to his headphones and flicked through the folders till he found classical. Debussy. "Poetic Impressions". Perfect. Play.

Ross closed his eyes and leaned back in the hard chair of the kitchen. The ebb and flow of the piano seemed to touch his hair and stroke it up the back of his neck. He let his mind float with the music, sometimes drifting down stream, sometimes being caught in little eddies and back-currents, momentarily going nowhere, before the gentlest touch of the musician's fingers would nudge him round to dreamily meander down-river once more. His perception became a lower brain function, guided and nurtured by the tender melodies, written over a hundred years ago, but still as fresh as the imagined brook that cooled Ross's mind and allowed his conscious thoughts to swim free.

The solution beckoned to him, tantalizingly out of reach, but there nonetheless. Strain too hard and he'd miss it... snatch, and it would elude his grasp. The trick was to float on as though nothing mattered, and let the idea drift towards him, borne along by the succulent beauty of Debussy's harmonic vision.

And there it was! It was staring him straight in the face. Timorously, he opened his eyes and stood. Gently, as though balancing a book on top of his head that he couldn't risk dropping, he shuffled through to the office where Kris was installed behind the desk.

"Cassandra". Ross's headphones named the workbench for his solution as they established their Bluetooth link with the powerful PC.

Ross turned and walked, still gingerly, back to the kitchen. Kris hadn't noticed he was there. He had been utterly engrossed, so much the better. Ross needed to write this down before it melted away to a sticky mess like a dropped ice-cream on a hot pavement. The problem, as Kris had eruditely pointed out back in Glasgow, was that people sell shares to buy other shares... or cars... or houses... or drugs... or rubber gimp masks... or anything. Spotting the to-and-fro was the trick.

Ross opened the output folder for various runs of his program, and trimmed each to cover one year, starting January 95, ending December the same year. He loaded each line of results into an Excel table, one column each and looked at the result. Nothing.

He selected the whole worksheet and clicked "transpose" to rotate it through 90 degrees; columns to rows, rows to columns. Still nothing. On a whim, he selected the data again and created a 3D surface graph... along one axis, a pattern, but total chaos along the other. Still nothing.

He needed to reanalyse the data based on costs, not individual quantities or valuations. He needed to see where one chunk of money was being realized and the same amount of money was being spent. Ross saved his current program folder under a different name "FT-FT-Analysis_Quantity" and got to work. Less than an hour later, Debussy still making love to his ears, Ross had a prototype.

The original sine-wave analysis of the share price was now overlaid with a similar analysis of the cash equivalents involved. He could see the rate of change of share price, and the moving quantities that were driving those changes... perhaps he was imagining a pattern forming; it was like he was staring at the sky long enough for a face to appear, and then wondering if his mind had overlaid the idea of human features on the clouds.

He rubbed his eyes, suddenly aware he'd been staring at the screen without blinking for far too long. He needed to sort the parallel graphs into an order that would show him where the movements were... and it would need to be done iteratively throughout a time-run. That would take a great deal of processing power, more than the feeble little laptop. That would take Cassandra... but far more problematic, was prising Kris out of the command seat.

Ross decided to delay facing that particular temper tantrum and concentrate on the immediate theory. He truncated the data to one month, and narrowed the field of comparison to a few large publishing houses. It allowed him to write and test a simple bubble-sort algorithm, but it was painfully slow: he'd need something a bit snappier, even running on the big PC, to deal with the quantities he was facing.

Something was still bothering Ross. Here he was dealing in moving waves, rolling fluctuations, volumes of buy-and-sell... what was being sold? Who was selling? Who bought from who? Who sold to who? What was their sales pitch?

Pitch! That was the key! Literally!

Kris had already programmed Cassandra to dissect sound frequencies into their component parts, and he'd recombined those to allow the musical pitch to be placed where and when he wanted it within the acoustic model of his father's office. So... what was the difference? Shifting frequencies, movement, volumes, waveforms... it was all there in the stock-market data. He could reuse Kris's sound modelling to listen to the music of the FTSE, the DAX, the NYSE... OK, in the aftermath of the GFC, that might sound like a funeral march, or worse, the theme tune to a slasher-horror, but in theory, it was worth a go. If Ross could adapt Kris's program, better still, if he could persuade Kris to show an interest and get involved... maybe instead of splitting the sounds of music and gaming and spatially placing them in the room, maybe they could divide up the sounds of the cash registers and listen to where the pennies dropped.

"Whatcha doin'?" Kris's footsteps had been masked by Ross's headphones.

"It's called work. I didn't think you'd recognize it."

"Hmmm... ", he glanced to the ceiling. "Nope. Can't say I'm familiar."

Ross explained the idea as best he could. Kris listened in attentive silence until almost the end.

"Mate, if I spent a week eating nothing but alphabet soup, I'd shit out more sense than that."

"Yeah, " Ross agreed. "But that's 'cause the colon is the only punctuation you ever got the hang of."

He turned back to the screen, crestfallen that his idea had fallen on deaf ears. For once, Kris offered an olive branch. "OK... look. It might work. But, you'll need to normalize the quantities against the total dollar amount in the market at any one time. I mean, young guys with their first bit of spare cash, fancy a flutter on the stocks... put cash in. Little old ladies, suddenly realize the pension isn't enough to put food on the table... take cash out. The total worth of the market is always going up and down. If you want to look only at movements within the market, you need to factor out the 'cash in-cash out'."

"OK. I get it."

"See? You only need to ask." He preened.

Kris was definitely going to be a project manager one day. He'd done nine tenths of bugger all, come up with one blindingly obvious idea that Ross would have got to anyway, and now he was taking the credit. It was only a matter of time before he started using words like "harmonize", "synergy" and "pro-active".

"Great. So… can we?" Ross looked hopefully at Kris.

"Can we what?"

"Get Cassandra to chew on this for a while."

"Em… right now? I'm kind of in the middle of something. Give me half an hour."

Ross turned back to the laptop and started hacking around with his code to get the normalization function working.

Summer daylight lasts a long time in the north of Scotland. The high latitude drip-feeds the last rays over the horizon well into the evening. Children giggle as their elongated shadows dance like giant puppets at their command, scenery stands out in crisp contrast as the warm light snags and catches on edges and corners, revealing details that normally go unnoticed when the sun is high in the sky. Nevertheless, it was long after darkness had well and truly drained the life out of their surroundings that Ross crossed himself like the good Catholic he had never been and hit the "run" command.

This was their first shot with live data. Kris's father still toyed with stocks and shares, but had gained a respectful caution for over-exuberant speculation. Nevertheless, he had plenty of monitoring programs, and still maintained subscriptions to market updates.

Kris had been extracting historical stock data as a substitute for doing any real work. He had already dumped file after file to the laptop, as much as anything to keep Ross off his back. It was akin to a student beavering away at a text book with a fluorescent marker pen, putting off the actual learning bit by fooling themselves that marking sections for later work was worthwhile. It isn't. Never has been. But it salves a guilty pre-exam conscience.

"OK. Nothing much more we can do now."

"Yup, " Ross agreed. "Just need to wait and see."

140

"Spliff?"

"Spliff."

Next morning, they watched the high speed graphic playback of the results over a cup of tea. A textured surface of parallel lines bucked and shuddered like the blanket on a honeymoon bed. Ross couldn't help noticing the similarity... sure enough, when the money is moving, someone is getting fucked.

"Nice." Kris sipped his tea. "Good colour choice." He praised with all due sarcasm.

"But what does it show us?"

"Well... nothing much really, except that it kind of works... with a couple of glitches..."

"Uh huh... but when do we become multi-squillionaires?"

"Well... the dotted overlay is pretty promising. When it's green, the predicted result is close to the actual result. The closer it gets to red, the further from the mark we're getting."

Kris leaned in to watch the shifting graphs more closely. "Yeah... not bad, I guess. Kind of looks like tartan." He put his mug down on the glass desk top. "What's that there?" He tapped the screen at a broadening oval of pink, rapidly colouring itself to a blood red, pooling, cooling and coagulating like the outflow of an abattoir.

"This was a test run. Remember. We limited it to tech-stocks. That... I'm guessing..." Ross looked at the date line. "Yeah. That's the dot com bubble bursting." He ran his finger to the date edge of the 3-D chart, first quarter 2000. "You know how we normalized the calculations against total dollar amount in this market?"

"Of course. A stroke of genius, I reckon." Kris glanced sideways for a reaction but got none.

"Just next to the date here... that's the total dollars in millions. You can see round about here, the total worth plummets... which means either assets are being taken out in a selling slaughter, or the net value is nose-diving... or both." He ran his finger down the screen. Kris tutted and leaned forward to wipe the finger grease off with the sleeve of his shirt. "To be honest... I don't know what's cause and what's effect. The price dives 'cause everyone is selling, and everyone is selling 'cause the price is in free-fall."

Kris considered this and gestured to the screen again. "OK. So why's the green section getting lighter?"

As the death-throws of the dot com bubble were flowing forwards in time, the green shade indicating accurate predictions of the program was fading to a bilious yellow.

"That's probably a whole load of companies going belly up and falling out of the market. There were a whole load of start-ups back here…" He pointed to a lush and verdant patch, a deep rain-forest green, full of promise and growth potential, but doubtless hiding hitherto undiscovered poisons and predators.

"And by here, " he continued, "they were all dying off." Sure enough, the fertile landscape had given way to parched and stunted crops, a few stalwarts eking out a subsistence living, but no fat left for the harsh winter to come. Ross tracked along the time line as the carnage reds coalesced through blighted yellows to vibrant greens over a period of a few months. "The problem is, though, that once the program starts getting things wrong, it takes a lot longer to recover the accuracy than it took to lose it… that doesn't make any sense…" He glanced at Kris. "I mean, once the data is back on track, it should all add up again…"

Kris folded his arms. "So fake it… cheat…"

"What's the point in…" Ross paused. It wasn't worth the argument. But, maybe outlying data could be filtered out… maybe a subset of the market just didn't behave with the same mechanical logic as everything else. OK, so a little preselection of the test data, narrow the field, then get the code to do a sanity check and dump out any anomalies; it could work. After all, the divergent data wouldn't flow with the rest of the markets, so maybe it did make sense to cut it out to start with; there'd be no overall benefit in taking it into account.

Two hours of effort by Ross, with scant encouragement from Kris, the pre-filter and sanity checks were ready.

"OK. Let's give it a go," suggested Ross. "I'll plug the Euro-zone banking stuff into the laptop. You feed the American and Chinese banks into Cassandra."

"That ought to be even enough. There's fuck all money left in Europe these days. I reckon Cassandra will still be quicker. Bets? Oh, and stop it before the Brexit referendum... it'd probably blow every chip on the motherboard."

"Yeah, good point." Ross giggled. "Put the mortgage funds and the UK banks into Cassandra as well, then you've got a bet. An evening of beers at the 'Hairy Minge'?" Ross was talking about his nickname for the 'Thirsty Midge' pub in the village. He'd mistakenly called it while sat at the bar one evening and had nearly been barred altogether.

A ceremonial countdown from three to one, and the race was on.

# Chapter 18

"You got somewhere to go?" Johnson challenged the utterly defeated little guy wedged between himself and Rafferty.

It had been a reasonable enough request. The aircraft was at its stand, the seat-belt light was out, every other passenger was already on their feet and recovering bags. There had been the usual race to be the first to release the seat-belt, the victor congratulating himself at obviously being the most experienced, well-travelled sardine in this particular airborne tin.

The rules are simple. As soon as the seat-belt lamp extinguishes, as soon as the last photons of its light bounce off your jet-lagged retina, flick the restraint catch open, jump to your feet and stand, neck forced into a right angle by the overhead locker for a further fifteen minutes while the crew get round to opening the door. Bonus points are available for opening the seat-belt as soon as the parking brakes are applied, before the light is extinguished, but penalties are docked against anyone who scans around smugly to see if any other passenger has noticed that you're daring to break the law of the lamp.

Charles De Gaulle airport was clothed in darkness, a few waiting rooms and offices punctuated the bland façade of the Terminal 2 with an emotionless fluorescent light.

"I… I… I'd just like to stretch my legs. It's been a long flight." The painfully polite little man from seat B grinned ingratiatingly. Johnson was reminded of a sad apologetic little puppy; he was no animal lover. Troy watched the little man with an expression of distaste for an aggressively long time before turning away, relishing the chance to tarnish another life with a little unpleasantness.

Frustrated at his own bullied impotence, Monsieur Dervailly in seat B would vent his "I should have said" on his wife, even more cowed and subservient than he was. Their nine year old twin girls would fret over mummy's tears. They, in turn, would be tired, sullen and withdrawn in school. A concerned teacher would request an informal visit from a social worker. Nothing out of the ordinary would be found, but an almost imperceptible crack of suspicion would exist for ever more between Monsieur and Madame Dervailly.

Troy Johnson had done what he did best, and he had not the slightest notion of the damage he'd caused, nor would he care if he did. He'd played his little game, the repercussions and resonance of his rudeness had ruined four innocent lives.

Inside the terminal, Willis searched the departures board for their connection.

"Couldn't we have flown direct, man?" Johnson had joined him, searching for the ongoing flight. He was running his gaze down the list of arrivals so it was a safe bet he wouldn't find their final destination. "Where the hell is Glasgow, anyhow?" He pronounced Glasgow to rhyme with 'anyhow'. It set his companion's teeth on edge.

"West coast Scotland. Overnight there… we'll be on the first tee in St. Andrews by lunchtime. This is going to be awesome." He grabbed the holdall by his feet. "Terminal 1, gate 12. C'mon, buddy."

Johnson shrugged, an impressive move given the architectural dimensions of his shoulders, and followed as Rafferty headed for the transfer bus.

# Chapter 19

"Man, this is the life, huh?" Rafferty grunted as he bent to replace the ball on the tee. The delicate scent of the recently trimmed grass rose to meet him. "Whaddya say, Troy? Ten bucks a hole?" He settled his grip and waggled his hips, just as he'd watched them do on the televised US Masters. Jerking the club skywards, he didn't so much as swing and follow through as bludgeon the ball, tee and all, into submission.

Troy traced an optimistic parabola towards the green, then back tracked to where the ball had slithered to a halt. It was close enough to hear the squeak as it continued to spin on the wet ground. "Tell you what, Willis. Make it a hundred a hole." Johnson smiled, licked his finger and mimed scoring a stroke on an imaginary card; 'one'. "Oh... Florida rules, by the way. That's a dick-out." He continued.

Rafferty was beginning to suspect he was being sharked. It seemed Johnson wasn't the fairway virgin he'd claimed to be when they started talking about betting on the outcome. "No way. This is Scotland... home of golf. We play Royal and Ancient rules here."

Troy plucked a club from his bag and twirled it, majorette-style, through his fingers. "Why do you think these guys wear skirts, man? It's so they can play the dick-out without getting all cold and shrivelled up." He placed a tee and ball together into the ground in one fluid movement, his club tucked behind his back for balance. "And..." he ordered. "You know the rules. If your tee shot doesn't make it past the ladies' tee..." He considered Willis's lay. "And by my reckoning, you're at least 5 yards short." He addressed the ball, raised the club and swung a perfect arc, his spine curving elegantly, momentarily morphing his gorilla physique into something with a more feline suppleness.

"So," he continued, "Zip down, dick-out." He spun the club to point the grip at Rafferty's crotch. He knew his ball had carved the fairway evenly down the middle, and was thirty yards or so from the green. He saw no need to track its flight.

"Fuck, man." Willis unzipped his eye-watering yellow plaid trousers and rummaged around to find his reluctant member. He faked a good-humoured laugh, but was only pretending to be in the holiday spirit. The two regular golfers who had been elbowed off the tee by the Americans tutted loudly as they waited their delayed turn. From the looks of the fat one's swing, they'd be waiting a while.

Johnson silenced them with a glare that dared them to make an official complaint. He turned back to Rafferty. "Anyhow... a little pecker like that, nobody'll see it unless they're close enough to blow it."

"Now, there's an idea. Where d'you reckon we get some action in St. Andrews? I could do with a bit of executive relief. I reckon I'm all tensed up... need a looser swing."

Johnson looked past the club house to the town. Left to right, it occupied only about twenty degrees of the horizon. The sky beyond was darkening with an approaching North Sea storm. Shafts of weak sunlight slid under the glowering clouds picking out a few acres of forlorn summer.

"Shit, buddy. You could try the retirement home. That's about the only place I saw with chicks as we drove through. Some of them might just about be grateful to get one last screw from a stud like you."

Rafferty took aim for his second attempt to persuade the ball towards the green.

Fourteen shots later, the pair were approaching where Johnson's ball had lain undisturbed for the best part of half an hour. His gaze meandered back along their erratic path from the tee. Open wounds in the fairway marked Rafferty's mostly forward progress; the resulting divots lay where they had fallen.

"You know, Willis. I needed this break."

"Uh-huh?" Rafferty was red-faced with a mixture of exertion and frustration, perhaps with a side-order of embarrassment.

"Yeah. My old lady... she's been giving be earache for months now."

"How come? I thought you pair were in hog heaven."

Johnson had already selected his club and was leaning on it, waiting for Rafferty's next assault. It was no longer clear if he was aiming for the ball or the turf. "Yeah, that's what I thought. But remember we up-scaled from the apartment last year? Bought the place by Lake Arbor?"

Willis swung at the ball. The head of the club stopped dead in the ground about four inches short. The vibrations of the impact jangled the length of the club and through his arms. Vision blurred by the tremors, he tried to focus on his partner. "Yeah. We been there. Helped you move your shit, remember?"

"Right... right." Johnson mused.

"And fuck, but you had a lot of shit..."

Johnson ignored this. "Anyhow. We got mortgaged up... it was tight, but we were on top of it... but Cindy wanted a new kitchen. The old one was fine... know what I mean? Then a bathroom... then the drive needed new asphalt... then the Hasslebachs next door... they got a new car... so we can't be doing with the old Impala no more..."

Willis finally connected and sent the ball another few yards closer to the green.

"So, we got a house now... so the bank got security on us... they were hurling money at us... we got another loan... 'Free up the equity' they said."

Rafferty pointlessly slid his club back into the wheeled bag and strode with purpose to his new position. Johnson didn't bother moving. "You know... their loan brochures? You ever see them? They got pictures all over of nice houses, cars, boats, gardens, holidays, even clothing stores, JC Penny, Abercromby.... We sat there in the bank... Cindy sees that brochure... I know I'm sunk."

"Yeah, I hear ya. Mirabelle did the same to me."

"I mean... in the name of God... the K-Mart ain't allowed to have candy near the checkout no more in case kids see it and start screamin'. But the bank, they can put this stuff in front of my wife and they know and I know, and they know I know... she'll throw a tantrum till I cave in... and I can see the bank manager watching, waiting for it... Cindy sticks out her lip, bats her eyes, and he pounces. Throws the form at me... before I know it... he's got me by the balls."

"Damn straight, buddy. It's a fuckin' crime." Rafferty managed to scare his Slazenger 12 marginally further greenwards.

Johnson squared up for his second stroke. "But you know the worst of it?" He made a gentle chip, leaving a simple putt for a birdie. He straightened to quiz Rafferty with his gaze.

"You know the worst of it?" He repeated. "The worst of it is that now we're in debt up to our eyeballs... I gotta work overtime just to keep pace with it, and Cindy is giving me brain damage about never being home for her... spending all my time at the office. She's beginning to think I've got a piece on the side... like I'd have the spare cash for two of them."

Rafferty shrugged. He wanted to relax, not stir up the hornet's nest of Troy's marriage.

"And to add insult to fuckin' injury..." Johnson was gripping his club with both hands. The sinews on his neck stood out till he looked like he would snap its carbon fibre shaft. "We were doing fine in the apartment. The mortgage was winding down. We didn't need a bigger place... but Cinders got into all those friggin' 'life-style' magazines about renovating a period home... selling it on..."

"Don't tell me. She forgot it costs to rebuild a place like that?"

"No, man. She knew fine. But she reckoned I'd be the one wiring it up and fixing the shingles. Like I got time for that on top of the job!" Johnson crouched to read the lay of the green. He squinted up at Rafferty. "So there's me... working my nuts off just to stay ahead of the interest... I get home, she's picked out another new colour for the living room, and I gotta paint that too." He stood. "It's damn good thing we're out here... otherwise the next bit of gardening I'd be doin' would be a hole about six feet deep, by about 6 feet long."

Rafferty stared at the back of Johnson's head while the big man curled over his putter. He seemed to be serious.

"You know..." Troy retrieved his ball from the hole. "Thinking about those loan brochures... you know like cigarette advertising got banned, and then they started putting disease warnings and pictures on the boxes?"

"Yeah. Didn't stop me, though."

"No... well, it wouldn't would it? No... they should do that with the loans. Ban the advertising, put pictures of repossessions and guys working overtime... with a Surgeon General's notice: Warning- Debt causes Death."

Rafferty took a deep breath of the air; its burden of softly scented moisture reminded him that yet another shower of rain was approaching.

He coughed a rib-cracking bark as his lungs shouted for a cigarette. His body suddenly realised it was at least an hour since he'd last lit up. He hacked and retched, all the while working his jaw, till he had a decent sized mouthful of bilious looking phlegm to dollop onto the ground between his feet. As it fell, a glistening string of mucus hung from his lips, an adhesive link from his mouth to the blob of sputum. The cooling spit-wad slowed its descent till Johnson was convinced, even hopeful, that it would recoil, choking Rafferty as it fought its way back down his throat. At the last minute, the membrane parted company and let the oily morsel drop. A remnant connected Rafferty's shirt and chin. He pulled it free, causing a gelatinous web to fan out between his fingers.

Johnson, hardened as he was by witnessing, and even participating in a range of military-related atrocities, struggled not to gag as he stared at Rafferty licking the sticky residue off his hand with barely disguised relish.

"Yeah, you're right." As he spoke, the last dregs of the recovered phlegm strung out between his teeth; it burbled in his throat giving his voice a plummy quality. Johnson looked away as Rafferty continued. "Debt is lethal... but it's totally legal. Used to be a crime, now it's repackaged and sold on as an asset."

"But better in the red than dead." Johnson turned to watch a few grey clouds being chased across the horizon by their bigger, blacker, angrier cousins.

The incessant drumming on the hood of Rafferty's cagoule was driving him to the edge of madness. The micro-fibre nylon wasn't keeping him dry, it was just ensuring that when the pounding rain did nail its way through the fabric, it couldn't get back out again. Needles of water pierced the flesh of his face, driven by a force greater than mere gravity. The sky was hurling every drop of rain that it could muster in an all-out assault that went beyond weather.

How the squall could be so cold and yet still remain liquid was a question forming on his blue lips, but his face, numbed by the astringent buffeting would not cooperate. For the first time in years, the jowls that hung in loose folds around his cheek and jaw felt tight and trim, shrinking and hiding from the percussive barrage of every weapon that east coast Scotland could appropriate from the North Sea. Despite the fact that he and not Johnson had heeded the weather warnings of the cheery little hotel receptionist, he was no better off than his partner.

Troy was running ahead of Willis, his jeans stuck fast to his legs, the muscles outlined in blue denim. The red tourist-tartan jersey flapped around his thighs, stretched and weighted down by its load of frigid water. He had his shoulder dipped into the wind, a quarterback fending off the crushing tackles being dealt out by the tempest.

The clubs clattered in the trolley-bag skittering along behind Rafferty. One danced free and tumbled to the mud. He slithered to a halt to retrieve it.

"Leave it!" Johnson ordered.

Willis was starting to get brain-freeze. How in the name of hell could rain fall upwards? It didn't matter how he turned his head, he was being pummelled from every angle.

Mud-spattered and soaked, the big man crashed through the club house entrance, sliding to a halt on the tiled lobby floor as the doors swung back outwards letting Rafferty slip through. A puddle was already forming around Johnson as he panted and shook his head sideways to drain the water from his ear.

"Sirs," the clubhouse manager stood with his hands clasped below his waist. "If you would mind waiting here for just a moment, just to keep the carpets in there dry, I'll fetch you towels and perhaps a little warming drink?"

Johnson was about to round on the waist coated man. Rafferty stepped in. "That'd be great, buddy. How about two large malts? Something with a bit of fire to warm us up?"

The manager cracked his face into a smile that instantly disappeared leaving no trace it had ever existed. He'd heard this particular whisky-based joke at least a dozen times daily in the last fifteen years, and it hadn't even been funny the first time.

Rafferty turned away from the bar window, leaving mist and mucus where his nose had been pressed. "Shit, this is not stopping."

Johnson merely grunted into his whisky glass.

"Troy. I said it's not stopping."

Rafferty slumped back into his wing-back chair and watched his colleague steaming, both literally and figuratively, on the opposite side of the open fireplace.

"Troy... I said..."

"I heard you," he snapped, without raising his eyes from the flickering logs.

Rafferty stared into the flames for a moment, figuring out how to broach the subject. "So, listen... I was thinking."

"Hah." In one syllable, Johnson made his opinion clear on Rafferty's thoughts.

"I was thinking," he emphasized. "We can't golf in this, there's no action in this crap-hole of a town... no poker, no pussy, the only bars are full of college kids... We're gonna need to make it look like we're not totally wasting our time... what do you say we go and find this Slighe D'Ahla place, grab some snaps, anything... something to show them back home that we been good little boy scouts... huh?"

Troy continued to stare, unblinking, into nowhere, the only motion in his face that of the dancing firelight. He knocked back the last of his malt in one throw, and pulled himself to his feet. "Alright. Let's get it over with." Turning to the bar, he clicked his glass on the countertop and rounded on Rafferty. "But I'll tell you two things for free. First... I'm gonna have a long, hot shower then get me into some dry clothes. Second... if I'm not tasting scotch or pussy, or both, by twenty one hundred hours tonight...." He sighted along his finger directly between Rafferty's eyes, clenched his jaw and pointedly closed his raised hand into a fist. He spun on his heel and marched from the bar, the menace of the uncompleted threat diluted by the flatulent squelching of his sodden shoes.

# Chapter 20

"Fuck you too, pal." Ross yanked the front door shut behind him. The impact of his dramatic exit was diminished by catching the loose harness of his rucksack in the front door, causing it to gently swing open again.

He turned and pulled the errant strap over his free shoulder to square the pack on his back. His last view of Kris was the smug bastard standing there with a pitying grin on his eminently slappable face, slowly shaking his head, pronouncing his superiority over this maladjusted, odious little creature before him.

Ross turned on his heel and marched down the steep slope of the driveway. His feet slid forwards, squeezing his toes against the fronts of his untied boots, his load jogged uncomfortably on his shoulders, but there was no way he was stopping to sort himself out until he was well out of sight and out of earshot. He swore he could hear Kris laughing, actually laughing at him.

That grating sound of his derisive snigger pinballed around his brain, never quite escaping. It ricocheted through his mind, rebounding off the bumpers, each impact triggering painfully memorized images of Kris's smirking face as the injustice score crept higher.

And still the hard steel of what Kris had done, how he had feigned sympathy for Ross's situation, let him cry on his shoulder, all the while laughing behind his back... still that hard steel ball tumbled around, skipping down the wire rails of his brain, ringing bells and buzzers.

It would roll to a slow halt, stuck like the lump in his throat, till it was fired back into play again by some unseen trigger.

From time to time as Ross stomped on, that cold, hardened, steel ball of pain would briefly disappear, dropping into some void on the pinball table of his mind, only to pop out of a different hole, flipping his thoughts back to the here and now. Someone or something was reloading the ball, pulling the plunger, controlling the paddles, tilting the table, keeping the ball in play... Kris was a player, no doubt, but Ross harboured the suspicion that he was doing it to himself.

It wasn't just that Miranda had cheated on him. It wasn't even that she'd fucked his alleged friend... or he had fucked her... or, fuck it... they had fucked each other, willingly and with malice aforethought.

No matter what happened now, she would be forever spoiled...

It would be like biting into a crisp, juicy apple only to find the flesh more yielding than expected, softened by a hidden bruise.

It would be like looking forward to a tasty breakfast only to find some other bugger had dipped his buttery knife in the jam, or even in the Marmite.

It was that Miranda was now physically flawed, soiled and defiled by Kris.

It was that the lips that Ross had kissed had most likely been vacuum-sealed around parts of Kris that Ross didn't want to think about.

It didn't matter that all this had... had... had, Ross struggled to bracket his disgust in a single word... had *happened* after the last time she and Ross had been together, it still left a nasty taste in his mouth that he couldn't spit away.

The timeline: Ross and Miranda, drifting apart, separation, Kris and Miranda, passion, infidelity... the sequence of events didn't matter. Ross felt betrayed.

Was that even what happened? Was there any infidelity? If Miranda has already left him, she hadn't cheated on him. Was he betrayed? Damn right. Kris had betrayed his feelings and his trust. Miranda had betrayed the memory of their time together by dragging someone else, his so-called friend, into bed before the sheets were even cold.

Would it have been better if it had been a stranger? Maybe. It definitely couldn't have been worse.

Was there something he should have done? Did he do something too much? Too little? Did he do something too soon? Too late?

It was the duplicity, though... of both of them. The humiliation that they were having a good laugh at his expense. That Kris had barefaced invited him to the cottage with the sole purpose of ensuring he and Miranda couldn't talk, couldn't compare notes.

*Station Road... looks promising,* thought Ross. Sure enough, a scar through the hillside to the west of the village hinted at a track. Unnaturally symmetrical shapes breaking the landscape were probably railway bridges. The black and white street name bolted into a recess in the stone wall meant he was a few hundred yards and the price of a ticket from being on his way back home, assuming it wasn't his father's home now. The thought of his father gave him an alternative focus for his anger, but at least the old git had never shagged his girl, as far as he knew; Ross almost welcomed seeing what state his old man had left his flat in.

Rounding a sweeping bend in the road, the pitted sandstone of the ticket hall swung into view, its sashed windows invisible behind the plywood covers nailed into place as a temporary measure while the building underwent renovations. From the looks of it that had been some time ago, and the renovations had never got past the planning phase.

Ross's steps slowed as he approached. The station hadn't seen a train in thirty years, and the inn that had taken over the premises hadn't seen a guest in about ten, while the low roofed afterthought of a hotel bar tacked onto the side hadn't seen a drinker in five.

157

The brewery sign above the door had not been illuminated since the electricity had been cut off, and its Perspex had become chalky with the passing seasons. To the left of the door, one of the makeshift pine shutters had been prised free and the window behind it cracked. Ross imagined kids too young to drink in the town's only remaining pub planning a raiding party to hunt for leftovers. They had probably scattered at the sound of the breaking glass, momentarily scared witless at perpetrating an actual crime in this sleepy little backwater town.

Ross could see them meeting at a predetermined rendezvous, giggling nervously and telling each other tales about what they'd seen or heard, who had broken the window, rehearsing alibis, lying about what they would have done if a grown-up had caught them. Ross could see all this in his mind's eye because he'd seen it all before.

The run-down pub with its faded event posters and the tarnished ambitions of its proprietor.

The gangs of bored kids with nothing better to do till the bar that had served their parents would take its toll on them too.

The heart of the community ceasing to beat.

His steps slowed and finally halted.

# Chapter 21

"So you decided to come back then, eh?" Kris heard the front door open, but didn't bother to leave his post at Cassandra's helm. He had tiled a selection of windows, date-synchronized, each displaying the high-speed playback of various test runs of their algorithms. It was a petulant attempt to carry on as normal despite the fact he was now on his own.

He knew he was technically in the wrong, but he was buggered if he was going to admit that to Ross. He hadn't forced himself on Miranda, just made it difficult for her to refuse. She had become ever-so willing eventually. She wasn't Ross's property. She was a grown woman, certain parts of her impressively grown, in fact. She made her own decisions. She decided on Kris. Kris and Ross were mates. If Ross couldn't see past his loss to the value of their friendship, then he was just being childish, and Kris could do without that in his life.

There was no answer from the hallway, just a muted shuffling; the sound of someone trying to be quiet but managing to make a more intrusive noise in the process.

Kris felt the need to assert his position over the aggrieved Ross. He stood and pulled himself upright to an authoritative stance. He marched to the hallway, tipped his head back and closed his eyes in the infuriatingly condescending pose he always assumed when talking down to someone. "So? What's your problem now?"

No reaction from Ross.

He cracked his eyelids open a fraction to peer down at his erstwhile friend and saw nothing but the lower half of a charcoal grey suit; as his eyes flashed open, he realized the suit was filling the narrow hallway from wall to wall. The last of the evening sunlight which should have illuminated the room from the open door was almost totally obscured, a corona blurred the edges of the giant figure blocking the only exit from the tiny cottage. Kris's mouth gaped wide to cry out but no sound came to his aid. His eyes peeled wide in alarm took in the scene in one hideous glimpse of comprehension. The last thing he saw was a fist like a Christmas ham swinging towards his jaw.

His brain, lapsing into unconsciousness would not remember the details; not the grey suit, not the gargantuan man compressed into that suit, not the impact. When he eventually woke, memory loss would be at the bottom of his list of concerns.


"Hey, mate". Ross waved at an elderly man struggling to walk a reluctant dog on the opposite side of the street. The man stopped, but only because his dog was pulling back on the lead.

"Excuse me, mate." Ross continued. He smiled to show he wasn't a threat.

"Is there a bus stop anywhere near here?"

"Eh... oh... em..." The man seemed lost in thought, concentrating on his dog's stoic effort to urinate on every upright surface in reach.

"Eh. Yes. Em... it's... no... wait... it's more like..." He faced each point of the compass in turn.

"Go back down that way... to the main street... turn left... when you get past the little shop, it's about a hundred yards."

"Great. Thanks," lied Ross. It was exactly the way he'd just come from.

They both watched in quiet contemplation as the little terrier eloquently defecated on the pavement. The dog tried to waddle forwards either to escape from the malodorous pile, or to ensure it was evenly laid across the path, optimising the chance of adhering to the maximum possible number of unwary shoes.

Ross silently challenged the man to clear up after his dog, but he merely shuffled off, shoulders bent, head down.

Ross continued to stare at the cooling mess before hefting his rucksack once more and turning to look for the bus stop.

# Chapter 22

Floating upwards through the thick syrup of his oblivion, Kris's awareness was returning. It could have been minute by minute, maybe hour by hour, but a vague perception of his surroundings was definitely approaching; there was a voice at the edge of his senses. He wasn't sure if he was hearing it or feeling it, following it or losing it. There were words, but only identifiable as such by the rhythm of sounds. No meaning, recognition or direction was available to Kris just yet.

It was pretty clear he had got massively stoned and passed out. The last thing he was sure of was sitting in front of the computer, trying and failing to reach Miranda on Skype.

There was no sense of elapsed time.

No feeling of presence.

Nothing to fill the dark cavity of his failed recollection.

No memory of falling into the living room sofa. From the textured surface he could just make out under his hand that was probably where he found himself now.

Texture… That's a start… but one step at a time… Kris had suffered major marijuana whiteouts before, the tunnel vision and loss of sense of self brought on by seriously overdoing the wacky-baccy, but he'd never had it this bad. He knew if he could just hang on to one little piece of reality, he'd come back OK.

He stroked his fingertips across the surface of the couch, seeking reassurance that he was returning to the real world again.

Shit, he'd never had spliff give him a hangover before. His head ached, and stiffened his neck in protest as he tried to turn. There must have been booze involved somewhere along the line. The dull throb in his brain, beating in time with the pressure waves pulsing from his shuddering heart told him it must have been cheap Tequila, or even worse, Australian lager. Eyes still closed, he rolled into the corner between the cushion and the back of the sofa. The darkness there offered sanctuary from the harsh light that permeated his eyelids.

Muffled footsteps in the carpeted hallway, approaching.

"See? He's coming round." The sound of movement in the office paused. A second pair of feet made their way to the living room.

"See?" The same voice continued. "I told you. I didn't hit him that hard."

"Maybe. But it was a bit unnecessary, don'cha'reckon?" Even with his head in the angle of the couch, Kris was aware that the light was dimming. Something was between him and the bare bulb overhead.

"I thought he was going for a concealed weapon." Johnson parroted the standard get-out clause.

"OK. Duly noted. It can go in the report." Rafferty sighed. *Although, I'd hoped we could avoid actually writing one,* he added silently.

Kris rolled onto his back, put a hand across his eyes and ventured a glimpse at the world outside his head. "Wha..tha… fuck… who… what?"

Two faces he didn't recognize were peering intently into his. He felt like a sample in a test-tube, about to be picked up and shaken by the mad scientists who were currently subjecting him to such close scrutiny.

"Nope. No point. Give him ten minutes before we get started. He's still out of it." Rafferty stood upright.

Johnson turned to the corner of the room, grabbing Rafferty's arm to bring him to impromptu conference. He whispered. "What's the deal? We just need to grab that notepad in the hallway and get the fuck out of here. If we go now, he won't even remember we were ever here. Nothing to worry about."

"Listen." Rafferty was suddenly serious. "That PC…"

Johnson glanced in the direction of his colleague's gesture towards the office.

"There's some serious shit on there. He's got a couple of things that we do need to worry about. And I mean 'we' as in you, me and Uncle Sam… and 'worry' as in 'game-over if we don't' kind of worry."

Johnson slid his head back on his bull-neck and raised an eyebrow. "What? That scrawny little turd-weevil there?"

"Looks like it." Rafferty turned to look down at the groaning Kris.

"What's he got? The ISIS phone book? Weapons of mass destruction?"

Rafferty paused, unsure how much to tell his sidekick. There were only two of them on this, and by rights, they should have been a couple of thousand miles away taking snaps of an oil-field, not taking 5-irons to a difficult lay in the rough. He made up his mind. He was in charge of this little spree, and he'd be the one to cop the flak if they got found out. The best way out of this mess was to bring something home that'd give the boss a boner. Rafferty sighed. He needed the big guy's help. "Worse. He's got a track on some of our instruments. Weapons of cash destruction."

Johnson's face remained immobile, a sure sign that he was completely in the dark. Rafferty debated with himself if Johnson needed to know, or if he would even understand.

"Look. Just go with me on this. We need to know what this streak of piss knows… and why he's fucking around in shit that's none of his damned business. Capiche?"

This was much more Johnson's home turf. "Capiche."

165

"Right… wake him up…. Wait! Not like that!"

The big man's hand was already raised to slap some good morning into Kris. He froze in mid-swing. "Awe… no?" Johnson looked like a kid who'd been told there was no more ice cream.

"No. We need him to answer a few questions. Sit him up."

Johnson gripped Kris by both shoulders and bodily lifted him clear of the sofa before pushing him back into an upright position. Kris squinted through the harsh light: two men. He recognized neither; one standing, the other on his haunches in front of him. At least, he might have been squatting. He was still about Ross's height even in that position. Ross! Where was he? Who were these two?

"Who are you? Are you doctors? Did someone call you?"

"Yeah, that's right, boy." The smaller of the two men drawled. "Doctors. I'm Doctor Shutthefuckup, and this is Doctor Ballbuster." His accent was unidentifiable to Kris's ear.

"Look", Kris mumbled, still dazed. "I'm really grateful for you coming all the way out here, but I'm OK. Just overdid it a little last night."

The larger man squatting put his hand on Kris's knee, offering reassurance. He squeezed… and kept squeezing. Kris felt the gristle of his kneecap being ground against the end of his femur. He smarted and tried to push himself up and away. The giant's grip was implacable.

"No. I can definitely feel that." Kris whined. "See? I'm fine. Honestly."

The smaller man leaned in towards Kris. "Buddy. We ain't doctors. We ain't no surgeons neither…. But we're going to perform a little procedure on you anyway. It's called a factectomy."

"A… a… what?" Kris was fully awake now. These two were definitely bad news. The big man was terrifying for obvious reasons, but the smaller of the pair… he was discretely sinister. Far more fear-inducing for the utter certainty that he would do whatever he felt necessary to get what he wanted. Worse, he might do something totally unnecessary just because he had it in his power to do so.

166

"A factectomy. We are going to extract the truth from you. Sometimes, it's a fairly painless operation... sometimes..." he paused for effect. "... sometimes... not so much." He grinned, a yellow-toothed rictus of malignant pleasure that had nothing to do with sharing a joke, but alarmingly, everything to do with amusement.

Kris flicked his eyes around the living room seeking a way out of this. He scanned his mind for an explanation. There was a large bag of weed in the kitchen, but not even the bored Highland police would come all the way out here for that. Still, his paranoia told him otherwise. A chill of impending catastrophe shivered through his mind. "I'm not kidding. You've got the wrong guy, or... or... or house, or something." His eyes, round and pleading, were starting to water.

"Yes, well." Rafferty crossed his arms. "They all say that. But I gotta be sure... so, tell me from the beginning... what's that computer doing in there."

"Huh? Well... it doesn't fit in the living room, and it's better having a separate office. You know... a bit of distance between work and relaxing." Kris was babbling. "... It helps you to put a..."

"No!" Rafferty screamed. On cue, the big man slapped Kris open-handed across his cheek. It was an adept blow, not enough to do damage, but enough to promise damage if the correct answers were not forthcoming.

"Wrong answer!" Rafferty took a step backwards and put his hands behind his back. It gave the impression that he would not restrain his enforcer, that anything that happened now was not his doing, that he was keeping his hands clean no matter what came next.

"What," he took a breath and continued quietly. "Is that computer working on?"

"What?" Kris felt his voice to be embarrassingly high-pitched. "It's a project for university."

"No!" Rafferty yelled once more.

Kris had already learned the lesson and winced, his face turning from the impending blow. It landed in his stomach. The breath flew from his body, punched out with a force that he could not have imagined possible. He could not refill his lungs. He buckled forwards, gasping like a beached fish. A chest that didn't seem to belong to him any more gave an involuntary spasm, he heard himself grunting an "nnhhh nnnhhhh" sound as he fought to regain control of his breathing.

"Wrong answer!" Rafferty advanced quickly on Kris and grabbed his hair. The boy felt the fire in his scalp as his head was yanked back for the man to look him in the eye. Kris's torso was fighting to remain curled, protecting his gut from another impact. His head was struggling to follow the pull, reduce the tension on his hair. Between the two, his brain was desperate for a way out.

"But... but..." Kris was actually starting to cry now. Hot tears welled in his eyes. His voice was a mere lump in his throat.

"Now tell me... what is that computer doing?"

Between the fear and the pain in his diaphragm, Kris struggled to talk. "Hnnhh... hnnnh... honest..." He was genuinely sobbing between each syllable. He felt his nose fill with mucus, salt saliva ran down the back of his throat. "Honest... I swear... it's a uni project. It's looking for patterns in the stock market. That's all."

He felt the tug on his hair relax and he reflexively curled around his pain-wracked gut. His head tucked down. The iron grip on his knee was released.

Silence, broken only by the convulsive gulps of air Kris was managing to grab. He wanted to vomit.

Not a word from the two men, so out of place in the modest living room of his parent's holiday home.

Kris looked up through his tears. Both men were staring at him waiting for more details. "Look. If you don't believe me, go and look at the assignment. It's printed out on the desk."

"Uh huh. All in good time." The man with the yellow teeth grinned again. "First... you're going to do some talking then we'll check. If you fuck up, you will be fucked up. Got it?"

Kris felt a thin veneer of ill-advised bravado overlaying his fear. The worst of the stomach blow was subsiding, but a hollow, hungry feeling lingered behind.

"Who are you anyway? You're American, huh? What are you doing here?"

The massive guy in the dark suit growled, "We're just here to play a little g..."

The other man put his hand on his arm, stopping him. "We're just here to play a little game with you. It's called '20 Questions', except you don't seem to have understood the rules." It was his turn to squat in front of Kris. He raised his hand. "We..." he lightly cuffed Kris's face. "Ask..." another smack to the opposite side. "The... questions... you... provide... the... answers." Each word underlined by a slap, alternating left and right. Not hard, but cruel in their intention to demean and degrade, weakening Kris's will with each blow. He winced and sobbed with each impact, his eyes flinching.

"So... last time." Rafferty leaned in close and whispered. He wiped the snot and tears from his hand on Kris's thigh, lingering a little too close to the crotch. Kris recoiled.

"Tell me... what is that computer working on?"

Kris fought for control, struggled to find an answer that might satisfy his tormentor. "Honest. It's a university project."

Rafferty raised his hand and sniggered when Kris flinched. That seemed to be enough for him.

"Seriously." Kris struggled on. "We take stock market history, run some programs and measure how accurate the predictions would have been. That's it."

"Kid. You've either got balls like an elephant, or you're fucking stupid. Do you expect me to believe that?"

"Why not? It's the truth." Kris bawled. "It's the truth. I swear it."

"Then why are you targeting that set of stocks? If you're just running analysis for an assignment... why that particular set of stocks?"

Kris stopped dead in his crying. "What? What stocks? We're just trying numbers."

"Enough!" Rafferty stood quickly and turned to Johnson. "Find somewhere we can put this piece of crap." He backhanded Kris without looking round. The student never even saw it coming. "Let's see if he can think of something more convincing. I want to have a look for myself."

The tumbling of bottles and junk in the hallway told him that the big man had found the narrow broom cupboard. He was emptying the cramped space to lock Kris away. Nothing would be left behind for the student to turn into a weapon, nor for him to 'A-Team' his way out of there.

As a boy, Kris had hidden in the cupboard for games of hide-and-seek with his mother. He never suspected she had been 'unable to find him' for so long, grateful as she was for the temporary peace and quiet. He was convinced he was always the winner. This time, he was definitely going to lose.

# Chapter 23

By the time Ross found the town's only bus-stop, nowhere near where the elderly dog-walker had promised, his mood had oscillated so often between fury, frustration and failure that he felt physically sick. Throughout his forced march, he found himself silently mouthing a litany of cunning put-downs that he should have unleashed on Kris. He became aware of his fists clenching, his teeth grinding, as he visualised lethally effective choke holds and devastating body blows that would have dropped Kris to the floor, defenceless against the onslaught of Ross's righteous retribution. In his mind, Kris became a mindless punch-bag, unable to retaliate or weather the raw power of Ross's vengeance.

By the time he passed the Thirsty Midge, he was wound up as tight as clockwork. He toyed with the idea of a pint to calm down, maybe with a whisky chaser, but with his current run of luck, the bus would come and go as he stared into the bottom of his glass.

Barely visible through the marker pen proclaiming "Josie 4 Rob 4 Ever" Ross struggled to make out the details of the bus times. The destination was Glenfinnan, not Glasgow, but it was a start. Whoever Josie was, and whoever Rob was, Ross sarcastically wished them luck;

"4 Ever" was an awfully long time, a lot could happen to turn "4 Ever" into "2 Little 2 Late".

"Aw, for fucks sake!" Ross peered obliquely into the plastic timetable holder.

When the buses had been privatised with the promise of more choice for the consumer, outlying, unprofitable routes like those serving the Highlands had been trimmed right back. Ross, the would-be consumer, now indeed had a choice; he could either walk or stay where he was. There was not another bus until, he rechecked his watch, Tuesday. He checked his watch again. It was now Saturday.

Tuesday! Fucking Tuesday! Who the hell wanted to go anywhere on a Tuesday!

Ross turned away from the timetable, and quickly snapped back to check again, just in case it had changed in the last few seconds. He spun too quickly and the inertia of his rucksack carried him past his balance point, dropping him neatly on his rear among the discarded cigarette butts and flattened wads of chewing gum that accumulate anywhere humans regularly stand and wait. He drew his legs to his chest, wrapped his arms around them and squeezed his knees to his temples, staring into the space between his feet.

The evening summer breeze breathed on the back of his neck and played with the short hair sticking out of his collar. He hunched his head further down till he could block his ears with his knees leaving the only sound he could still hear that of his own blood pumping, gradually slowing down as he rested. He stared through the ground, his eyes misting over, as he wondered if he could slow his own heart down enough that it might just forget to beat again. It would be a gentle cessation to the grief. He could just sit there till he faded from the world, forgotten and unmissed. His backside was numbing on the cold ground, telling him that the blood flow was indeed stopping in at least one part of his anatomy. It could have been two minutes, but more likely twenty that he sat before he was capable of thinking of anything else other than just ceasing to be, before he concluded that if he was going to cease to be, he'd find oblivion easier to face with a belly full of beer.

# Chapter 24

From his makeshift cell, Kris could hear the two intruders moving around his father's office. They weren't ransacking the place; they had been trained that the initial order and positioning of evidence was as important as the evidence itself. Theirs was a measured, controlled and methodical search, professional and precise, not fearing discovery; put everything back where it originated and plausible deniability was assured.

A suggestion of light filtered under the door, but did nothing to illuminate the cramped confines of the storage space. It was little more than a recess in the wall next to the front door. The large man had patted Kris down before placing him in the cupboard like a piece of meat in a refrigerator. He'd taken the boy's Bic lighter but there was nothing else of interest in his pockets.

The mixed scent left behind by the various cleaning products and polishes favoured by his mother transported Kris briefly to a happier time when he'd felt the protection and love of a nurturing family, a love he had seen no need to return. He ached for that protection now.

He was in trouble that he didn't understand, and that was the worst kind. There was nothing for him to work with. If there was no context, there was no way he could weasel his way out of whatever mess he'd been dumped in. There was no story to twist with self-preserving falsehoods and nowhere else to point the finger. He was on his own: lost, alone, and locked in a cupboard.

The vague blur of light at the bottom of the door divided itself into three equal parts. A pair of feet had approached.

"Hey, Kid." It was the deeper of the two voices, probably the bigger guy.

"What?" Kris sulked.

"What's the screensaver password for that PC in there?"

"Fuck you." Kris spoke quietly in resignation.

"I guess I didn't hear that too good. Wanna try again?" The door handle rattled noisily.

"Fuck you. All in lower case: 'fuck' 'underscore' 'you'." There was nothing for Kris to hide that he could think of. His emails? Who cared? Mostly jokes and photo-shopped images, nothing secret and nothing of value. His bank account? These guys weren't after money.

"Smart." The feet departed.

Kris could see nothing, cocooned as he was in impenetrable blackness. It matched his despair.

The spit of light dribbling under the cupboard door did nothing except ruin whatever night-vision he might be able to garner if it were total darkness. He screwed his eyes shut and covered them with both hands, the same position he'd used when it had been his mother's turn to hide all those years ago. Perhaps if he could get a minute or so of total blackout, his night-vision would let him inspect the cupboard for anything that might help his current predicament.

He was fearful of feeling around in case of knocking something over. The bad guys might still be standing within earshot for all he knew.

Turning his head away from the door, he uncovered his eyes. Nothing. There was a suggestion of shape at the corner of his vision, but when he turned to look directly, it vanished.

174

Kris's face was really aching now. It was more than just the slaps. He'd taken a real blow to his jawline, a couple of his bottom teeth felt a little looser under his questing tongue than they should have. Maybe he'd fallen, or been dropped on his face. No. Wait. One of the voices had said something about hitting him. Christ, what with? A cricket bat?

Backtracking what he could recall of the last 20 minutes, Kris was surprised to find his brain attempting to analyse what was happening. The fear, maybe even the darkness, let his sharpening senses contemplate every possibility of a way out of this.

Hold it! He nearly slapped his own forehead at the revelation, stopping himself just in time before aggravating the already present stinging.

They'd taken his lighter, obviously, but he still had his watch. A 100m waterproof diver's model that had been no closer to the ocean than a splash from washing his hands… it had a backlight. Dim, true. But in the tarred black of the cupboard's interior, it would be an incandescent beacon of hope.

Kris quietly twisted over to sit with his back to the door. He carefully guided the movement of each limb, slowly, inch by inch, terrified of knocking over some discarded bottle or broom that would alert the two men currently dissecting his father's office and computer.

Bringing his two hands together in a position of prayer that he would have mocked in other circumstances, he slid his right hand over the left and up the wrist, probing for the light button on his watch. At the last second before depressing the metal tab, he realized he was staring at the watch. He would need both his night vision and the faint glow-worm of the backlight to stand a chance of seeing anything useful in his prison cell.

A sickly yellow blush coloured the bare floor boards of the cupboard as Kris angled his wrist to scan its confines. He methodically tracked the shred of faint illumination across the floor and worked his way up the wall to his left in a narrow ladder search pattern.

Nothing on the floor in that corner except a couple of off-cuts of carpet, saved aeons ago to repair some predicted future damage.

The climbing light picked out the underside of rough wooden shelf, the wood unpainted and unvarnished, it's rough surface discernible even by the over-stretched backlight of the watch.

A glint of metal briefly reflected before sudden darkness. Kris froze and felt his heart stutter before he realized that the light would only run for three seconds anyway. He tried not to move his left arm while he pressed the button once again. He sought out the elusive sparkle of steel, tracking around where he thought he'd been looking.

There! Again! It was a small curve, about an inch in diameter. And another. They dangled beneath the handmade shelf like the steel earrings Kris used to wear before he'd opted for the more radical wooden spacer hoops he sported now.

Fuck it. Cup-hooks. His mum's contribution to DIY was to stick them anywhere she thought she might want to hang a mug, brush or a bucket, and then promptly never use them again. Damn near every wooden surface that wasn't actually furniture had sprouted these miniature grapnels.

He continued his search: two more shelves, perhaps a third suggesting itself at the limit of the light's range. Kris scanned the yellow patch back down to the bottom corner of the back wall. Even in his anxiety, he realized that the best chance to spot something useful would be a methodical raster of his surroundings. Partitioning his little oubliette into strips of concern would ensure that nothing would be lost by frantic random flitting here and there.

The back wall offered nothing bar a couple of old towels hung on the omnipresent cup-hooks. The wall closet was barely deep enough to house more than buckets, brooms and an ironing board. His worryingly competent captor had pulled all those into the hallway ensuring nothing was left behind for Kris to even contemplate turning into an escape plan.

The fact that the cupboard was only about six inches wider on either side than its door had meant that the previous owner had installed shelving in the otherwise wasted space. Shelves that now stood out like the rungs of a ladder climbing to nowhere on the cupboard's third and final side.

From his muscle cramping position on the floor, Kris couldn't see onto the tops of the shelves. He would have to stand up, there was no option. But, it would have to be done in utter silence. Touch the door, and it would rattle on its hinges. Bump a shelf, and it might cascade whatever it supported onto the floor. Any noise would invite investigation.

Kris gingerly slid on his bottom to the corner of the cupboard, letting his legs elongate as far into the opposite corner as possible. He briefly contemplated Ross being here. His smaller stature would be easier to manipulate in such a cramped space, but above all, if Ross was there, it meant Kris wouldn't be.

Shuffling his shoulders against the jamb, desperately trying not to touch the door itself, Kris shrugged his way upwards until he could get his feet down to support his weight. Delicately, left hand outstretched towards the back wall, he eased his body vertical. Wary of bumping into some unseen piece of detritus, he pulled both arms tight to his chest, found the light button on his watch, and began a methodical scan of his surroundings from this higher perspective, working left to right.

A short stick, its end coated in paint, a few cleaning cloths. The charred, grease-spattered metal grill from the brick barbecue optimistically built on the patio, stood on end, festooned with burnt fat since Kris's last visit. A gentle buzzing sound, overlaid with evenly spaced ticks, tempted him to look right, but he held his resolve and continued his line-by-line search.

Immobile to his tentative grip, the shelves themselves offered no solution, screwed to L-bracket supports, in turn, firmly fixed into the walls.

The back wall: resolutely unhelpful.

Turning right, working along each shelf in turn, Kris saw a deck of cards, a chess set, a pack of wax crayons bought for his 8 year-old self to keep him occupied during another of those long, wet weekends for which Scottish summers are famous. He had scored a vengeful vortex into the kitchen wall in bored protest, snapping the orange crayon in the process.

Now, the light fell on the source of the buzzing. The electricity meter and fuse box. Kris's first instinct was to reach out and shut down the power to the whole cottage, stopping the two intruders in their tracks. He stayed his hand as he considered the possible outcomes.

These two had come all the way to deepest Argyllshire. They had already made it clear that they were looking for something. A mere power-cut wouldn't stop them. They would just dig Kris out of his cubby-hole, turn the power back on, and kick seven shades of shit out of him for his trouble.

The watch was growing dim, warning Kris that its battery was not intended to drive the light for such an extended period. He let its timer extinguish the LED. The image retained on his retina seemed brighter than the lamp itself; it faded to nothing, and took with it Kris's hope.

Almost unconsciously, he reached under the shelf, probing for one of the cup hooks. It twisted free from the damp pine fairly easily. Kris gently eased it into the right hip pocket of his jeans. If he sat down carelessly it might well stab him in the thigh, but as an idea coalesced in his mind, it seemed like a risk worth taking. Sliding his hand along the shelf bottom, he located and retrieved another cup hook, and another. Both were stashed in the same pocket. The shelf above yielded three more that he slipped into his left hip pocket. He now had a serviceable set of spikes for each fist. Not quite Ninja kubotans, but close. He could thread his fingers through the hooks leaving the pointed screws outwards. Make a fist and it would be a fist with claws.

# Chapter 25

As the key rattled in the lock, Kris realized he was gripping the pockets of his jeans, protecting their illicit cargo from discovery. He hurriedly hugged himself as though against the cold and squatted, not wishing to raise the slightest suspicion that he'd been up to anything. Blinding light engulfed him. The bulb in the hallway was only 60 watts but after half an hour in near total darkness, it stung his fear-reddened eyes.

"Up." Johnson commanded.

Kris held the door jamb and timidly got to his feet. He made a show of rubbing life back into his numbed legs.

"There." The giant continued, pointing into the office. He stepped back to let Kris pass in front of him.

Rafferty stood as Kris entered the room. It was not a courtesy gesture. "Sit."

Kris glanced between the two men, eyebrows high, seeking pity in either face. There was none. He sat in the chrome and leather office chair. It felt unpleasantly warm, recently vacated by Rafferty, warmer than if he'd been sitting there himself.

"Now," Rafferty leaned his butt on the edge of desk at right angles to Kris, deliberately crossed his arms and turned his head. "Do you recognise this?"

He flattened a single photocopied sheet on the desk top, and rotated it towards Kris. Instinctively, the boy reached forward for the paper.

"Hands off. Just read."

Kris placed his hands in his lap, leaned forward and read the first line to himself: "Dear Mr President USA". It wasn't in Kris's nature to confess, but he sensed that it was the right thing to do this time. "Eh... yes. It's... it's... a letter..." he stammered. Was this what this was all about? A joke fucking letter?

"And?" Rafferty stared hard as Kris glanced between him and the other man.

"We wrote it..." Kris started to relax. Perhaps this wasn't so serious after all; a simple misunderstanding, a joke gone too far. They'd probably sit around and laugh about it later.

"Yes, we know that," interrupted the bigger of the two men. He took a step forward as he spoke. "The paper matches the pad next to the phone out there."

Rafferty jumped on the opportunity. "We?"

"Yes, we... you and me..." countered Johnson, confused.

"Not you. You kid. You said 'we'. Who is 'we'?"

Kris didn't hesitate. "We. Me and Ross. He's a friend of mine."

Rafferty leaned closer. "And where is this 'friend' of yours?"

"I don't know. He's not here."

The bulk of the larger man loomed large as he bent over the desk. Kris leaned back in the chair. "Kid. The paper matches that pad. The letter was written here. There are two beds here. Both have been slept in. That means someone else is here." He leaned closer, owning the space between himself and Kris. Despite the width of the desk, he could easily have stretched out a hand to grab Kris's throat. "So... where is he?"

"Honest. I don't know. He left this morning."

"Pint o' heavy, pal." Ross was already counting coins onto the sticky bar top.

The bar man shoved them back. "Next time, mate." He winked.

Was it that obvious? Was he really so transparently a hard-luck case?

He felt like hurling the coins, plus a hefty tip, across the bar at the young man's kindly smile, but he mumbled a thanks, his voice snagging in his throat, and went to find a dark corner to brood in.

While Johnson held Ross's full attention, Rafferty was toying with the PC mouse. He rotated the monitor and snapped a question at Kris, catching him off guard. "Tell me what this means." He stared hard at Kris while the student looked at the screen. A text file was open listing somewhere between 20 and 30 acronyms, each a few characters in length.

"They look like stock symbols." Kris offered.

"I am aware of what they look like. What do they mean?"

Kris glanced back at the larger man looming in the doorway. "I'd need to look them up. Like GOOG would be Google... only that's not there..." He rocked back in his seat as Rafferty twisted like a viper to face him more squarely. "It's just an example!" He yelled, hands in a defensive position.

"I know that. But why these particular codes?"

"Honest! I don't know! The program spits that out."

"No! Wrong answer!" Rafferty screamed. He turned to his colleague. "Hold him down."

Before Kris could move, two huge arms pinned him into the seat from behind.

"Why'd you write the letter, runt?" Kris felt the voice rumble through the chair back more than he heard it.

"I... it... was a... joke... we... didn't mean... to..." Kris was trying to turn his head to address the answer.

A loud bang yanked his attention back to the front. The meat of Rafferty's palm had slammed hard on the desk, his silver ring clacked on the glass in echo. "Now. Let's try again. Why these codes?" The ticking of Rafferty's single piece of jewellery against the table top as he drummed his fingers counted down the last reserves of his patience.

Kris was mortally afraid. Physical pain was one thing, but being restrained smacked of being worked on, like a cadaver on a slab; a state he didn't have much hope of avoiding. "I swear it's true. I don't know. I didn't write that bit."

"Right. Let's assume I believe that. Who did?"

"Ross, but he's not here anymore. He left this morning. I told you."

"Uh-huh. So where is he now?" Rafferty stepped from the table to face Kris. He used the toe of his shoe to tap the boy's feet apart, separating his legs.

"I have no idea. Honest!" Kris tried to close his thighs but Rafferty had placed his foot between his knees.

"Now listen to me. I could reach down there, grab your nut sack and twist till you sing like a canary…" Kris felt the back of his neck begin to sweat.

"But… a little faggot like you might enjoy that… and I don't want to get no faggot-mess on my hands when you blow your load in your tightey-whiteys, do I?"

Kris shook his head convulsively, keen to show how co-operative he was being.

"So. Far easier for you to tell me. Who is Ross? And where is he now?"

"Please…" Kris knew he couldn't satisfy this lunatic, no matter what he said. The man's eyes flashed with a psychotic passion. "Ross is my lab partner at Uni."

"Partner, huh? As in gay marriage stuff? I knew you was a queer hawk the minute I set eyes on you." Johnson joined in from behind the chair.

"He left this morning. He'll be trying to get back to Glasgow."

"How?" Rafferty asked, clearly enunciating the word.

"No idea. Bus, hitchhike, train… we're in the middle of nowhere here. For all I know, he's still stuck in the village."

182

"That's not helping us," warned Rafferty. He slid the heel of his shoe up between Kris's thighs, till he could place a little pressure on the trapped boy's scrotum. "How do we find him?"

Kris hesitated. Should he lie to give Ross a chance? Fuck that. He, Kris needed to fully cooperate if he was going to get out of this. "He's about 5 foot 6, black jeans, red jacket, Scotland top... I mean a blue football shi... soccer shirt," he translated for the American audience. "Carrying a ruck-sack. Black hair." Kris babbled.

Rafferty stood hard on his testicles. A couple of seconds reprieve while Kris thought he'd escaped the pain before a sickening, hollow agony pervaded his lower torso. It crept into his stomach and nauseated him. His eyes filled with tears till the down-lights of the office ceiling turned to stars. And still the solid grip held him fast to the back of the chair. He had no chance to ball his body for protection; the pulsing ache begged him to curl up but to no avail.

"Now." Rafferty withdrew his foot and continued as if nothing had happened. "I don't know if you're lying or not. But consider that a decent example of what's to come if I find you are FUCKING WITH ME!" He screamed the last three words full into Kris's face. Flecks of foaming spittle peppered the hairless skin of the boy's cheek. "So. One more time." He shuffled himself along the desk in front of Kris to a more comfortable position. "Why... these... stocks?"

Kris's mind raced. Clearly there was some significance. He just had no idea what it could be. Ross had been error checking the program as some stocks had coughed up some wild anomalies that threw off the rest of the analysis. Maybe these were test cases, or the divergent cases that were being filtered out. He could barely summon the oxygen to answer. "The only thing... they might... be... if they were giving bad results, maybe... Ross filtered them out... maybe he isolated them to find out what was going wrong."

Rafferty seemed to genuinely consider this possibility. He watched Kris intently for a few seconds then put his head on one side. It was an oddly affectionate gesture, out of place in the circumstances.

183

Kris could feel the man's reptile gaze slithering over his face and body.

"Nice tattoo." He tilted his head further as he took in the artwork on Kris's arm.

Kris sniffed back his tears. "Eh?"

"Nice. I had one... got it in the navy. Had it removed though." The statement was unnerving in its inconsequence, delivered as a conversation piece, just two acquaintances passing the time of day. He looked over the back of the seat to the big man. "I'd like to see the rest of that. Get his shirt off."

Johnson slid his grip back to grasp the collar of Kris's shirt. Without apparent effort he tore it cleanly in two leaving only the remnants of the sleeves at the shoulders.

Rafferty leaned in more closely to inspect Kris's chest. "Very nice work... very nice indeed."

The big man leaned over to take a peek. "Yup. That's a good tat, man."

The stench of rotten lamb, garlic and cigarettes filled Ross's nose. The hot liquid mucus blocking his nose, evidence of his recent tears, was no defence against the onslaught of Rafferty's breath. "Yeah, looks good on you. What do you reckon, buddy?" He continued looking over Kris's head. "I think it'd look better hanging on the wall of my hunting lodge. Huh?"

Johnson laughed. "Could be... but you'll never get that all off in one piece."

The smaller man stroked his chin in contemplation. Kris could hear the rasp of three days' worth of stubble. "Maybe not. I've done a back before and a few little objets d'arts, but never a whole arm. But, I reckon if we slice it here..." he trickled a yellowed fingernail down Kris's sternum and under his right breast. "And round here..." He continued to trace under the boy's armpit and into the crevice between his flesh and the leather seatback. "And we'd need to open it up anyway..."

Kris screwed his eyes shut as he felt the finger nail drag its way down the underside of his triceps. He longed to pull his arm away but was frozen in the cryogenics of fear.

"Otherwise I won't be able to flatten it out to frame it. Shame to cut those pictures though."

His brain couldn't grasp this. Was this demon proposing to flay the skin from his body? Just to get some new artwork to hang next to the heads of felled deer and wild boar from previous hunts? Or what did he hunt? Was Kris just the latest in a longer line of human quarry?

The man pinning him down leaned further over to look. "No. It'd be OK. They're all in boxes. You could just work round the edges." He was referring to the cartoon frame surrounding each of the miniature tableaux.

Kris realized he was no longer a human to these monsters. He was just flesh to be carved up and displayed. He was just a temporary assemblage of meat, fillets ready for a butcher's iced window tray.

"True... true." Rafferty sucked air over his repulsive teeth, a professional tradesman through and through. "In fact, we could just take each frame out one by one. That'd be more fun now, wouldn't it?" He smiled benevolently at Kris.

This couldn't be happening. Kris shook convulsively, more than the mere shudder of a sudden fright. It was genuine, bone-deep fear, gripping the fibres of his heart, tumbling through his brain, taking command of his spine, loosening the slender control he still had over his body.

Kris sprang up as the grip on his shoulders was released. He stumbled forwards out of the seat, bolting for the door. There was no plan. Just escape. Nowhere to go... just somewhere he was desperate to leave. Two steps and he was airborne, tripped by Rafferty's outstretched foot. He landed heavily on his chin, arms outstretched, bare chest braking on the wooden floor as he slid to a painful halt. A heavy force on the small of his back announced that a foot was pinning him down.

"Not smart. It's time you went back in the closet to think about what you've done." The weight was lifted from his back.

Kris's scalp was once again cruelly ripped as a claw hand pulled his head upwards. He desperately piled his own hands on top, trying to take the weight off his hair. Half dragged, half jumping, he was on his feet. Whoever was pulling his hair was almost lifting him clear of the ground as he was propelled towards the broom cupboard; his feet skipped and danced across the ground as he ran to keep up.

Thrust into the back wall of the little cupboard, Kris stood against the wood where his face had impacted, arm still held up beside his head in an effort to ward off the blow. The door clicked shut behind him with a delicate finality. The lock was turned and the key withdrawn.

# Chapter 26

Options. Options. Options.

Ross watched the foam gently slide back down the inside of his glass; the widely spaced tidemarks hinted at the rate at which he was demolishing his beer. Each mouthful delineated a significant drop in level every time he steered his pint back to the circular table top. He put the glass down, but never let it go.

Options. Options. Options.

Before he drank himself into a coma, he blearily concluded he had to figure out what he could do, which options might be open to him.

In descending order of preference, but increasing order of likelihood, the top ten were:

One: Find some hot looking local lass to trap off with for the night. Comfy bed, a decent shag, wake up to a blow-job and breakfast. Start the journey with a spring in his step.

Two: Find some dodgy looking local lass. Drink enough till she looks half-shaggable, stumble into bed at her place, fall asleep. Wake up to embarrassed regret. Sneak out without waking her up. Start the journey in a hurry.

Three: Ask around if anybody is driving back to civilisation tonight. Start the journey with the risk of being killed by a drunk-driver.

Four: Stumble out of the bar at closing time. Find a hedge to sleep under. Wake up (hopefully) in the morning. Start the journey covered in cow-shit.

Five: Stagger back to the cottage. Sleep in the garage. Start the journey before Kris wakes up.

Six: No idea.

Seven: Nothing.

Eight: Start walking. Just walk all night. Start the journey now.

Nine: Still nothing.

Ten: Drink himself to death. Start his journey to the other side.

Somewhere round about number one hundred in the list of acceptable choices: Wander back to the cottage. Admit defeat to Kris. Endure about an hour of his supercilious gloating. Crash out. Try to start the journey in the morning, but more likely repeat today's attempt verbatim.


Kris pressed his forehead into the wood panelling. In the dark horror of the cupboard, his imagination would not let go of the prospect of his skin being peeled from his flesh, living or otherwise. Nothing in his past could give his mind a shape for the pain he expected. Instead, his memory sought for any reference, any trace that might make sense of its current distress.

In his head, he heard the slick glutinous sound of a barbecued chicken wing being separated, the muted reverse kiss of a dry mouth opening, a Band-Aid tugging at his skin until the adhesive gave way and ripped free. His mind's eye saw flesh and fat parting like the clinging layers of a pizza as a slice is lifted, stringing cheese and rich tomato sauce in its wake. He replayed scenes from "House" and "E.R.", watching, unable to press stop or pause, as fibrous muscle was exposed then rolled back to reveal the glistening pearl of bone beneath.

It is the last ditch attempt of a human mind on the edge of the precipice to scan its memory and experience for possible solutions, to find a way out. Kris's mind was trying everything; everything that his limited experience could relate to witnessing his own skin being stripped from his arm, but he couldn't wrench his focus from the hideousness of the act itself.

For most of the evening, the smokers had been wandering outside in ones, pairs and larger groups. Now that last orders had come and gone, they didn't return.

Ross had grabbed a half-pint and a whisky, a "hauf 'n a hauf" as Greg the barman had called it. He sucked one generous mouthful off the top without lifting his pint, then dropped the whisky, glass and all, into the beer. As it sank slowly to the bottom, Ross's head sunk with it till his chin was resting in the sticky spillage on the table. Before long, Ross and the barman were the only two left in the place.

Greg reached behind the one-armed bandit and jerked its plug from the wall. It was only now that Ross realised it had been beeping out an abrasive little anthem for the last few hours; the sudden silence clanged shut around him.

"C'mon, mate. I've got to get home," Greg pleaded. He gathered Ross's collection of empty glasses and pointedly nudged the remaining glass towards him. "C'mon, eh? Ten minutes while I drain the pumps."

Ross gently became aware that someone was talking to him. He tried to neck his beer/whisky, get to his feet and shoulder his rucksack, but found he could only handle one task at a time. The gas bubbled in his stomach, bloating it painfully, as he knocked the rest of his drink down in one.

He didn't quite know how he got outside, but he found himself swaying slightly in the pub car park, twisting into his rucksack straps, trying to guess the direction back to Slighe D'Ahla. The garage floor seemed pretty enticing. If he was lucky, maybe there'd be something soft like a sun-lounger, or even a pile of tarpaulins or anything.

"Awe, bollocks." Ross said aloud. He stopped in his tracks when he noticed light streaming from the cottage, piercing the darkness of the hillside above his line of sight.

Kris must still be awake, maybe loading the crippled car. Surely he couldn't be planning to drive it home. Maybe there was a truck coming for it in the morning. It wasn't worth salvaging, that was for sure.

Ross allowed himself a little chuckle when he imagined the roasting Kris's mum would give him when she saw what was left of the Fiesta. "Fucker needs a thrashing anyhow." Ross looked down and toppled forwards a few steps till his feet caught up with his misplaced centre of gravity. "Fuckin' thrashing... that's what he needs. Fucker..."

He weaved onwards up the middle of the deserted road. Any approaching cars would be announced long in advance by their headlights, main beam, this far out of the town. He'd have time to make it to the grass verge.

# Chapter 27

"Man, this is getting us nowhere." Johnson seethed. "Some vacation, huh? It's beginning to feel a lot like work."

Rafferty settled back into the office chair and put his feet up on the desk. He reached under the seat squab and toyed with a lever rather than answer his colleague.

"What's the big deal anyway?"

The chair suddenly dropped a few inches as Rafferty released the height mechanism. He rallied and maintained his dignity. "I told you. He's messing with stuff that's none of his business. We need to know why, what he's found and who else knows."

"If he knew anything at all, he'd have told us already. You saw him. He's damn near pissed his shorts. Anything at all... he'd tell us his own mother was sucking cock in a line-up, and he'd have got us a family discount too... he's nothing."

"The kid knows something he's not telling us."

"What are you going to do to him? He's had enough, man."

"Relax. I'm calm. I'm OK." The older man looked anything but. His olive skin was flowering red around his cheeks and bulbous nose, the veins of his neck stood out, visible as bulges in the folds of excess fat. Rafferty flattened a creased black and white photocopy and held it out at arm's length to Johnson. He glanced over, but didn't take it.

"Yeah, the letter. So what? You already told me we're being jerked around. It means nothing."

Rafferty withdrew and refolded the sheet using the fingers of one hand. "I know that, you know that, and he knows that... so it's something we all know. What did they teach you in Guantanamo?"

"Eh... Ay-rabs don't like rock music? Oh, and start with something you already hung on them... build on that." He snapped his fingers, turning the movement into levelling a finger at the letter.

"Uh-huh. And... it's easier to let them think you're going to damage them than to actually do it... harder to prove in court, too."

Johnson stared at Rafferty who winked back at him playfully.

"OK. But back in G-land, we had a sound-system, state-of-the-art too... there were all kinds of sound-effects." Johnson gazed back into his recent past wistfully. "It was beautiful, man. Alphabetized. There were folders full of it... electric shock, screaming in who knows how many languages... gun-shots, crying, beatings, rapes... you name it... you could even sequence them... just crank it up outside the cell, play it like an orchestra... let their imagination do the dirty work."

"Yeah, I know. They never knew if they'd be next. Happy days, huh?" Rafferty gazed at the floor. "The shocks were my favourite. I used to get Old Man Harper to turn the dimmer down on the lights... fuck, I thought I'd die laughing."

Both men paused to consider the sacred art of mental torture.

"I always wondered if those screams were real or play-acted." Johnson put his hands in his pockets and raised his shoulders.

"Best not to ask, buddy... best not to ask." He tapped the side of his nose confidentially. Rafferty knew no more than Johnson but liked to maintain an air of being party to privileged information.

Both men got to their feet.

"So, what's it to be? Good cop, bad cop? Bad cop, worse cop?"

"Can I be bad cop?" Rafferty pleaded, hands clasped together at his breast. "Pretty please? Oh, say I can, please?"

Johnson grinned widely and nodded. "It's your gig. Take it away, maestro."

"No way, man!" Rafferty over-enunciated from the office doorway. "That little fuck wrote this letter! The pad's still there on the table!"

"Yeah," Johnson agreed. "But it's nothing to do with the PC."

"That's not the point. He's jerking us around. Who does he think he is? Fucking with the US? We don't take that kind of shit from nobody!"

"Not any more anyway... But not the face this time. We might need photos."

Rafferty grinned and gave the thumbs up sign. "Photos for what? Do you think I want his corpse identified?"

"No, but maybe we gotta ransom him or something. Maybe stop someone else talking... we might need to show he's in one piece."

Rafferty paused and bit his lip to stifle a giggle. "Yeah, I didn't think of that. But they ain't going to ID his balls."

He turned his face to the hinge side of the cupboard door and hissed, "They'll need to find them first..."

Johnson shook his head and mouthed silently "too much".

Nevertheless, the breathless sobs from within grew more rapid, underscored by a desperate, pitiful mumbling.

Rafferty tugged on the big man's shirt, directing him back to the office. "Give him an hour or so," he whispered. "Let him chew on that then we'll go again. Keep him awake, he'll be putty by the morning..."

It was Johnson's turn for the comfort of the office chair, although he was barely able to jam his massive frame between the chrome plated side bars. He leant sideways, feigning an air of nonchalance, to flick through a copy of Angling Times, but couldn't find a satisfactory position. He gave up and offered the seat to his colleague, glad of an excuse to show deference without actually capitulating.

The older man unnerved him. Johnson could definitely tear his colleague's arms off in a straight fight, but he somehow felt he still wouldn't comfortably turn his back on the resultant cripple. There was something indefatigable, something persistent about Rafferty. He had the mindless task-focus of a hive insect with the empathy and compassion to match.

Occasionally, Johnson glanced from the pages he wasn't really reading at the middle-aged man. His body had gone to seed, flaccid and pendulous from a lack of exercise, but under the off-white, over washed shirt, beneath the sagging folds of flesh, there was a potent choleric energy. Rafferty's unfocussed irritation at the world around him occasionally released little shocks, temporary build-ups of static electricity that needed to be fired off before they accumulated to something more destructive. It seemed like he was charging himself up, just looking for a lightning rod to find a path to earth.

Pulling the stout iron key from his hip pocket with one hand, Rafferty used the other to swing the heavily painted lock guard away from the key hole. In the darkness of the cupboard, the spike of escaping light lasered a spot on the back wall. Kris raised his head to watch the dust motes swirling, choreographed to dance by his breath, as they were briefly illuminated before dispersing into the darkness.

The lock mechanism tumbled over and Kris began to sob convulsively. The brave dignity he had hoped to show all but evaporated.

As the door was pulled open, he tipped forward onto his hands and raised his head, pleading with red-rimmed, blinking eyes to the pot-bellied figure standing before him. "Please... please... I don't know anything... this is a mistake... I p-p-promise."

Rafferty said nothing. Years of interrogation sessions, first in training and then in the field, had taught him that disorienting the subject would lead to this eventually: locking them up, dragging them out, locking them up again; a little violence, the threat of a lot more violence, turn up the voltage; get them talking once and they wouldn't stop. He felt no pity for this object grovelling at his feet. He'd been through worse himself.

"I'll tell you anything you want to know... please... l-l-let me go. I never saw you... you were never here..."

Rafferty thrust a piece of paper under Kris's nose. "I know you'll tell me," he hissed. "So tell me what this is all about."

The mottled monochrome glinted under the hallway bulb. Kris's eyes, still stunned by the onslaught of the light after the blackness of the cupboard, wetted by tears, could not make out more than a few vague shapes. He blinked to clear his vision.

Clearly the pause was too long for the impatient man. "Tell me!"

Kris edged forward on his knees and tried to focus on the single sheet of paper. It twitched with the elevated pressure of the man's pulse.

A darkened patch near the bottom of the sheet looked like a pencil drawing of a meteor crater, heavily shaded to black at its centre. The page was dappled in shades of grey like a poor quality photocopy, impossible to tell if the marks were reproduced from the original or were aberrations of the copier itself. Characters on the page, they might as well have been hieroglyphics, swam into relief and assembled themselves as characters as Kris's eyes adapted to the light and cleared themselves of tears.

"Dear Mr. President USA…" he read.

"I… I can explain…" he stuttered, raising his eyes to Rafferty's implacable face.

"Glad to hear it." Rafferty squatted to stare hard into Kris's eyes. "Begin."

"It was a joke. Me and Ross… we wrote it for a laugh."

"So, you think it's funny to play a freshman prank on the government?"

"But…"

"Don't you think we've got better things to do than go running off on a wild-goose chase to the butt-hole of nowhere for a joke?"

"But…"

"But nothing. You've wasted our time, kid. Do you have any idea of the resources that have gone into tracking this down?"

"Why?"

Rafferty was caught wrong-footed by Kris's inherent curiosity. It surprised Kris himself, considering the circumstances. "Why what?"

"Why bother? It's just a letter."

"Procedure, kid. Procedure. We gotta follow these up." Rafferty sighed, his face softening. He was just another cog in the machine, same as Kris. He was as much a victim as the kid was.

"Look," he laid the copy of the letter flat on the floor between them, cards on the table time. "Since that fuck-head Snowden, we can't do the electronic snooping stuff no more." This was a lie, Rafferty knew. The intelligence agencies of the world, not just those of the USA, had to make it look like their information came from pursuing leads, like in the old days. There were whole departments just stumbling over each other to lay fake tracks, diverting attention from the digital sources.

Kris snorted his derision, but rapidly turned it into sniffing back tears when he saw the spark of anger flash in Rafferty's eyes.

"So... any non-electronic intelligence... well, now we got budget to chase it down. If we don't spend the budget, we don't get it next year. You know how it is."

Kris didn't but he nodded anyway. "And you came all the way to Scotland to check this out?"

"Like I say, kid. It's budget review time. We don't use it, we lose it."

A silence fell between the two, each waiting for the other to fill it. Eventually Rafferty broke the stalemate. "Now. Tell me. Why did you write this?" He picked up the paper only to drop it again in demonstration.

Kris relaxed a little. "I told you. It was a laugh. We were a bit wasted... never really meant to send it... it just sort of... happened."

Rafferty remained granite faced.

Kris continued. "It's true anyway, if you think about it. We've got, or at least we had oil... it's gone now."

"Uh huh." The man sounded unconvinced.

"And England took it..."

"Right..." Rafferty was encouraging Kris to keep talking. He tapped the letter.

Anxious to show willing, Kris continued. "And, it didn't seem fair. They were robbing us blind, and we got nothing. Me and Ross... we just got talking, and it all got out of hand."

Rafferty leaned back, considering the situation.

"I'm sorry." Kris hung his head.

The man leaned lower to catch the boy's eye. Kris's head lifted, as though levered upwards by the force of Rafferty's stare.

"OK. Now we're all singing from the same hymn sheet, tell me some more about your project through there."

Kris glanced at Rafferty's accusing finger. "I don't know what else to tell you. It's a project, that's all. Why are you so interested?"

"It's my job. Now. Who else knows about it?"

"Just me and Ross, I guess."

Rafferty stood. "You guess? Guess again."

He placed his foot deliberately against Kris's sternum and propelled him backwards into the cupboard. Through the locked door, Kris could hear Rafferty's voice as he walked away. "You'll stay there till you come up with some names for me, kid."

# Chapter 28

"I'm telling you, man." Rafferty leaned back into the leather chair; it tipped accommodatingly on its springs. "That kid knows something."

Johnson rubbed sleep out of his eyes and pressed his simian knuckles onto the glass desktop opposite. "And I'm telling you he doesn't. He's stumbled into this. He has no idea what it is or why it's jerking your chain. To be honest... neither do I." He stood upright.

The seated man steepled his fingers under his nose and paused. "Maybe he doesn't know what this is about... but either way, we need to shut it down. This is the wrecking ball that brings down the house of cards."

Johnson had turned to peruse the shelves once more: accountancy records, statute books, tax law. A scant few were familiar to him: international titles and bound periodical collections like 'Time' and 'The Wall Street Journal' for the most part. "What in the name of Clinton's wiener are you talking about? He's hacked a chunk of code that looks like it might be sort of OK at guessing the markets... so what? That's been around for ever. "

"I know. But this, " he waved his hand at the monitor, "has chewed up and swallowed the data, and spewed out the bits it couldn't digest. These...," he peered at the list of stock codes, "glitches here... they're not glitches."

Johnson circled the desk and placed his hand on the seat back. It dipped to one side under the force as he leant down to inspect the screen.

Rafferty glanced at the side of the big man's face. He saw not the faintest glimmer of comprehension. "These are the companies and funds that ran the sub-prime mortgages."

"So?"

"So... that's kind of what triggered GFC... eventually."

"Uh huh. Meaning what?" Johnson's brow furrowed as he tried to peer through the codes to whatever deeper significance Rafferty had spotted.

"Meaning, that kid, or rather his little game of Battleships here," he pointed at the graphical program outputs, now frozen, "has identified the depth-charges that sunk the fleet."

Johnson craned further into the screen, forcing Rafferty to tip sideways in the chair. "I still don't get it. That's common knowledge. A fuck-load of investors got a fuck-load more greedy than usual... bought up a fuck-load of bad debt... and lost a fuck-load of cash. So what? They had it coming... about time too." He straightened. "And anyway, everyone knows the shit-storm started with the mortgage companies. Why are you all juiced up about this kid's software?"

Rafferty rubbed his temples with his knuckles as he held the weight of his head, elbows on the desk. "Because... the test data he was using... it came from the months before the crash... his code here... it coughed up these guys..." He clasped his hands and pointed with both index fingers at the list of stocks. "It spotted the charges before they blew..."

"Charges?"

Rafferty looked askance at his partner. Was he really that naïve? "OK..." he sighed; he was going to have to walk Johnson through this, step by painful step. "Where did those investors get their fuck-load of cash from?" He waited in vain for a rational answer. "Take your time... think it through."

"Previous profits?"

"And?" Rafferty strung the word out, singsong style.

"And... they borrowed more?"

"Right!" Rafferty beamed indulgently at his star pupil. Johnson crossed to the low bookcase beneath the room's only window where he sat down. The shelves creaked under his weight, presaging imminent collapse.

"They borrowed... that's called leveraging. If you can make a hundred bucks by investing a thousand... you can make a hundred thousand by investing a million. Only..."

"If you don't have a spare million lying around, you borrow it, yeah?" Johnson interrupted.

"Yeah. You borrow it from... from... anybody...?" He didn't wait for an answer. "A bank... or an investor... or anybody with a fat wad of readies burning a hole in their pocket."

"Duh... obviously. So why has this got your back up? It's what happens."

Think it through, dumbass... think it through. Rafferty silently instructed the big guy. Eventually he realized he was going to have to put the song sheet in front of Johnson and help him with the words. "Where does that pile of cash come from?"

"They earned it?" Johnson hazarded a guess.

"Oh please." He spat at the floor in disgust; the glutinous oyster of yellow phlegm glistened as it wobbled to a standstill. "Earned it? These are stock brokers, banks and investors. They didn't earn it. Do you reckon they go down a mine and dig it out? Do they flip burgers at the weekend to save up their nickels and dimes?"

The big man shrugged.

"They might have got paid... but no way in hell that bunch of freeloaders earned it." Rafferty stood, in full lecture mode now. "No... where did the cash come from? What is it that NYPD's finest say? Cui bono? Who benefits? Follow the money, find the bad guy." He paced out from behind the desk to stand, hands behind his back in front of Johnson. "Where does all US cash come from?"

"The Fed... Federal Reserve," stating the one fact he really thought he knew.

"Right. And where do they get it?"

"What do you mean? Where do they get it? They don't get it from anywhere... they already got it. They got mountains of gold... that's the money."

"Yes... but they don't hand that out when they give you a dollar bill, do they?"

"Well... no. That'd be a bit impractical. Walmart don't take no gold when you want a carton of beer."

"No. Exactly. You get a little bit of paper that says, 'honest... we've got some gold somewhere, just can't seem to find it right now... sure it was round here some place.'" Rafferty made a show of patting his pockets and glancing around.

"That piece of paper," he pulled a green note from his wallet and waved it, "this piece right here is a promissory note. It isn't inherently worth any more than we believe it to be worth."

"OK. But the Fed and Uncle Sam tell us it's worth a dollar... so I believe them... thankfully, so does Walmart."

Rafferty began to pace the room, his heels clicking on the wooden floor, occasionally muffled as his steps encountered the rug. "Let's say that's true for a moment. But..." he paused and rotated to face Johnson. "Do you think that for every dollar out there, there's a dollar's worth of gold in Fort Knox? Huh?"

The big man bent forwards to rest his elbows on his knees. He clasped his hands together as if praying that the fiscal fairy tale he'd believed in his whole life might still hold a grain of truth.

"Nope. I tell you now. The Fed Reserve can lend out 90% of what it holds... it only keeps a fraction of its handouts as a reserve. That's the law. The US government doesn't own the Fed. It's just a customer. When Uncle Sam needs some cash, he asks the Fed for a loan."

"And what happens when he pays it back?"

Rafferty snorted in derision. "Yeah, right. Pay it back?"

202

He continued, ignoring the ridiculous implication. "So… if Mr. President wants to inject some cash into the economy, he goes and borrows some from the Fed." He could see this was not making an impact on Johnson. His faith in the folk lore of finance was not yet shaken.

"Look." Rafferty grabbed the notepad on the desk and hunted around for a pen. Johnson obliged, handing him a hotel biro from his pocket as he stood up to watch. Bending to the desk, Rafferty began to sketch out a cash-flow. "The government here," he scribbled a cartoon eagle, looking more like a chicken, and enclosed it in a box. "They want some pocket money."

"The Fed here," he drew a box with a dollar sign in it. "They say they've got a million, but thanks to the 10% law, they only need to keep back 10% actual funds. So… they can lend out nine hundred thousand; they only need to hold onto a hundred G." He connected the two boxes with an arrow.

"So… that's OK. Isn't it?" He started to look a little panicked. His forlorn hope fluttered like that of a child told that grandma is very sick.

"Not really. They don't hand over the cash… they just write a little I.O.U. The government then puts that in their own bank. So, the Fed actually has a million, and the government pretends they've got a chunk of it, although, in reality, the actual cash never moved."

Rafferty clicked the pen twice to retract and expose the nib before drawing a third box surrounding an ungainly looking sedan. "Now… let's say that Detroit, "he tapped the image of the car, "they're going under and need bailing out. They phone Uncle Sam and beg for a bit of breathing space."

Rafferty drew an arrowed line from the government to Detroit. "'Just a few bucks till pay-day… honest, boss.' And the government says 'No problem… dem fine automobiles represent freedom for the public, jobs for the masses and votes for us…'" He mimed putting his thumbs threw imaginary braces as he stood up, the willing philanthropist. "So… the government, finding themselves with a prescription for the new wonder-drug 'miracle-cash'… oh, and remember they're still bound by that same 10% law… they just write a cheque. for 810 hundred thousand. Once again…"

Johnson interrupted and stabbed a finger into the diagram. "So there's another eight hundred or so just come out of nowhere."

"Exactly. The banks did the same thing when they started feeling the pinch." He held out a begging hand as illustration. "Now… what do banks do when they get money? They make money by sharking it out…"

"So… every time someone borrows money, if only a small chunk of that needs to actually support the loan… the rest is imaginary?" Johnson's eyebrows shot into his hairline.

"Right."

Rafferty started drawing a list of names tagged with ever decreasing numbers.

Fed: 1000000

US: 900000

Bank: 810000

Investors: 729000

Mortgage holders: 650-something 000

Initial cash: 1000000

His mouth moved silently as he did the mental arithmetic.

Total 'money': 3 million and change

"Look… there's a little piece of gold here…" he tapped the word 'Fed', "and by here," he tapped the last line, "it's mutated into 3 times that much. This goes on and on."

Johnson was following Rafferty's pen like a cat following the dancing light of a torch. "That's no problem. We've got 3 times as much cash… everyone's happy… everyone's rich."

Rafferty sighed and laid the pen carefully parallel with the lines of the A4 pad. "Really? If sea-shells were money, what's the value in a seashell? You can just head down to the beach and collect yourself a new pickup truck or a condo… or a dental plan. Supply and demand. If there's a lot of something, its value plummets."

Waves of enlightenment, whipped up by the gathering force of Rafferty's explanation, suddenly crashed on the shores of Johnson's understanding. "So, more dollars floating around, mean each dollar is worth less? No wonder I can't fill the freezer no more."

"Right." Rafferty spun the pen on the pad by twirling it with his finger tip. "Stuff isn't getting more expensive... they like to tell you that, but the reality is that your dollars are worth less... only a matter of time before they're worthless."

He glanced at Johnson to see if the pun had triggered a neuron, but sadly not. "Now... add into this the interest on each of these loans. Where does the money come from to pay that back?"

Johnson took the pen clumsily in his pork sausage fingers and drew a vertical arrow heading towards the top of the page. He added the word 'Interest' and a % sign. "Nowhere. It can't exist till... somebody..." he slowed to a stuttering halt. "... borrows... it."

"Once again... 100% correct. Therefore, loans can never be repaid... period. I mean, individual loans, yes, well... some of them, anyway... but the sum of all loans? No way. It can't. It's built into the system." Rafferty sighed and stared into the middle distance. "You know what the sickest thing about it all is?" He didn't wait for an answer. "That trickle-down theory of Reaganomics... it sure does work... just... not for wealth, only for debt."

Johnson wrinkled his forehead.

Rafferty carried on regardless. "The rich and the big corporations? They feed their debt to the next rung down... wait. You know what's even sicker? They re-packaged the debts, covered them up in gift-wrap to make 'em look pretty, and sold them on as assets to each other!"

The big man tentatively raised a hand to ask a question; Rafferty pre-empted him. "Yep... not only are Joe Schmos like you and me drowning in mortgage arrears... but some bread-head somewhere figured out even that was worth something and sold us all on as collateral... it's like we're cattle at a round-up, just waiting to be sold on and branded..." He fixed Johnson in the eye. "The good old U. S. of A. is sunk. It's going down... with all hands on deck. The weight of debt, money that never even existed in the first place, is drowning us, and still the band plays on." His shoulders sagged as he continued.

205

"We can't pay back what we already owe. We're the biggest sub-prime mortgage there is… and we don't even have a house the bank can repossess to cancel the loan. We have nothing, and we're still printing money like cheap newspaper."

Rafferty slumped back into the office chair. "Worse… we're printing the National Enquirer… it's all fabrications and conspiracies and… and… and boob-jobs and UFOs …" He forced a brave smile. "Unsupportable Financial Operations….Yeah, sure we can raise the debt ceiling and keep borrowing, if anybody'll still trust us, but that doesn't solve anything… it just postpones the inevitable."

Johnson stared at his companion in disbelief, not at what he was hearing, but at what he saw: there were almost tears in Rafferty's eyes as he contemplated the destruction of all he held dear. "This can't go on," he added quietly. "Get him back out here."

# Chapter 29

By the time Ross could see the whitewash of the cottage, a watery silver in the reflected moonlight, the security lamp had gone out. He paused until he was sure Kris wasn't coming back outside again, and quietly walked on. Rounding the last corner before the final debilitating climb, Ross thought he could see another car, bigger than the tortured Fiesta, blocking the driveway. "Shit. His dad's here."

Bonn senior must have come to drag the prodigal son back home.

There was no way Ross was going to brave the pair of them together. No matter what Kris had done, his dad always backed his little boy against anyone else; apart from Mrs Bonn, that is, when Mr Bonn would suddenly remember some work he had to do and would sneak off to the office.

Ross weighed his options. The chances were that Kris and his dad would stay the night and set off in the morning. And, if Ross turned up at the cottage right now, he'd be subjected to a whole night of Kris and his dad taking turns to pick on him, particularly while Kris's dad was still fuming about having to come and pick up his son. However, if Ross 'turned up' first thing in the morning, the chances are they'd both be a bit calmer and he'd be able to cadge a lift back to Glasgow. At worst, he'd cop a bit of flack on the journey home, but as he'd be relegated to the back seat, he could always pretend to be asleep.

In silence, Ross picked his way over the paving of the driveway, seeking out the flagstones to avoid being betrayed by the gravel, eased open the garage door and used the thin moonlight to find a pile of sacking where he could unroll his sleeping bag. Ross unpacked his headphones and leaned into a fragment of light to find the on switch. As he fitted the earpieces, he twisted to find a shred of comfort in the sacking, each movement wafting a musty scent of disuse, coal dust and potatoes over him.

"Show me." Rafferty hissed into Kris's ear.

Kris hovered, legs bent, his backside half way to the seat. He froze momentarily, then edged into the seat.

"Who else knows about this?"

"Ah... nobody... just me and Ross." Kris leaned towards the desk.

"Show me. Open your email. Inbox."

Kris complied immediately; Rafferty brushed him to one side tabbed down through each mail in turn, pausing till he read each title.

"Who's that?" He stabbed an accusing finger at the screen. Ripples flowed out across the LCD from the point of impact.

"My advisor of studies. He was answering a question about sort algorithms."

"And that?" He indicated a mail folder titled 'Randy'.

"Miranda. That's this girl I... I mean Ross... was seeing. I call her Randy."

"And is she? Randy, I mean?" Johnson suddenly appeared interested.

"Ah. Not really. I don't know, I mean. It was just the once..." *One night, four times, and once bent over the kitchen table in the morning for good measure*, Kris added to himself. Despite his current predicament, he felt the twitch of an impending erection painfully pressing against his y-fronts. He needed to adjust his swelling penis through the pocket of his jeans, as was his habit in such a situation, but it might precipitate a search of his pockets; they'd find the cup-hooks.

"OK. And that's your pal's girl? You are fucking low."

Kris hung his head. "Yeah. I know. Sorry."

"Open it."

Rafferty stepped sideways for Ross to take the keyboard. He placed both hands in the typing position as he clicked the enter key with his little finger.

"'Hi Kris,'" Rafferty read aloud. "That's you, huh?"

Kris nodded warily.

"If she's seeing your buddy, why's she writing to you, eh? Let's see, will we?" He read on. "'Sure, why not. I haven't heard from Ross, so I guess he really doesn't care. Have you heard from him? I can get the Fort William train first thing in the morning, then jump on a bus. I'll get into the village at about 10:45. Can you pick me up?'"

Miranda's grammar was always careful and precise. Even in these days of text message abbreviations and Twitter, she had never relinquished her education or background. Kris liked that in her. It made him feel like a bit of a rogue, a bit of rough for the posh girl.

Rafferty looked sideways at Kris. The boy felt hot colour climbing his neck. "I thought this Ross kid was here with you?"

Kris hesitated. "He was. He kind of... em... found out about me and Randy. She didn't know he was here."

It seemed like Rafferty got the picture. He read down through the conversation. "Hey, buddy. Check it out. Lothario here has been poking his best friend's girl. Look. 'That was awesome last week. I'm up at my parents' holiday place. Got the place to myself. I'm so lonely... ;-)...Wanna come up for a return match?'"

As the man glanced over to catch Johnson's eye, Kris gently pressed the function key to activate the desktop microphone. The red line through the relevant icon on the taskbar winked out.

"Who'd have thought he had it in him?" The big man was standing, arms folded, blocking the door in case Kris tried to make another bid for freedom. "And she's on her way here?"

Kris nodded.

"Johnson... maybe you'll get some action after all..."

Kris winced.

"What else?" Rafferty pressed on. "Who else have you talked to about this 'project' of yours?"

Kris obligingly tabbed down through his inbox, stepping further back in time. Rafferty occasionally stopped him to give a particular email closer attention. "OK. And the outbox."

Once again, Kris willingly tabbed over to his sent mails. Perhaps if they knew the information had already spread beyond Kris and Ross...

He realised he'd get one chance, but timing was everything.

The art of the conjuror is not really sleight of hand; it's making sure the audience is looking at the wrong hand.

Kris reached for the mouse with his right hand, leaning across the PC keyboard as he did so. With his left, he simultaneously keyed ctrl-alt and R. This was another little tweak he'd installed for his father. Just as his old man had recorded meetings with clients, Kris was now committing everything in range of the microphone to disk, saved every few minutes as the buffer filled. It might be futile, but a tiny part of himself, that element that was rapidly vanishing, was still grasping at straws.

The spoken word, recorded, evidence... Maybe he'd get a chance to send some of the audio files... Maybe it was nothing more than a desperate act of defiance, trying to do something, anything... Maybe it would just be a last chance to salve what little conscience he had, uttering a final apology for... for... for everything... everything that had brought him here. It would probably never be heard, but at least he'd have said sorry.

Eventually, after checking the contents of a few relevant mails, Rafferty was satisfied that only Kris, Ross and their advisor of studies had any inkling about the project's methodology. Furthermore, it looked like the isolation of the rogue stocks was a recent development. However, the advisor, probably on holiday somewhere, had the method. He could easily reconstruct the results.

"OK kid. You're going back in the closet. Me and him, we gotta think about this some." *Or at least, I'll think about it... Troy just doesn't have the tools for that kind of job,* he added silently. Rafferty guided Kris by his upper arm.

# Chapter 30

The muffled discussion wasn't quite penetrating the confines of the hall cupboard, but Kris could hear the pace winding down and the volume dropping. A decision was being reached. He swallowed forcefully, competing with the rawness of his own throat. He needed a decision of his own.

The relatively gentle questioning about the letter... God, he wished he'd never sent it... he'd just wanted to see Ross's reaction when he'd confess to posting it, just wanted to show-off how devil-may-care he could be, nothing more. The questions about the letter though... that was the calm before the storm. Kris was positive.

Steeling his resolve and tensing against the tremor in his hand, the terrified student gently slid his fingers into the right pocket of his jeans. The serrations of the first screw thread brushed the prints of his middle finger as he reached deeper. The pointed end of a second hook crow-barred its way under the nail and pried the keratin away from the raw flesh beneath. Kris barely stifled his yelp of pain, bit his lip and swore silently, the agony made hell-born by his inability to yell out.

Convincing himself that he would imminently be dragged out for more questioning, Kris individually fitted cup-hooks over three fingers of each hand. They hung loosely, points outwards, but when he clenched his fists, the hooks aligned as an extension of the metacarpal bones. By tightening his grip, the points could be brought to attention.

The best, and only, chance would be to leap forwards as the door opened.

Kris strained his ruptured mind to fill in the blanks, rehearse the scene he would soon play out for real.

Only one of the intruders would come to collect him, assuredly the bigger of the two. To open the door in the narrow corridor, such a giant man would need to press himself hard against the wall opposite, or step to the side. That was more likely. But which way?

The cupboard door opened away from the front door of the cottage. Would the captor block the front door, or stand in front of Kris to guard his movements?

Fuck. Kris couldn't focus through his fear to even make a logical guess. What would this bastard do?

He'd want to see what the prisoner was doing. If the big man stood to block the front door, he wouldn't be able to watch Kris, and there'd be a barrier, albeit a flimsy hinged door, but a barrier nonetheless between the two. No. He would definitely face the boy.

Kris's best chance was a sudden lunge, maybe knock the giant backwards, and then spin to fire himself out through the front door. If he could just make it to the village...

The cupboard was shallow, but there was just about enough room for Kris to force himself backwards into the corner between the wall and the floor. He took his weight on one foot and steadied the other against the wall, a sprinter ready in his blocks. The tendons of his thigh reminded him that there was a finite limit to the time he could hold this position, and probably a shorter time he could still affect the spring-loaded leap to freedom he had planned. The element of surprise would be somewhat diminished if instead of seeing a set of barbed fists bearing down on him, his captor witnessed no more than Kris, ignominiously rolling onto the hall floor, crippled by cramp.

He would get one chance.

If this went wrong, they'd use his balls for batting practice, then feed him what was left. The older one of the two would probably neatly slice Kris's nut-sack open at the seam, pop his testicles out like peas from a pod, and force them down his own throat. What did the Ozzies call them? Bush-oysters?

If this went wrong.

If this went wrong?

Was it worth the risk?

What if he gave them everything? Just gave them the computer, the code, the lot... help them find Ross... would they let him go? Would they cut him up anyway? Would they at least show him some mercy? What could he offer?

If this went wrong... if this went wrong.

He had to do all he could to stack the deck in his favour. The deck! Yes. Distraction and diversion! When Kris did his rabbit from the hat act, a little misdirection might be all the difference between safety and supper served a la scrotum.

He leaned forward, taking a little weight with his forehead against the door, and twisted his shoulder up and back to finger the shelf for the pack of cards. Kris's hand brushed the towel he'd used earlier; worth a try too.

Yes. It was coming together.

When the door opens, throw the pack of cards from one hand, the towel from the other, leap forward, spikes out. A mad banshee wail for good measure, and he'd be off and running.

If this went wrong?

It was going to go wrong.

Kris knew it. Minus his shirt, he was getting cold. Muscles in his legs that he was not previously aware of were warning him... it's going to go wrong.

His shoulders sagged, and he pressed his forehead into the chipped shellac paint of the door. Robbed of the faintest of hope, Kris let his whole body soften and sink into the crevice of the cupboard floor. The circulation had well and truly ground to a halt behind his knees, his feet were a fading memory.

Kris tried to unfold his legs, but his limbs weren't co-operating. He could just about inch his head up, but only at the expense of compressing his neck back into his spine. If he could turn his head sideways, he could maybe just slide on his cheek until he got upright. He laid his face against the door and begged his legs to push. Slowly, each inch an irascible dispute between his mind and his muscles, Kris fought his way up the door, shrugging his shoulders to walk up the door jamb. Chips of paint grated his cheek, flicking irritating grains into his eye, an eye wide open in fear despite the lack of anything to see.

He was stuck.

His butt was jammed into the back wall, knees bent at an unmaintainable angle, and his face was flattened into the painted wood. With his vertebrae contorted into an impossible s-shape, he could neither move up nor down. Like a plastic ruler, bent to its limit, the tension had to give; his spine had to straighten, or snap in the attempt.

His arms were now dangling, not quite able to reach the floor to push, his shoulders were held in the meagre gap between the wooden uprights of the door frame. He dropped the pack of cards he'd previously congratulated himself on finding, and let go of the ancient cloth with his other hand, flinching from its unpleasantly rough, inflexible surface, now rancid to his touch. It hung there, snagged in the cup-hook of his ring finger. *Typical*, he thought. *I can't even throw in the towel.*

He flailed his arms, but with his biceps securely restrained by the door jamb, he could do no more than flap loosely at the elbows. He shamefully recalled the Thalidomide jokes he used to make at school. Not only had some pharmaceutical giant racked up an unfeasible profit at the expense of kids that had been born deprived of proper limbs, but Kris had reserved himself a place in hell for the mimes he'd forced on his embarrassed class mates. They'd been a dress-rehearsal for the predicament he found himself in now, handicapped and helpless. If he could have raised a fist to shake at the God he often vociferously denied, he would have.

"Vengeance is mine", saith the Lord... and Kris was starting to believe he could hear His voice, or if not His voice, then a spiteful sniggering, muffled behind His hand.

The lull in the discussion in the office grew longer, dragging on till Kris strained to hear the merest trace of a human presence. With his ear pressed hard into the dense oak of the cupboard door, the tick of the electricity meter and the tap-tap of his heartbeat were trading places, indistinguishable and inseparable, back and forth, one then the other.

The wood was a sounding board, dulling yet amplifying both, resonating till Kris was no longer sure if his pulse drove blood or current around his body.

Gradually, his physical rhythms merged with those of the house, flowing together, choreographing a tormented waltz, tick tap-tap, tick tap-tap, tick tap-tap. His numbed feet could not step, his strained legs could not dance, his trapped arms could not reach out to hold a partner.

Mesmerised by the insistent tempo, dizzied by lack of sleep and with the flow of his carotid artery limited by the unnatural angle of his throat, he felt his consciousness fade once more. Seconds, minutes, maybe hours drifted by; he'd lost all track of time. As his awareness slithered from his weakening grasp, his thoughts constructed music, faintly at first, but gathering strength. His mind, so bruised by the brutality it had already endured, was retreating, falling back to a stronger position, ready to gird its loins.

Overlaid on the swaying three-four time, another pattern, an imploring two-step syncopation began to assert itself; faintly, imperceptibly at first, biding its time till its inevitable crescendo and domination. Waiting, holding back, advancing then retreating, forcing its way to the fore.

A slap of light woke Kris from his trance. The door burst open. He cannoned forward, a spring wound and held against impending fatigue, abruptly released. Arms outstretched, he pitched into the hall, knocking a body to the ground.

Regaining his senses far more quickly than he would have imagined possible, Kris tried to roll away. The cottage door was achingly close. The village was a sprint away. He twisted and bucked to flip over, landed on his back, and reached out along the hall floor with his left hand. He scrabbled in the rug for purchase, trying to pull his body to freedom.

Something grabbed at his right hand, pulled at his fingers and held him firm. They were being bent backwards against the joint, a move designed to disable his whole arm, nerve against bone, sinew against its limit.

He felt a bellow of pain shudder through him. But the voice was not his. It had shaken loose from the body next to him. They were now lying side-by-side, close, even intimate. He had felt the noise rumble through the floor.

He jerked his right hand, heedless of the threat of dislocated knuckles, a bestial shriek stopped him dead.

Tentatively, he turned his head to squint along the length of his outstretched arm. His hand rested palm-up on the yellow-and-white checked tea-towel. Square-by-square, the pattern was disappearing, fusing into a luxurious, claret-red as blood wicked into the cloth and permeated to its hemmed edge.

Kris pushed himself up on his left hand and slid backwards on his bottom till he was looking down in horrified fascination. The flesh of his fingers blanched white either side of the three metal rings anchoring his hand in place, through the cloth and into something twitching beneath. That same cloth was now thoroughly soaked down one side, a red so deep it was almost black. The remaining half flapped angrily with the huffs of furious breath panting from the unseen face beneath. He could no more stop himself than he could break free. In terrified slow-motion, he reached across with his left hand to grasp the corner of the tea-towel.

The floor boards vibrated under him as the crashing footsteps of the other man, alerted by the noise charged from the office.

Each footfall bounced both Kris and the prone body.

Each bounce yanked Kris's hand against the cup-hooks.

218

Each yank jolted another scream from beneath the tea-towel.

The boy felt the force restraining his index finger ratchet down as the hook broke free from its anchorage. He could sense the vibration of the threads as they progressively tore free, unzipping one by one.

Kris froze as he touched the edge of the cloth. He stared into the narrowing eyes of the older of the two men, slowing to stand above him.

He now knew who was lying beside him.

# Chapter 31

Johnson clamped his fist around Kris's wrist, preventing any further movement of the hooks buried in his face, and gripped the waist band of the boy's jeans with his other hand. Without apparent effort he stood, and Kris was lifted clear of the ground to be transported back to the office chair.

With an unexpected delicacy, the two fingers still held by the cup-hooks were extracted, leaving the saturated tea-towel stuck, firmly anchored in two places, and gummed by cooling blood across half of the man's face. All of the malevolent fury pent up in his huge frame, focussed through the single visible eye. The giant straightened, looming ever larger in front of Kris, leaned back against the table and slammed his foot into the boy's body; heel-to-toe, the sole of the shoe flattened Kris from his stomach to his throat. Just when he thought the chair would topple, the older man righted it from behind.

Kris watched in horrified fascination as the colossus before him began to unscrew the threaded metal from his face; the man's venomous stare never wavered, never moved from Kris's eyes.

The first hook bounced once and tinkled to a standstill on the opaque glass of the desk. It left droplets of ruby red against the snow-white of the surface, and an echo in Kris's ear.

The second hook, attached higher, was causing more of a problem; it was either lodged into bone, or into the gap between teeth. Either way, the man was having to apply significant torque to remove it. Yet still, his fury burned an almost visible line in the air between his eye and Kris's; he didn't so much as blink.

As the last hook tumbled to the desk, a fresh trickle of blood ran under the cloth and onto the once-white shirt collar, straining against the bulging muscles and throbbing veins of the man's neck. He deliberately peeled the towel downwards from his forehead, folding it back on itself. Millimetre by millimetre, a second eye was uncovered, impossibly carrying just as much hatred, and as much twisted purpose as its counterpart.

The entry point of the highest hook snagged on the towel, pulling the cheek out and down, attached by a ragged fold of skin entwined in the thread of the cloth. The man still did not deviate from his purpose; even as the flesh and face parted company, the bloodied visage was revealed at a constant, agonisingly slow rate.

Twice more, the swab of cloth, its faded pseudo-tartan now utterly indistinguishable through the coagulation, tore a string of skin from the tattered face. Kris tracked the sodden cloth as it fell to the floor between his feet. His eyes reluctantly traced the contours from the lower slopes to the peak of the mountain of barely human fury before him.

A roll of parcel tape was clenched in a scarred fist a few inches from Kris's eyes.

The frayed face risked a snarl: "Tie him up."

With his wrists and bound to the armrests, and his ankles tied backwards behind the metal uprights of the chair, Kris strained to hear the muffled conversation in the hall. The older of the two men had walked the other, with little resistance, out of the room. The last thing Kris could make out as they left was "Don't you lose control now. We need him to talk," before the rest was lost behind the thick oak panelling of the door.

A chance. Alone... for how long, he didn't know. Minutes at most, but not long.

Kris fought at the tape on his wrists. He bunched his fists and tried to push against the chair, then against his bindings, but they were too tight to gain any purchase. He twisted his body to get his teeth to his hands; he switched from one to the other in futile panic. If he could just snag an edge of the tape, it might be enough to start a tear... he only needed one free hand and he could peel the rest off, but he might have only seconds.

He whimpered in fear and pain as his ribs and spine twisted and contorted... just an inch or so short. Willing his head forward, he felt the muscles of his neck shudder with exertion, his eyes bulging with the constriction of his breathing.

If he squirmed down in the seat, maybe he'd find a better angle. He slipped forwards, knees on the ground, his ankles being cruelly bitten by the base of the chair. At least now his head was level with the tape on his wrists. If he could just twist back enough to reach the taut section between his wrist and the metal support...

"Nope. I don't think so, my friend."

Kris stared up through tears of pain and exertion at Rafferty.

"If you ain't gonna play ball, I reckon I'll need to truss you up good and proper."

Kris felt himself being lifted back into the seat from behind. An arm reached over his shoulder to grab the roll of parcel tape from the desk. Behind him, the bigger man cursed as he tried to get a fingernail under the edge of the tape; a squeak descending in pitch to a howl as a length was paid out, before a wide band pulled Kris's forehead back, securing him once more to the back of the chair. The tape spool, still attached, swung behind the seat-back, and tapped patiently on the leather.

The terror-stricken student ignored the tape yanking at his hair. He strained his neck and pushed back with his left shoulder, willing his head to turn. He could feel the adhesive across his forehead begin

223

to slip as the sweat that slicked his brow started to loosen the glue. And still the layers binding his head to the chair back would not fully give way. He could hear the follicles being plucked from his scalp, now rooted in the tape, not his flesh, but he had no perception of pain... yet.

Levering himself left and right, using his shoulders for power, the back of his head as a fulcrum, he was making headway. Degree by degree, he was regaining the ability to turn his face. If he could push his cheek into the headrest, get his upper arm between the chair back and the rest of his body, he could force his way down and under the tape.

Simultaneously, Kris clenched and relaxed his fists, forcing his fingers back under the heels of his palms, stretching and relaxing the bands of tape that held his wrists to the arms of the chair. He had no hope of breaking the tape, but if he could just stretch it, maybe fatigue it, maybe roll it over or find a weakness, he could free his hands. He froze as the two men came back into the room. Rafferty carried a brown canvas bag with stitched leather handles and a zip that had long since ceased to close. Kris's eyes peeled wide as he strained to look to the doorway. He felt the tendons of his face twinge as he forced his eyeballs sideways; patches of his vision darkened as the strain on his retina became unbearable. At the very periphery of his field of view, Kris was sure he recognised his father's tool-bag.

He let his gaze flick forward, but not for long. He could not direct his attention away from the bag while he tried to remember the contents: a few underused items, mole grips, a cheap screwdriver with the point chipped, pliers, a small carpentry hammer, an incomplete set of blunted drill bits, some loose tacks and screws.

Forcing his gaze forwards, a dull ache in his eyes from holding them in such an unnatural position began to throb with his already racing pulse.

Rafferty dropped the bag to the floor. It landed heavily. Something solidly metallic clattered lower still, dragging out the sound in the otherwise silent room. Only the cooling fan of the PC hummed tunelessly, unperturbed.

The big man squatted on the opposite side of the bag to Kris and peeled the handles backwards, relishing the moment of revelation, delaying his satisfaction to heighten the eventual pleasure all the more. "Do you read the bible, kid?" He asked without looking.

Kris tried to shake his head, but the tape only afforded him a quiver of movement. Bible-bashers and God-botherers were people looking for someone else to blame, somewhere to point when it all went wrong. At least, that's what he'd always said. He never actually believed the Good Book might be his salvation.

"Leviticus 24, 19. 'And if a man cause a blemish in his neighbour; as he has done, let it be done to him. An eye for an eye, a tooth for a tooth.'" Johnson extracted a hammer from the bag. It was a toy in his massive hand as he hefted it, testing its weight. He laid it on the floor to one side, apparently rejected.

"Actually..." he continued, matter of fact. "It's a misunderstanding. It doesn't really mean tit-for-tat, nor nothin'." He pulled out an uneven rack of drill bits for detailed inspection. He turned the plastic holder slowly to check the points of each tool in turn.

Kris let out an involuntary whimper. The sound of his own broken voice unnatural in his ears.

"Something you want to say?" Johnson paused and glared hard, holding Kris's line of sight for a count of five. "No... it doesn't mean I have to do to you what you did to me." He laid the drill bits next to the hammer. "It means that what I do to you should be less than you did to me. The original text went more like 'an eye under an eye'. Did you know that?"

Kris shuddered. He could not shake his head, but his body was convulsing in its place.

"Ironic, really..." The big man mused. "It was originally intended to stop escalations... like... make sure the punishment doesn't exceed the crime, so there's no further pay-back..." He paused. "Kinda funny... now that it's been mistranslated... just one word different... all

kindsa people use it to justify all kindsa being crappy to each other...
totally not what was the original intent."

"Now. I ain't a vindictive man." Johnson retrieved the hammer
and the largest of the drill bits as he gained his feet. He grunted with
the apparent effort of lifting his own muscle mass. "But kid... you
messed me up. We've been pretty fair with you, and you do this to
me?"

He ran the blade end of the drill bit along the line of his jaw as he
stalked towards the immobilised boy. Kris hadn't thought his eyes
would open any further but as he stared and stared, the chewed metal
of the blunted drill end gripped his focus. He watched it bounce over
a torn flap of skin marking the insertion point of one of the hooks'
screw threads.

Outside in the garage, a soft voice whispered "Cassandra" in
Ross's ears as the Bluetooth connection to the office computer was
established, but he was already too far gone on a cocktail of beer,
whisky and exhaustion to notice. He grunted, rolled on his side and
settled into a fitful doze.

"So, how do we add this up? You stuck me, what, three times?
So... do I stick you... twice?" The giant bowed till his face was level
with Kris's, turned his hands palm up, the hammer in one, drill bit in
the other, and mimed a set of scales settling out. "Maybe just the
once?"

He turned to Rafferty. "Open his mouth."

"Hey, c'mon man. Enough's enough."

"I said, open his mouth!" He squealed the last word, control
evaporating in the face of Rafferty's reluctance.

Kris turned his head left and right as he tried to evade the smaller
man's grasp on his chin. He clamped his teeth shut and ground the
molars together.

"Kid. If I'm prepared to knock out your teeth, it don't make no
difference to me if I gotta go through some flesh first. Like I said,

you stuck me. I can stick you and take your teeth at the same time. I'm at peace with my God for that."

Kris felt his intestines first freeze, then liquefy as he tried to lower his bottom jaw. His lips remained sealed.

Rafferty saw his chance and looped a band of the packing tape over the boy's jaw from behind. He pulled hard, down and back, and Kris's lips parted like a surgical wound. He could feel the edges of his mouth peeling away from each other, lightly gummed with the salt left over from the tracks of his earlier tears.

The tape was sealed unforgivingly behind the back of the chair. Kris heard his own jaw lock in place. The unnatural tension in the muscles to either side of his head opened his ears; the pressure equalized with a gentle pop that only he heard.

"Listen, kid." Rafferty came round the chair to face him. "Nobody wants to do this. Tell us. Who else knows about this software?"

Kris felt a trickle of his own saliva escape his mouth and run down his chin. He was powerless to catch it. He tried to nod, but couldn't move. He tried to beg, but his voice was a guttural collection of indistinct vowel sounds. He tried to stretch his fingers out in supplication, but neither man was watching his hands.

Rafferty leaned closer. Kris tasted his foul breath, the stench of festering meat and cheap, bitter coffee. The odour dissolved in the moisture of Kris's mouth until he felt that if he swallowed, he would be permanently infected with a reminder of this man, ever present, overpowering every other taste he would ever experience.

Rafferty moved his head to inspect Kris's face. He drank in every detail, savouring the terror that seeped from every pore. It was visible, refracted and magnified in every drop of sweat. It was audible, soughing on every panicked breath rasping over the boy's throat. He could smell it, even taste it, as he edged closer, close enough to plant a rapist's kiss on the youngster's brutalized lips.

He held his position. Kris held his breath.

Rafferty snapped out of his momentary rapture and spun on his heel to walk to the door where he knelt down by the bag, his back to Johnson and the boy. "Listen." Kris's jaw was so out of its natural alignment that it dulled his hearing. The man's voice sounded further away than it actually was. "Don't break his teeth." It sounded almost pitying. Kris desperately tried to nod his agreement.

"Why... the... fuck... not?" Johnson spaced out the words between each heaving breath. His shoulders pumped up and down, driven along with his chest by the adrenaline rushing through his system.

"Because," Rafferty stood, turned and held out the rusted mole-grips. "If we pull them out whole, we can get a silver dollar for each one we put under the pillow."

Johnson advanced on the restrained figure below him. "Tell you what. Just let me give it a try. I'll pay you a dollar myself."

He rested the tip of the drill bit against the gum-line of one of Kris's upper incisors and pushed it into place. Kris felt the gum snick open. He darted his tongue up to the twisted edge of the tool piece. It felt a hundred times its size in the violated sanctuary of his mouth; the taste of fresh blood indistinguishable from the steel of the makeshift chisel.

Blurred, in the corner of his eye, Kris could see Rafferty shrug and turn away. The man blocking most of his field of view held the hammer halfway along its shaft and placed the head against the blunt end of the drill. He adjusted and settled his grip, twisting his wrist and elbow to find a comfortable swing.

Kris lifted his eyes to Johnson's once more, pleading, begging.

The giant man blinked once as he met Kris's stare and lifted the hammer to try a tentative aiming stroke, testing his delivery. The jolt of the light tap jarred along his jawline, repercussions throbbing out through his skull, waves in a pond, fading but not quite dying away. Last to react were the minute bones of Kris's ear, jangling to a nauseating standstill.

Johnson rested the little finger of his left hand across the boy's upper lip, ensuring the relative position of the drill bit would not be shifted, and lifted the hammer high behind his head. It paused in its arc, briefly outlined against a dapple of morning sunlight, before changing direction.

# Chapter 32

The first crack melded into Ross's alcohol-fuelled dreams; his subconscious seamlessly blending the snapping of a twig under his stumbling feet into his nightmare scramble through dense woodland. His mind assimilated the available sensory information to populate an ever more vivid landscape with detail: the headphones clamped across his head became branches grabbing at his hair; the musty scent of the potato sacks evoked the decay of a forest, lumber rotting and returning to the earth; his legs, restrained by the sleeping bag, tried to run, dodge and weave, and told his imagination that the surrounding air was thickening to tar.

As he approached wakefulness, his twitching became ever more frantic. Panic flung his eyes open. His gasped in a breath and held it. He was aware of his chest deflating as he exhaled. His breath condensed to steam in the reluctant watery light that filtered through the barely translucent garage window.

The second crack hammered through Ross's ears, straight into his spinal column. He jerked bolt upright.

A viscous gurgle enveloped him; the gagging, retching sound was everywhere.

He twisted left then right to find the source of the noise, and felt the earpieces shift. He flipped one side of the headphones off his head. The volume abated and shifted.

"That's enough." A distinctly American accent spoke.

The boy unzipped his sleeping bag and freed his legs. He stretched to unknot his back, and allowed the pent-up hangover free run of his head. Squeezing his eyes shut against the pain, he could hear the voice continue. "I said that's enough."

Ross didn't recognise the track but it could have been Pink Floyd, probably post-Roger Waters, trying a bit too hard to be an eccentrically malaised middle class. He pulled on his boots and stuffed the still-warm sleeping bag into his rucksack. "OK... get it over with." He advised himself. "Deep breath." Leaving his gear behind, he eased himself out of the garage and around the nose of the battered Ford. Artificial light spilled out through the office window. That and the damaged car reminded Ross that Kris was getting a well-deserved roasting. Might as well enjoy the show while he could; he'd be on the receiving end himself soon enough.

Placing his feet deliberately, he sidled his back along the cottage wall. Pivoting around his shoulder, he squinted around the window frame. Two figures standing and one seated, head tipped back. Both the men on their feet were intently focused on the man in the chair. Tied to the chair!

Ross flattened himself back against the wall.

He twisted round and slid sideways to risk another look. The bigger of the two men, and he was significantly bigger, was bending down to their captive. Kris! It was Kris in the chair! A rivulet of blood spilled over his chin and down onto his naked chest, tracking along bands of tape, darkening the edge.

The smaller man opened his mouth to speak. Ross jumped as he heard the words directly in his ear... as though the window protecting him from the scene beyond had evaporated. "Johnson! Troy! Are you listening to me? I said enough!"

The bigger of the two jerked as he became aware of the speaker's presence. He stood upright and seemed to grow even larger.

"That's better. We might still need this piece of shit to help us find this Ross guy."

He recoiled at his name and dropped to his knees in the dirt beneath the window. The chill damp of the earth soaked into his jeans.

The big man let the hammer drop to the ground and reached behind Kris to rip the tape from the head rest. Outside, beneath the window sill, Ross couldn't help but put images to the sound: a stab to the torso and a slicing of flesh.

"OK, happy now?" Rafferty kept his eyes on Kris, but spoke to Johnson in an exasperated singsong voice.

"Yeah..."

Kris pitched forward as far as his remaining bindings would allow. He spat blood and shards of enamel into his lap. His tongue couldn't be held back from probing the splinter of tooth still wedged in the torn gum. Every breath wheezed across the exposed nerve, drawing a fresh scrape of pain that scrawled along his jaw, into his temples, and accumulated behind his eyes.

"Glad to hear it. But..." Rafferty squatted in front of the boy, ducking to catch his gaze. "It still doesn't get us closer to finding the other one."

He lifted the boy's face by its chin, stared and let it drop. Kris's head lolled drunkenly.

"I mean... this place is butt-fuck Idaho... there's every chance he's still in that little piss-pot of a village."

"Ya reckon?" Johnson seemed to have calmed down.

Rafferty stood. "If he's gone, he's gone... but I got a gut feeling he's not too far away."

Now he put a finger to the bigger man's jaw, and turned the head, inspecting the damage Kris had inflicted. "Yeah... Like the whole town's half the size of that shopping mall on Gateway... It's worth a try."

"Right. Let's get on it."

231

"No... I'll go. You stay here, just in case he shows up. Maybe clean yourself up a bit." Rafferty could see one of the punctures was pretty deep and still oozing a reasonable amount of blood. "Get a Band-Aid on that, or something. Then you're gonna work through that computer. Get some names and addresses... anything. Maybe his buddy did hightail it home. We'll track him down eventually."

Kris's whimper caught Rafferty's attention as he tucked the laptop under one arm. He glanced down at the limp student, then askance at Johnson. Maybe by the time he got back, there wouldn't be anyone left capable of answering questions.

"Cut him loose. He's coming with me. I need someone to make an ID. I'm gonna go find something I can use to make sure this one don't run off again."

Squatting with his back to the mildewed whitewash of the wall, Ross fought to keep his breathing shallow. His headphones were relaying what was going on in the office. Logically, they couldn't hear him, it was one-way communication, but the conversation was so clear in his ears, he felt as though he were an invisible presence in the room, having to dodge around the unseeing men to stay out of reach.

His body puckered when the older of the two Americans voiced his sense that their quarry probably wasn't far away. He turned hesitantly, side on to the wall ready to sprint; ancient spider webs and their captive insect carapaces hanging from the window sill caressed his scalp and tugged at his hair.

"Get some names and addresses... anything." Ross stopped dead, his breath frozen in his throat. The hard drive! A simple string search would turn up his full name, that's assuming Kris hadn't already told them. Once they had his name, they'd search Kris's email history... address book... everything. They'd get his home address, or maybe even his parents!

This couldn't be happening.

Maybe Kris had already given them everything. But if he had, why were they bothering to look in the village? Either Kris had kept his mouth shut, or they didn't believe him... or maybe there was something urgent about all this. Either way, he had to get his hands on the hard drive, if only to buy time.

The cottage door creaked open. The Audi unlocked by remote. Ross barely caught his balance, crouched on the balls of his feet, and knocked one side of the headphones away from his ear. He slithered down and flattened himself behind an upturned plastic trough. The door was out of site round the corner, but the nose of the car was visible. Someone crossing to the passenger side might glimpse his wide eyes and pale face.

One pair of footsteps striding across the driveway; another, more hesitant, uneven, feet dragging.

A single car door opened. Shuffling, grunting. A few words, but impossible to understand from Ross's position.

Engine started, door closed. The nasal whine of a car moving at high speed in reverse. A spit of gravel as the wheels changed direction on the loose surface. Gone.

Ross exhaled through pursed lips and gently pushed himself back to a crouch.

A metallic banging shook the air. He froze.

The thumping briefly accelerated, quietened then stopped to be replaced by drumming water as pipes rattled into life. Ross felt his bladder twitch in sympathy.

Sighting along the cottage wall, he watched steam begin to percolate from an extractor fan outlet. It gathered beneath the roof overhang before overflowing upwards to dissipate into the chill air.

"Nobody knows the trouble I've seen..." A mellifluous baritone luxuriated from the shower, punctuated by gasps of pain. Johnson was cleaning his injuries, soapy water nipping at the wounds. "Nobody knows my sorrow..."

This was Ross's chance.

He risked raising his head below the windowsill and realised he'd be much less visible looking from the side. He inched his hands up the wall as he stood, and sidled across until he could see into the office.

Nobody.

233

The PC monitor scintillated bands of colour as the algorithm executed. A stack of text ratcheted up one side of the display.

This was his only chance. With one American gone, the other singing in the shower, he could sneak in, grab the hard-drive and be out in a minute. Seconds later, he'd be lost in the hillside ferns.

Another glance into the office; the door stood ajar. It was now or never. The more he hesitated, the less time he'd have to get in, out and away. He edged round the corner of the building, expecting the growl of the returning Audi any second. Or worse, that the song might end as the water stopped flowing.

"Nobody knows but Jesus..."

The bathroom was between the open cottage door and the office. Ross would need to get past it... twice... before the big man's ablutions were complete. He removed his headphones and folded them into his jacket pocket.

Easing his body across the threshold, he could see the bathroom door was closed. Even out here in the middle of nowhere, while allegedly on guard, the American had put prudish conservatism before duty and had sought privacy. Nevertheless, Ross laid one foot timidly onto the floor, then the other, and gently willed himself towards the office. Stepping round the detritus ejected from the hall cupboard, and the pool of blood dried into the floor, he felt his centre of balance wobble out of reach. Rotating on one foot, his other leg swung out behind. One arm up, and one down, he swayed in a ballet choreographed in equal parts of indecision, gravity and inertia. He caught the cupboard door jamb on rigid fingers and held his breath.

"I have my trials here below... Ohhhhhhhhhh yessssssss, Loooooooord..."

Ross didn't know the song, but there was only one more chorus to go. With his eyes on the bathroom, his unbidden fingers spidered over the wood until he could reliably push back and lower his elevated foot.

He glanced back at the cottage door. The office was closer. He was past half way.

234

From the entrance to the office, Ross could pick out speckles of velvet red against the frosted white of the desktop. White shrapnel dotted here and there; one fragment dead-centre in a circle of blood like the bullseye in a target.

A sudden metallic thumping behind catapulted Ross through the door and under the desk: the one place in the room he couldn't be seen from outside.

"Ohhhhh, glory, Hallelujaaaaah."

The last syllable dragged on as the water dripped to a halt. Ross thought it would never end, and prayed that he'd be right.

Silence.

Only the computer fan, blowing heated air across the sweat on Ross's brow, made a sound. It was almost soothing... shhh, shhh... it'll be OK. He sucked a breath of roasted dust. Balled up under the desk, his face was wedged against the back of the PC.

The shower curtain rattled along its pole.

Ross opened his eyes. The muddle of cables, power and peripherals, were directly under his nose. He tried to twist to see under the desk and along the hallway. The chrome frame of the chair blocked his view.

He turned back to the cabling. There were two finger-thick power cables: one for power into the computer, a second for power out, feeding the monitor. Without thinking, he flicked the master power switch. The fan wheezed to a halt; the haze of light from the monitor permeating the desk winked out.

All the time, straining to hear any sound from the bathroom, Ross edged out from under the desk and jerked the power cable out of the screen. He shot back into hiding as a pair of feet squeaked from the tub onto the bathroom linoleum. His heart thundered against his ribcage. He darted one arm back above the desk and grabbed the external hard-drive. Something he could hold in one hand, slip into his pocket... something so seemingly benign... and yet it held his life in the balance.

The Leatherman bounced off the hard-drive in his jacket pocket. He gripped it to prevent it rattling on the casing. It felt reassuringly solid in his hand, but with about an inch of a blade, there was no way he could fight his way free with that. However, it might buy him enough time to make a run for it.

He laid the monitor power cable on the floor and sawed at the junction where it disappeared into the plug. The plastic outer sheath split quickly exposing the blue, brown and yellow insulated wires within. Clasping the blade away, he unfolded the miniature scissors. The click was louder and more distant than expected. He stopped dead. The bathroom door had been unlocked.

A pair of feet slopped towards the kitchen. The fridge door was pulled open; the clink of a bottle.

Ross pried one of blades between two of the wires and snipped. The second and third were easier to access, but as the plug came loose, it bounced to the floor. The noise was unbearably loud to Ross's ears.

Breathing faster, the boy forced the tool down between the exposed wires to cut a slice into the outer cover. Cutting one, two then three inches, he guessed he would have enough length of wire to grip and separate them. He pulled with as much force as he could muster in the confines under the desk. The outer sheath stretched and split. Back to the little clippers, he stripped the plastic off to reveal a thumb's width of copper.

Drawers were being opened in the miniature kitchen; cutlery rattling as the man rummaged around. The click of a bottle top bouncing across the room, gulping, and a long, grateful sigh.

Not daring to waste time trying to close and open the various blades for something more appropriate, Ross used the flat of the scissors to lever the plastic pedestal away from the metal base on one side of the chair. He forced the exposed live wire into the gap and let the plastic snap back into place, gripping the copper. He repeated the action with the neutral wire on the opposite side of the chair.

He desperately tried to picture the chair construction. He could only see the base from where he was, and now that the giant man was out of the bathroom, he couldn't risk checking. If it was one piece, what he was planning would make a loud bang, maybe a bit of smoke. It definitely would not give him the chance to escape.

But, if it was two pieces...

He edged back behind the PC and waited, finger on the power switch.

The dripping bulk of Johnson, towel around his waist, bottle in hand sloped towards the office. Breaking into song, his voice did not sound quite so rich without the hard surfaces of the bathroom providing a bit of reverb.

"Nobody knows..." He paused. He cleared his throat.

"Nobody knows the trouble I've seen, Nobody knows my sorrow, Nobody knows the trouble I've seen, Glory, Hallelujah." He shuffled a gentle two-step in time with the music.

Ross could see his feet perform a lazy, rhythmic swing as he reached the doorway.

"Sometimes I'm up, sometimes..." He pulled out the office chair. Ross clenched his fists as he watched the wires pull taut, resist and hold.

"I'm down, oh, yes Lord..." Johnson sat heavily on the word 'down', and giggled the rest of the line, appreciating his own timing.

"Sometimes I'm almost..." He wedged himself back into the chair.

"To the ground..." Ross flicked the switch. Grounded indeed.

Ross scrambled backwards, rolled and staggered into a run before he was fully clear; creased his skull against the jarringly solid edge of the table. Johnson kicked out, burying his foot in the small of the boy's back, punting him onto all fours.

Yelling without words, just sheer animal fright, Ross spun and skittered across the room on toes and fingertips. He careered into the wall, and cowered down where the floor met the skirting, arms wrapped around his head. He fended off a barrage of blows that never came.

Wheezing great sobs of air, reflexively making the most of breathing while he still could: "No... I didn't mean to..." He paused. Nothing. He risked lowering his arms, raised his head.

The man-monster was still locked firmly in the chair, quaking, eyes distended in apoplectic rage.

Ross tentatively placed a hand on the floor to his side, ready to push himself into a sprinter's start. He narrowed his eyes and focussed. The big man was crying; tears welling at the corner of one bulging eye.

Curiosity overcoming caution, Ross slithered his back up the wall till he was on his feet and began to edge round the perimeter of the room towards the door, tensed for flight. As he sidled round the table, Johnson remained immobile. He didn't track Ross's path; even the shudders that had wracked the huge body were suddenly stilled.

In the cloying silence, a metronome of droplets tapping to the floor below the chair counted down the time; seconds, minutes or hours... Ross couldn't be sure. He risked a glance and saw a pool of urine gathering between the bare feet, mapping the contours of the floor, seeking escape in the gaps between the boards.

"Happens to the best of us, mate..." Ross breathed, strengthened by the human weakness in this inhuman being.

Ross drew level with the desk, his hand crept out. He snatched backwards as his fingers brushed the cold glass surface. He gasped and froze.

Stealing through his slack mouth, lingering there on his throat with the last panicked breath, thickening, congealing and sticking to his teeth, a scent he was sure he knew well but which was so incongruent with his current situation, he just couldn't place it.

He did know.

Every Saturday morning from earliest memory, his mum... she'd... she'd made a fry-up for her growing lad: egg, beans, black-pudding, and Ross's favourite... crispy bacon.

He leaned in, taking another hesitant sniff, vowing a vegan life-style from that moment forth. There was something else... again... his mother sprang to mind; her hair being singed between the blades of a cheap set of curling tongs. By lowering his head, Ross glimpsed a sprite flitting on the edge of the desk light; a wisp of smoke trickling upwards from the oversized hand welded to the chromed steel of the chair arm.

Johnson was dead.

Ross stared in revulsion. He wasn't a killer, despite the evidence. His eyes were drawn to the ragged punctures on the muscled jaw. The edges of the wounds were already cauterised, sealed and curled like the skin of a roasted chicken. He gagged and turned his face into his own shoulder to cover his nose.

This couldn't be.

It couldn't.

He wasn't a killer. It wasn't in his nature.

It shouldn't have happened.

The PC power output was 240 volts, 13 amps maximum. It should have temporarily paralysed, yes. It would have hurt like hell, yes. But kill? No way.

But there sat the proof. Jammed tight between the arms of the chair, towel wrapped around his waist, still dripping wet from his shower. OK, the moisture probably made the shock more effective, conducted easily from the metal frame of the chair to the body, distributed the charge... but even so...

Johnson's heart, weakened by years of steroid abuse, maddened by the jolts of current, short-circuited into a final, fluttering seizure, had convulsed once, twice, and ceased to beat.

Ross suddenly noticed his hand reaching out in its own morbid fascination to touch the man's face. He stopped himself just in time. If there was smoke, there was fire... or at least, electricity. Ross reached under the desk to pull the main power from the PC. He threw the connector as far away as the cable would allow. It bounced and flicked, a viper in its death throws, its poison spent.

Turning back to face his victim... no he couldn't think like that... this brute who... no... it was self-defence... Ross inched his hand out to lower the eyelids. It wasn't an act of respect, it was one of self-preservation. There was no way he could function with those eyes carving the word 'KILLER' into his flesh.

The tear tracks were still fresh on the cheek, even still flowing. He'd heard that hair and nails seem to grow after death, but that's just an illusion. It's the flesh retreating. But tears? Had this man's lifetime of callous indifference finally overtaken him? Was this a deathbed redemption? Was he crying now all the tears he should already have shed, a last-chance penitence?

Ross felt his own eyes welling, not for the death he had brought about, but for his own sanctity, his lost innocence, for his hollow, broken future.

His fingers slithered over the eyelids and the cheeks on a greasy film of fluid; tears are not this viscous. He steeled and held his breath, blinked away his own tears and peered deeply into Johnson's furious left eye. Distorted by the convex of the pupil, reflected in miniature, was the face of Ross himself, tiny and alone in a hostile world.

There was no breath on his cheek as he dragged his gaze across to the right eye, an eye that was already fading; not losing colour, not fading to grey, but retreating, surrendering vitality as the body surrendered its heat.

Ross moved closer still. The drip-drip from below the chair slowing to a halt as he willed himself to look.

The eyeball had ruptured, its vitreous humour slowly draining, overflowing the socket, to glisten on the cooling flesh.

Repelled by the touch of his own finger, now slicked with fluid, Ross scraped his hand down his jeans, stumbling to the door. He bounced between the walls of the hallway, tripping over his own feet. Throwing himself over the threshold, he felt the bile rising in his throat.

Doubled over before he even came to a halt, Ross retched and convulsed, and hurled his stomach contents across the gravel of the drive. He spat strings of saliva, tried to pluck the glutinous remnants from his lip and tongue. Tasting the salt of Johnson's body fluid on his fingertips, his gut wrenched again; he heaved as though taking a body-punch and vomited afresh.

"Ah... and you must be Ross."

Ross tipped his head back, and through flooded eyes, could make out two figures standing next to a large black estate car. Rapidly blinking, he fought his spasming stomach muscles to stand upright.

"We've been looking for you, haven't we?" The speaker turned to his companion.

"Ross! Get out of here!" That was Kris, for sure... but there was a rupture in his voice.

There was a slap, and a muted whimper. "Oh hush now..." It was clear this was an older man, American accent... vocal chords weighed down by years of smoke. This wasn't good.

Ross crushed his eyes shut to clear his vision.

There was Kris, being led around like a dancing monkey by a chain through the perforations of his ear. At the other end of the leash, the organ grinder.

"Your friend here... he's been pretty helpful... but you and me need to have a little chat now, kid." The man grinned. He tipped his head to one side and looked at Kris. "Now you gotta stay put a while."

His captor slowly wound the chain around his fingers, settling the links into place. He bunched a fist. Kris flinched back, cowering, keening. For the first time, Ross noticed the shattered teeth, outlined by the darkness of Kris's mouth.

Sniggering, Rafferty pulled his hand out of the chain, and tied a loop through the remaining ball of metalwork. He flicked the handle of the Audi, threw the knotted end of the tether into the car, and slammed the door. He made a show of patting his pockets, and gleefully produced the key remote. The cheery double beep as the central locking activated reverberated around the glen and skimmed off across the heather.

The hazard warning lights flashed.

# Chapter 33

"So." Rafferty began. He advanced on Ross.

"You've been a busy little boy, haven't you?" Ross backed up a step.

"Truth be told, son." Rafferty continued. "So's your bro here..." He tipped his head back towards where he knew Kris was still shackled to the car; he didn't look round.

"You know he was poking your girl, huh?" Ross didn't reply. He felt the Fiesta at his back. The beaten-up little car rocked on its jack, its front wheel still lying in the dirt after the boys had abandoned trying to pull the wing back into shape.

He had nowhere else to go.

Rafferty walked slowly at Ross. He was as casual as if he were browsing a store. He paused. "Johnson!" He licked his tea-coloured teeth in anticipation. "Johnson... get your ass out here. Game on!"

There was no response. Rafferty cocked his head, and held Ross's stare. "Troy! Are you beatin' your meat? Get out here and..."

"He's dead." Ross's words stumbled from mouth... "He's dead."

Rafferty's grin remained. "I don't think so... but nice try." He placed his knuckles on his hips, and appraised the boy; a tradesman sizing up a job.

"Hell with it... you're nothing I can't handle myself. I'll maybe save him a piece... but then again... maybe not."

Ross was edging along the little Ford, creeping his fingers across the paintwork, trying to feel to the end of the car without taking his eyes off Rafferty. If he could find the corner, he could find escape. He was no fighter. Mind you, he was no killer either, but there was a carcass smouldering in the office room that proved otherwise. No, he had no illusions. He'd only mastered one special move in Tekken, and even that was only any use up to about level 3. His real-life special move was to run like fuck and he was fully reliant on that working.

If he ran, he could definitely outstrip this guy.

If he ran, Kris would definitely die.

And what? Ross owed him nothing. He risked a glance at his one-time friend.

Kris was slumped by the side of the Audi, his head tipped to one side by the tension on the chain tugging at his ear. Defeated, vacant, hanging like a carcass on a rack. All that was left was to gut him and parcel up the meat into the different cuts. It was clear: inside, the boy was already dead; only his body had to catch up with his shattered mind.

Rafferty shuffled another step towards Ross, kicking his heel on the driveway, almost dancing.

Ross's fingers found the edge of the windscreen, only a bonnet-length till he could clear the car and run for it.

Rafferty feinted to his left, giggling. Ross inched the other way. His fingertips were achingly close to the makeshift antenna... about 3 feet of clothes hanger, pinched and twisted to jam into the stub of the original factory unit, snapped off as the car sat roadside back in Glasgow.

With a skid of gravel, one foot sliding back under his lunge, Rafferty sprang forward. The slip bought Ross a vital reprieve; he spun away as the bigger man pummelled into the side of the Fiesta. It wobbled uncertainly, barely balanced, creaked and settled out.

Surprised by the boy's turn, Rafferty made a grab for his hair. He missed but latched onto Ross's shoulder, pivoting him on the spot.

Rotating on his heel, fighting for freedom from the grip, the boy whipped around, flailing for balance; the coat-hanger aerial was in his hand. It lashed Rafferty's face, opening a gash across one eye. His cheek split as the hook end of the metal rod snagged on the sagging flesh and ripped open a ragged track. The bridge of his nose parted, a neat wedge of gristle excised and left hanging on the impromptu crop in Ross's hand.

Rafferty howled, bestial rage and slicing pain fought for control of his voice. Semi-blinded, instinctively he snatched Ross's wrist out of the air and slammed it back against the car bonnet. The tendons in Ross's hand jerked his fingers open. The metal whip skittered away across the paintwork.

The American's free hand gripped the boy's throat and half-lifted, half-threw his frame into the air. Advancing one step, he used his inside leg to sweep Ross's ankles up and away. Rafferty punched his quarry down into the ground. If his grip hadn't been blocking Ross's throat, the impact would have driven all the wind out of the boy's chest. His vision shuddered as his head pounded into the driveway.

Rafferty snapped upright. He stomped his foot into Ross's throat before his quarry could so much as roll away. With both hands fighting to push at the sole of the shoe, Ross was as effectively restrained as Kris was. He fought to get his arms under his hands, just take the pressure off his windpipe, or even turn the shoe so its edge wasn't cutting into his throat...

The pressure eased. Ross trapped a breath, forced himself to swallow. The agony in his throat felt like he was choking down a broken bottle.

Silhouetted against the sky, Ross could just make out the man drag an arm across his face to clear the blood.

"Fuck you, you little shit!" Rafferty hawked a lump of tarry phlegm from the back of his throat and spat full into Ross's face. He felt it land, warm and shuddering, sticking to his forehead, stringing into his hair. He twisted, revolted, hoping to dislodge the hideous offering. It stuck fast.

Rafferty reached into his jacket pocket. His thumb was already on the release switch of the flick-knife as it re-emerged. It snicked open, slicing a blade shaped hole in the sky above Ross. At four inches long, the cutting edge occupied the whole field of Ross's vision.

Rafferty fought to master his choleric rage. He slowed his breathing, rotated his shoulders. He cricked his head left and right. "You little shit..." He repeated. "I'm gonna fuckin' gut you like a fish... nice and slow so we can both enjoy it."

He rolled the knife between his finger and thumb.

"It could take a couple of hours... maybe more..."

He let his gaze wander down the boy's body, stopping at his groin. "Or maybe you wanna know what it's like to be a woman, huh?" Ross pushed harder at the foot on his throat. "Yeah..." Rafferty barked a laugh. "Then maybe you'll know what your girl saw in your buddy back there!"

Rafferty's glare snapped back. Ross fought to return the stare, but snatched a glance past the man's shoulder. The American glimpsed a movement to his side and spun, his foot sliding off Ross's throat. He whipped his knife-hand out and back.

Ross rolled away; an explosion of air above him, an unforgiving clunk.

With his face buried in the gravel, one noise after another measured out in unnatural regularity.

A metallic slap, and the crumple of a body folding to the ground.

A shudder of a something far more solid landing flat, inches from his head.

Another body disassembled itself onto the earth.

And silence.

As his ears strained for more... a vague hiss and bubble, rhythmic, followed by a tap-tap, and a sigh. It repeated, slowing, fading.

Ross gathered his head and pushed himself up on his elbows.

Rafferty was down, the blood pooling under one temple was already staining the gravel rust brown.

A concrete slab, muddied and scattering nocturnal insects; obviously recently turned over.

246

And Kris. Ross dragged himself commando-style to the fallen boy. The flick-knife was buried to its hilt below the ribs, angled upwards. Blood sputtered and boiled around the blade. The handle tap-tapped on the earth, twitching twice with each weakening heartbeat.

Ross pulled himself to Kris's side. He reached out to touch the knife, but held back. He wouldn't know what to do anyway. He eased himself under Kris's shoulders and cradled the boy's head in his lap. Kris rolled into Ross's thigh.

The tattered remnants of an ear, ripped down the piercings; the regular holes where the stretchers had been... a cross between a shark bite and the edge of a sheet of paper, torn from a note pad. The centre remained attached to Kris's skull, draped with flaps and loose meat; it looked like some odd little bracket fungus, draining the life out of its host tree. Blood seeped from Kris's head into Ross's shirt, just gently arriving there, in contrast to the pulsating flow from the knife wound.

He reluctantly turned to the Audi. There, threaded on the chain, were the wooden spacers, previously mounted in Kris's ear. Remnants of lifeless gristle still adhered to the earrings. A few daubs of blood marked a bounce against the paintwork.

Ross looked back to Kris.

Livid lines in the skin signified where the ear had been stretched to the point of rupture. The flesh around each hole must have given way one after the other, opening like buttons popping on a shirt; Kris had gained his freedom piecemeal, and yet had not cried out.

A noise from Rafferty; the man's hand sliding down the car door. He'd landed and rolled, head under the vehicle, like he was simply looking for lost change.

Kris was pale... a blue-yellow that gave his face a greasy look. The handle quivered in his side as he began to shake.

Ross reached for the knife but stopped again. Part of him wanted to pull it out, but the foaming blood warned of a punctured lung... it was likely only the hilt that was stopping Kris from bleeding out.

Kris grimaced and gripped Ross's shirt as a fresh wave of agony rippled from the wound and out across his body. He whispered, fighting for a breath. "Ross... " There was a dribble of blood on his lip.

"Ross... I want you to..." His head sank while he gathered another breath... perhaps he really was working on one lung. He was definitely labouring. "Ross... please..." His eyes were begging.

"It's OK... it's OK... you're going to be OK..."

"No... Just do one thing for me..." Kris hissed.

Ross felt tears well in his eyes, and his throat caught. "Listen, you bastard. You are not going to die on me... not here... not like this..."

Kris opened an eye. Ross leaned closer.

"It's not that." He wheezed. "Just... give that fucker a good kick in the balls for me."

Ross eased Kris off his lap. He stood and walked away.

"Ross... Ross... where the fuck are you going? Don't leave me here like..." He gasped again. "Where are you going?"

Ross turned and scuffed the ground with his boot. "I'm taking a run up..." He took aim and began his approach.

Was there a hint of a groan from Rafferty when his testicles were redistributed? Maybe. Or it could have simply been air being dislodged with the force of the impact.

Ross stepped back out of reach just in case and surveyed the scene. The guy in the office was definitely dead, but Ross didn't want to go check the one here on the driveway. Although... he looked innocuous enough... just lying there half-under the car like he was helping the boys finish bodging the crash damage enough to limp back to Glasgow. It gave Ross an idea to make sure. He remembered seeing the warning on the jack when they lifted the car, something about the risk of working under a vehicle.

Could he pull the support out? It would definitely trap the American, but there was a risk he'd get trapped himself. Maybe a rope?

In the end, he settled for rocking the Fiesta back and forth until the jack finally toppled; it took a surprising degree of movement to overbalance.

At the critical moment, the car seemed to hang indecisively before sliding sideways and down.

A drawn-out crunch twisted Ross's head away and screwed his eyes shut. He leaned on the paintwork, pushing and willing the weight downwards.

The car ratcheted lower as successive structures of the skull withheld before surrender; the cartilage of the nose, the orbit of the eye, the cheekbone. A mechanical grind and click signified a tooth giving way; a viscous pop as the jaw decoupled, dislocated then collapsed.

Every sound was metallically amplified by the hollow panelling of the vehicle, transmitted up through the heels of Ross's hands, conducted via arm and spine, to resonate around his cranium as though he himself were gnawing on the bone, marrow and gristle that was being methodically compacted beneath the Fiesta. He could not pull his hands from the car until there was certainty, until all sound and motion was stilled.

Finally, the fissure, initiated by Kris's paving slab, blossomed open; the fractured sections of the parietal bone shifted, held and then collapsed with a noise like a plastic drinks bottle being stamped on. The sound spread out across the fields leaving only silence in its wake.

Even if this guy hadn't been dead when he hit the ground, he was now.

Ross's jaw fell open. He jerked upright, staring at his fingertips; one day, two bodies.

He stumbled backwards, trying to distance himself from his own hands. "Kris!"

Ross's focus shifted from his palms, where he could still feel the metallic chill of the car, between his fingers and down to the corpse. With the head out of sight, it was nothing more than a collection of stuffed clothing, the joints crooked at unnatural angles.

"Kris! Get up... We've got to get moving!"

He forced his head to turn, but his gaze lingered on Rafferty. "Kris... c'mon... get up."

Finally, Ross's eyes swivelled to Kris. He'd flopped over onto his back, staring into the distant steel grey of the sky. The beginnings of rain promised a downpour as droplets detonated on Kris's forehead, dashed against his cheeks, bounced off his unresponsive eyeballs.

The knife handle had ceased its twitching; darkened blood was being diluted by the gathering rain and washed to the ground, but was no longer being replaced by fresh outflow.

Kris's chest was still.

If he ever got to tell the story, he'd maybe come to believe it himself when he said he'd knelt at Kris's side, felt for a pulse, closed the boy's eyes. Truth was he just needed to be gone.

The two Americans were dead.

Kris was dead.

Ross jerked into autopilot action, and scrabbled at the Audi's door. His panicked hands couldn't gain purchase on the polished surface; his fingers tripped off the handle as it sprang away from his grasp twice... three times. The rattle of the chain, Kris's former shackle, still laden with bloody tissue and the wooden ear-spacers reminded him the door was locked.

Fumbling for the car keys in Rafferty's trousers took an effort of will that Ross hadn't been sure he could summon. He was sure he'd grabbed the man's slug of a penis through the pocket cloth. The boy felt the still-warm plastic of the key-fob and yanked his hand free as though scalded.

He ducked one arm back into the garage and grabbed his rucksack from behind the door, all the while watching Rafferty's corpse for signs of movement.

The reality of what had happened started to hit home. Ross snivelled and choked back on tears as he heard himself reassure Kris's lifeless body.

"On the way, mate... home soon... it'll be OK..."

Or maybe the words were for his own benefit... one part of his mind consoling and coaxing another. "Home soon... home..."

Sliding into the driver's seat, he glanced down and saw the laptop in the footwall. It was only then that he remembered the weight of the recovered hard-drive in his jacket pocket.

# Chapter 34

"Miranda!" Ross swerved as he tried to jam the brakes on, sound the horn and open the windows all at the same time. Hitting the wrong switch in the unfamiliar cockpit, he retracted the side mirrors instead.

The Audi mounted the kerb heavily just as Miranda was about to cross the road, laden down with her shoulder bag and newly purchased women's interest magazine... four quid for 300 pages... 70% advertising, 10% articles bemoaning commercial deforestation, 15% editorials claiming the reader is overweight, the remainder blaming men for women's body image problems.

She stopped abruptly, rocked back on her heels and regained composure quickly enough to start mouthing obscenities and throwing her hands in the air.

Ross flung his door open. One foot out of the car, half stood to yell across the windscreen. "Miranda! Get in the fucking car!"

"R.. R.. Ross? What the fuck? You could have killed me!" She pulled up, catching the look in Ross's eye. "So you're here as well? Are you and Kris having some kind of sick laugh at..."

"Miranda! Shut the fuck up and get in!" Ross as a kicked spaniel was the norm. Ross as a ratting terrier was an altogether unfamiliar concept.

Miranda yanked open the passenger door, threw her belongings onto the back seat and huffed herself into the car, rammed her seatbelt home and crossed her arms, shoulders hunched.

Ross stood on the throttle and the car leapt forwards, bouncing clumsily as it rocked off the pavement back onto the road. The tyres squealed in protest before the anti-skid kicked in. Ross put in far too much opposite lock, leaving the back end to fishtail twice before they careered off down the road. A handful of locals watched in slack-jawed silence; city-folk, definitely.

Miranda shot an arm out to brace against the dashboard; her other hand snatched at Ross's shoulder. "Ross! Calm it! What the fu... Watch it! Jesus Christ... you were about a foot off that tractor!"

He ignored her. Hunched hard over the steering wheel, throwing the car left and right round the bends in the narrow road, foot clamped down on the throttle, willing the pedal to sink through the floor, get them as far away as fast as possible. Their passage over cattle grids mutated from a rattle, to a buzz to a barely audible brief throb as the Audi gathered speed. A goodbye sign thanking them for driving carefully through the village zipped by unnoticed.

"Ross! Ross! You'll get us both killed! Please... " She willed her voice to relax. "Please, Ross... slow down."

He faded back to reality, seemed to become aware of a world other than the bonnet of the car and where it was aiming. He backed off, but they were still hurtling round the normally sedentary B-road.

"Ross... what the hell is going on? Who's car is this anyway?" She made a show of looking round to appraise the interior.

"Look. Miranda... this is bad shit. It's a whole pile of bad shit. I... " He didn't know where to start. "We just need to get away from here right now." His eyes were 50-50 between the road and the rear-view mirror.

"Miranda... I think... I... I might have... I... killed someone... maybe two..."

"What? That's not funny." She turned in the seat to stare him down; he was deadly serious. For the first time she spotted the swelling in his face, the tracks of blood on his shirt. "Did you have a crash or something? Was there an accident?"

Ross fixated on the road ahead; he'd slowed down a little, but was still determined to put as much distance between himself and Fanaidh Balaichen as possible, as quickly as possible. Tears were coursing down his face, gathering at his jaw line, to be shaken loose by the car jolting in and out of potholes in the unmaintained road.

"It's all fucked up, Miranda. I… I don't know. It's just all fucked up. What am I going to do?" His voice was cracking, warbling into higher and higher pitch, on the edge of breaking down altogether. He wrenched one hand off the wheel, ran the back of his wrist and forearm across his nose to wipe away the snot dribbling out over his top lip; in the same motion, he scraped the salt tears from his eye with the ball of his thumb. Grabbing the wheel again, his hand was now slick, he rubbed it twice down the thigh of his jeans; the fluid he'd removed from his face had already returned.

"Police. Talk to them. You have to… Accidents happen." She flinched as low hanging branches threatened to puncture the windscreen.

"It kind of wasn't really an accident. I sort of… look… it went too far." Unnatural pauses in his speech punctuated sobs, manoeuvres and close calls. "It was self-defence…" This was more for his benefit than Miranda's.

Ross couldn't get his mind to cope with the enormity of the events back at the cottage. It was as though some mechanism in his subconscious was parcelling up individual components, prioritising them and handing them back in chunks he could face individually.

"Are you…?" Miranda silenced. She swallowed. "Are you talking about Kris? What did you do?"

"No, I am not talking about Kris!" Ross screamed. "But…" A snap decision not to tell her Kris was dead… not yet. "But I might as well be. Thanks very fucking much!"

Now she knew: Ross knew. "That's got shit all to do with you." She retorted. "You and me... we're history. You know it. You can drop me off in the next town." She turned to stare out of the side window.

Ross fumed. She always did this, no matter what. Not matter what had transpired from the trivial to the terrible, she'd make a scene, pout, stomp off, and Ross would be left with his hand out like an organ-grinder's monkey, begging forgiveness for something he wasn't even aware he'd done, or even for something she'd done that would somehow be reconstructed to be his fault. It ends here.

"Listen! For once! Just listen!" She tightened in her seat and contrived to turn even further away from him. The confines of the car made it difficult, but she succeeded, as always.

"Miranda... it's not a question. It's a fucking order. You will listen!"

Rage bloomed in Ross as he sought the words he needed. Unbidden, his foot ground into the accelerator. The Audi kicked down a gear and lurched forward. He opened his mouth to speak, slammed it shut again, as the speedo crept past 70, 75, nudged 80.

"Ross! Slow down!"

The sinews of his neck strained against his clenching jaw as he willed the car on.

"Ross! Please! You're scaring me!"

90... 95... 100..

Both lurched forwards against their seatbelts as Ross stamped the brake pedal. The nose heavy car understeered into the corner, slithered left; into the next straight, charging on at Ross's command.

Two cars snatched past in the opposite direction. They barely registered in the boy's peripheral vision.

A third, far more obtrusive with its familiar two-tone white and orange livery, snapped Ross out of his mindless flight.

"Oh no... God no..." He breathed.

Miranda whipped round in her seat.

Ross glued his eyes to the mirror. "Oh fuck, no..." The brake lights of the police car were bright against the brooding darkness of the pine forest. Blue light sparkled briefly and was lost to a corner beyond the trees.

"Ross! Stop! You can tell them what happened!"

"For fuck's sake! One fucking police car in a hundred miles of here..." He wasn't ignoring Miranda; he just wasn't hearing her.

He yanked hard on the wheel as a corner sharpened to the right. The steering floated as the car skipped across the camber, momentarily losing traction.

A jolting left pressed both occupants hard against the turn. The straightening road slingshot them back across the cockpit.

Trees thrummed past the car, thinned and vanished. A siren howled somewhere on the road behind. Gravestones peered over a rising wall like voyeurs revelling in someone else's argument. The burial sites counted down from timeworn, almost blank sandstone, through the ages to modern granite and marble. Ross heard their chanting "Soon, soon, soon..." as the shout of the engine echoed back with the passing of each tombstone. Soon it would be his turn.

And he saw his chance.

The iron gate of the church yard stood open, the welcoming arms of a parent ready to comfort a sobbing child.

Miranda choked, torpedoing under the seat-belt as Ross braked.

If he could make the turn before he was in sight of the police car, he might find his sanctuary. Please, God...

As Ross prayed, the car kneeled forwards. Momentum bled off. 60... 50... 30...

Full left lock on the steering wheel; the Audi argued, then obeyed. Its tail end thrashed wildly, clipping the iron gate. The impact knocked the car straight, facing back towards the graveyard, out of sight of the road behind the churchyard wall. Ross killed the engine.

The bell-like toll of the impact continued to ring out inside the car, pulsing against their ears. It held, eking out the last of the note, blending with the rising scream of the approaching police siren.

"Down!" Ross grabbed the back of Miranda's head and forced her below the dashboard. He threw himself across her back.

257

The police car dopplered away into the distance. A leisurely creak from the rusted gate hinges bracketed the ensuing silence.

"Out! Now!"

The pair flung themselves out of the Audi. The lush scent of damp grass surrendered to the bitter incense of the roasted brake pads.

Ross half-crawled round the car, grabbed Miranda and yanked her to her feet. "C'mon!" He released her arm. "Shit, my bag!"

"Leave it!"

"I can't... if they find the car with my stuff in it... I'm fucked!" He threw Miranda's bag to the ground at her feet. Slinging the rucksack across his shoulders, he squatted and slipped the car keys behind the front tyre. Miranda raised her eyebrows. Ross glanced at her. "If the cops come back, they won't tie us to the car..."

The pair scuttled into the graveyard, Ross half-dragging Miranda. He slumped to the ground behind a mausoleum, his rucksack scraping down its eroded surface.

Miranda stood defiantly, but kept herself out of sight of the Audi and the road. "You fucking little shit! You could have killed me!" She balled her fists against her hips. "What the fuck is going?..." She snapped her mouth shut at Ross's stare, her shoulders heaving.

He drew a long delayed breath. "Listen... I... Fuck it..." He didn't know where or how to begin. "Just... give it a few minutes. If the cops don't come back this way..."

Miranda squatted in front of Ross, her hands clasped with her elbows on her knees. "Ross... Ross..." She forced herself to sound calm. "Look at me... Tell me what is going on."

# Chapter 35

He shrugged out of his rucksack and laid it across his outstretched legs. He explained; all of it... from the project, to the pub, to crashing Kris's car, to the cottage. Where had the Americans come from? No idea. No idea why. Just that he'd heard them working on Kris, and Kris giving them everything they wanted and more. He kept the student's death to himself for now; he didn't quite believe it yet... saying it out loud would make it true.

Miranda tried to interject, but Ross just kept talking. He didn't even pause when the subject of Kris and her came up... just kept talking. Words flowing past, streaming out like water from a breached damn; an initial leak giving way to a torrent as the first crack in the wall burst, surrendering the last futile resistance.

Ross was starting to shake. The adrenaline that had coursed through his body was turning sour, leaving a magnetic taste in his mouth.

"Ross!" Miranda nearly slapped him. "I can't believe you're saying this! If it's true you just killed a guy... what's got into you? What about Kris? You just left him behind!"

"He didn't make it either..." Ross watched Miranda for a reaction. "One of the Americans... he stabbed him... "

She rounded and glared at him.

"Honest!" Ross threw his hands up. "I'm sorry, truly. He's dead."

Miranda rocked on the balls of her feet, and placed a hand to the earth to steady herself.

It wasn't true. If she strained against her reluctant memory, she could still feel Kris's body on hers... in hers. He'd invited her to the cottage for more of the same, and she'd readily complied. This couldn't be some jealous revenge from Ross, could it? But as she swung towards disbelief, she could sense the truth in Ross's words. Kris was dead. In that moment, as she tried to remember his face, she couldn't see him; he faded to a featureless blank. The man that Kris had been no longer existed, not even in her mind. And yet, tangential details persisted: the vibrant colours of his tattoo, the scent of the expensive shampoo that he pretended he didn't use, his unwillingness to tune his guitar but persist in strumming the three chords he knew... but not his face.

Grief heaved Miranda between acceptance and denial; between guilt and absolution. As she fought to define an image of Kris, his loss pulled her into an echoing, dark cavity of shock. The further she tumbled into that cold void, the harder her mind pulled her back, tried to save her from accepting that he was gone. She almost convinced herself she hadn't had any more feelings for Kris than physical, and that was true... but right there... there crashed another wave of shame.

As the anguish pummelled at her afresh, her mind oscillated back and forth: belief, denial, acceptance, rejection... ever faster, till her consciousness became a conflict of vibrations. The harmonics would build until damped by reality, or until the structure of her perception shattered like a resonating wine glass.

Miranda stared into the earth, and on through its surface, until her gaze was pulled upwards by some external force.

Ross's eyes verified what he'd told her. She shuddered a breath in, and exhaled one long, steady sigh as her shoulders sagged. Turning her muddied hand, she stared at her palm for one, two, three seconds, and scraped the dirt off on the edge of the tomb.

"Listen…" Ross breathed. "The Americans are dead. Kris is dead. The cops don't have the resources to look closer… it's a done deal. We can get away…"

Miranda interrupted. "Ross… I don't know. You need to…" To what? Miranda's throat tightened, tears welled in her eyes, but not for Kris, only for herself, and a fresh wash of remorse seeped through her fragile internal defences.

They lapsed into silence, staring unfocussed into the ranks of tombstones. The monuments blurred and ran together like water colours as Ross's eyes misted over. He blinked the salt liquid away. "So that's their car…" Ross jerked his thumb over his shoulder. "And I don't know how long we've got it till someone reports it. We've got to get a long way from here while we still can." His voice faded with his hope. Only the breeze soughing through the sparse trees of the graveyard textured the stillness.

Ross waited for Miranda to respond, but broke the silence himself. "Listen. You can believe it or believe it not. I don't give a shit. If you want to walk from here back to Dumfries, be my guest. But I'm telling you… I'd be dead meat as well now. You too, I guess."

"What? What am I in…" Her words came from a long way distant.

"I'm guessing you were on your way to meet Kris?" Ross felt his throat close as he contemplated his ex and his ex-friend together. Miranda stammered a confirmation. He was beyond blaming her. "Right… So you'd be right in the middle of this… If the Yanks knew you were coming, there's a good chance they already knew who you are, and already passed that info on…"

Miranda's face blanched.

"They were working through the PC… they were reading emails, checking names and addresses… They had Kris's account… I think they had mine too…"

She opened and closed her mouth a couple of times, struggling for something to say in the face of the new Ross. His eyes remained

261

resolutely locked on hers. "We need to move. You drive. I need to check what the Yanks could have got... maybe they already reported me, Kris... even you..."

They inched towards the car, ears straining for the police siren... any traffic. Ross brushed his hand against the paintwork and felt the heat radiating off the engine. There was an awkward moment as they met at the front, both trying to take the same route round the other; the dance lasted a few steps before Ross grabbed Miranda by the shoulders and pushed her round him.

She turned the ignition. "It won't start!"

"It's an automatic... you need to have your foot on the brake!"

"Shit. I've never driven an auto before."

"Don't panic. Put it in drive... no... that's the indicators... that's the gear stick." He forcibly grabbed at an extra column switch behind the steering wheel. "Right... now just drive like normal... just brake and accelerator."

They made the U-turn and inched forward back onto the road; suddenly both were hanging forward in their seatbelts, the laptop and hard-drive flying out of Ross's grasp onto the floor between his legs.

"Tuck your left foot under the seat. You don't need to change gears." She'd instinctively gone for the clutch pedal, hitting the brake hard instead.

"Sorry... sorry... just... don't give me crap about my driving, OK?" She leaned forward over the wheel. The act of driving, something to do, anything, put Kris gratefully from her mind; mourning was lower priority than moving.

Ross didn't say a word, just retrieved the computer and continued booting it up.

"I saw that!" Miranda yelled. "You just rolled your eyes!"

He ignored her, and keyed in the password.

After an age, the disgustingly cheerful Windows wake up tone tinkled at the edge of hearing and the screen populated with icons.

Holding his foot off the floor to raise his knee, Ross's leg jittered up and down. Between that and the pitching of the car, he struggled to find the results file. Intermittently twisting in his seat to confirm the road behind was empty didn't help. Navigating through the hard-drive, his eyes stopped on an unfamiliar folder: 'In-Dicta'. He opened it before he could stop himself. Ranks of MP3 files announced themselves. He clicked one at random. "I can't hear it..." The tiny laptop speakers could not compete with the chatter of the engine or the grumble of the road.

"Can't hear what?" Miranda was concentrating hard on keeping the speedo at just over the limit, not below, that would arouse suspicion, but not so far over as to merit a tug.

"It's an audio file... there're loads of them. Dated today."

Ross glanced at the Kadron ICE system embedded in the dashboard, and back to the Bluetooth icon in the Windows task bar. 'Accept connection to Bluetooth device Kadron: Yes/No'... 'Yes'.

He counted down in his head; this usually took about five seconds... Nothing... he stared at the animated wave form, but could only hear the faintest of telephone voices. Reaching across the dashboard, he cranked the car stereo volume.

A metal clunk overlaid with a brittle crack saturated the car.

Miranda jerked the wheel, mounting the grass verge. The Audi bounced back onto the tarmac. "Shit! What was that?" She checked the mirror. "Did I hit something?"

"It's this.." Ross cued the MP3 back a few seconds.

"...me give it a try. I'll pay you a dollar myself." A richly American accent boomed from the speakers... a few breaths later, and the shatter of metal on ceramic... a pause... and a second impact, brighter in tone, higher pitched... then the distant thump of something heavy falling onto a wooden surface.

"That's enough." A second voice, older, world weary. "I said that's enough."

Ross hit pause and turned to Miranda. "That was..."

She cut him off. "Don't! I don't want to... don't tell me..."

He ignored her. "That's the yanks... I told you about..."

Ross scanned through the list of MP3s. Each was appended with a date and time, each was the same file size. He found the oldest. Kris's fractured voice crept into the car. "That's our advisor of studies...

These are all mails from him…" The high end sound system placed Kris's voice vividly in the car, directly between Ross and Miranda. A chill traced down Ross's spine. Miranda stared resolutely forward.

A discussion followed, mostly Kris and the older American with a few simian grunts from the younger. He was walking them through the emails.

Ross selected another file.

"… was the weakest link in the chain… bring them down, Europe follows. Who'da thought the Krauts would bail them out?"

The younger voice answered. "Yeah… them boxheads don't have it in them."

"I guess they're still apologising for Dubya Dubya Aye Aye…"

Next file.

"Nah… he's one of ours… Farage ain't even his real name… It's Franklin… Looks like this one's going to work out… Poor bastard, though… he even had surgery on his jaw to reduce his chin to almost nothing… now that's what I call devotion to duty …"

Ross looked up at Miranda. She was staring hard at the road ahead, pulling at her bottom lip with one hand.

He skimmed through the audio file.

"Maybe I'm not the sharpest tool in the woodshed," this was the younger voice. A snort of derision agreed. "But I don't get the deal… Why Europe?"

"Too big too fast, and it's inherently unstable… fractured. We can't touch China… Russia'll burn itself out… But the EU? That we can control… we need a footprint in Europe. Best way? Bring 'em down hard… crash the Euro… they'll be beggin' for greenbacks so hard they'll start singing to our hymn sheet… Post-Brexit UK… they gonna be our little bitch, at least…" A caustic snigger. "And the best part… they're all blaming the Russkies…"

"But you said we'd crashed the dollar ourselves… That's what this bit of code's pointing out… It's why you freaked so hard…" The younger voice was almost pleading.

"It's all in the timing… Step 1… We had to get dollars out of circulation, bring the value back up longer term. Best way… pass the national debts onto Joe Public, without them even spotting it happening... Even better... have them desperate fo' a piece of the action... Make it their choice... Easier to scam a greedy sucker..."

Ross stared at the laptop.

"That's what this bit of code's pointing out..." Did that mean the software Ross and Kris had built?

"The sub-primes?" The playback continued.

"Exactly... but this program these two nerds built..." Ross felt his body ice over. "It's spitting out a list of all our tools... Look... " The rattle of a keyboard like dice in a cup. "See? Fanny Mae... Freddie Mac... and most of the rest... AIG... and..."

Ross paused the playback and found the results file. There was no sign of either company. He clicked the rejects log, the list of stocks that didn't follow the maths and were isolated as bad data, discarded.

There they were.

"Holy shit..." Ross exhaled slowly.

"I don't get it." She confessed. "What's the big deal?"

"It wasn't... It wasn't an accident... None of it..." His words paced out as the concept coagulated in his mind. The information was Kris's dying legacy. He flicked back through the results files to the date of the GFC; one by one, or in suicide pacts, stocks, currencies, bonds... they all trotted obediently off the cliff.

Ross glanced from the screen and winced as Miranda narrowly avoided a sheep who suddenly decided that the other side of the road was a much better place to be.

"If it wasn't an accident, you can still plead self-defence... seriously... go talk to a lawyer first... my uncle Jeff... he'll listen...'

Ross stopped her. "No... I mean the big crash... the GFC... the EU coming undone... Brexit... none of that's an accident..." He fumbled a button and his window slid down; the imbalance in air pressure in the car made a rhythmic beating; it thrummed in his ears and woke the throbbing in his battered nose and cheek. The over-sweet reek of silage filled the car. Ross gagged, but Miranda breathed deeply. He raised his window and pulled the collar of his shirt over his nose and mouth.

They drove on in silence for a few moments, each lost in their thoughts, each watching different futures stretching out ahead, while keeping an eye on the road behind. Ross shifted uncomfortably in his seat, stopped fidgeting resting on one hip, and twisted towards Miranda.

The lives, hopes and dreams of untold millions of people... shattered to heal the ailing dollar. The shock-waves reverberating around the globe as jobs were lost, families rendered homeless, viable companies trodden into the ground. The only growth industries were debt collection and foodbanks.

Ross knew the ignominy of begging a loan from a friend. Was that better or worse than standing in line with your family to rake through a box of donated soup tins in the hope of feeding them? Hiding the shame of accepting anonymous hand-outs to put food in the bellies of those you had sworn to love, and those you had brought into the world? Lacquering a smile across your face... everything will be OK.

"OK." She conceded. "So if all of this really happened, what next? I suppose you want to sell it to the papers?" She snorted as she ladled on the sarcasm.

Instead of watching the road, Miranda turned slowly to face him; on reflection, maybe it wasn't such a bad idea. The mention of selling anything snapped Ross out of contemplating the heartache of charity.

She shrugged "Thousands, hundreds of thousands? More?" The car accelerated gradually as Miranda's mind's eye gazed at the money.

Ross leant forward, buried his face in his hands, closed the laptop with his elbows. He sat up, dragged his hands down his face and drew a breath. He frowned and stared out the window. Clouds were gathering. He popped the folding screen open and laid his hands to the keyboard. "You name it..." Reluctantly, he boarded Miranda's train of thought. "But... no. We've got to get the hell away from here. With the hard-drive... and the laptop... we're clear for now. Kris's stuff's still in the cottage... his blood's all over the place. But there's nothing left on the PC there... It could be weeks before anyone finds them... But, I guess once that happens, we can flog the audio to the media…" He was babbling. "It's a fucking mess there… it'll look like they all topped each other… believe me…"

Miranda sucked at her teeth. "I guess the audio's worth nothing till someone finds the bodies."

"What?"

Miranda pointed at the laptop. "Right now, it's just audio… it could be a film soundtrack, or a radio play… it's worthless…"

Ross looked down at the screen.

"But," she continued, "we can't say anything till they're found… it'd just implicate us… we need to wait it out…"

The engine settled into a consistent, easy burble as the road levelled out. Miranda eased back in her seat. "So what now?" She took her eyes off the road to Ross's fingers, twitching on the keyboard.

"I don't know… South… Get back to Glasgow." Ross hazarded. "Dad'll back me up. We can say we were at my place… you came to stay for a few days."

"And which way is South from here? We're in the arsehole of nowhere…"

"Just keep driving… this wee road has to go somewhere; it's getting better so we're heading to civilization. There'll be a sign for something."

Miranda stared out over the wheel.

It suddenly registered with Ross that she had said "we need to…". He plucked at the thread of hope. "Just think about it, Miranda… you and me… we're set for life. We just need a bit of capital to get going… yeah, maybe we can sell bits of the story… shop the Yanks to the papers… Anybody starts digging it'll corroborate what they were up to… I don't know what the going rate is, but it's got to be worth something…"

"Hmmm." Miranda was noncommittal, lapsing into silence. She plucked at her bottom lip as she always did when deep in thought. From experience, Ross would have equated it with him being in some kind of trouble, but he was staring at the gathering storm, unaware. A first few drops of rain began to smear the windows.

"Emm… actually… I was kind of hoping we could pick it up… get back together… we're in this together now."

She snorted in derision. "Why the hell would I do that?" She checked the mirror. "We weren't going anywhere… Ross… it was already dead before I buried it."

Ross teared up. Her words were so final.

"Listen…" Miranda tapped a finger on the steering wheel as she itemized the situation. "This has nothing to do with me. If it's true about the bodies, you're the one in the shit. OK. Let's say the police do turn up, and there is an abattoir waiting for them, what links me to any of this?"

Ross cocked his head and opened his mouth to speak.

Miranda continued. "Someone sent me an email… big deal. Proves nothing. There'll be a few text messages… nothing wrong with that. I can deny knowing anything about it."

Ross turned doleful eyes to her. "Yeah, you can deny it. But you do know. They must have talked about you too… with Kris as well… they knew you were coming… your name'll be on the audio files as well…"

"Yeah… maybe." She pressed a little harder on the throttle. "We'll need to ditch the car. It ties you to the Americans." She glanced down at the laptop. "And, yeah, it ties us… we're in it together right enough… now."

Ross's heart leapt. "Yeah, it does… but it could be days before anyone comes near the cottage. Kris's folks probably haven't even noticed he's gone yet."

"Which means," Miranda concluded, "Got to get away somewhere… get in the clear… Before anyone checks out the cottage…"

"Where?"

"Anywhere…" Miranda mused.

"Anywhere…"

"Yeah…" she whispered. "Set for life…" She breathed, as she twisted her bottom lip between thumb and forefinger, tugged at it and let go.

# Chapter 36

The waves whispered their rumours, hushed each other and lapsed into momentary silence, like old biddies pausing mid-gossip as the object of their disparagement approaches. They spoke in huddled tones of the boats, bobbing at their moorings, flaccid in their lack of purpose; they susurrated opinions on the bygone optimism of their purchase: a life of leisure, a life of toil, a life. They hissed and breathed of a body; a body they bore in turns, in grey solemnity to ragged shore line, to join a flotsam of unburnable wood, unwoven rope and decomposing kelp. They gasped, drew breath as the body rolled and moaned. Its arm fell across the pebbles, without muscle, without ligament... only bone was confirmed by the hinge at the elbow.

Ross retched on his back, a mixture of his own bile and brackish water dribbled back into his nostrils. He coughed himself upright as the liquid burnt into his sinuses and gnawed at the soft flesh of the roof of his mouth. He hacked and spat, retched again, and regurgitated another stomach's worth into the water lapping sensuously at his crotch.

Head hanging limp at his shoulders, he stared at the greasy slick of vomit cooling and coagulating, clinging to the inseam of his jeans. He watched, an impartial observer, as tendrils of mucus attached to his thighs, pulsing like jellyfish, sinuous and delicate in the harbour formed by his legs. The salt scent of seaweed stirred the odour of his own body fluids, not quite mixing, but wreathing round each other like milk poured into a spinning cup of tea; one moment, he was scenting the redolent air of childhood excursions to the coast, the next gagging afresh on the acid of his gut.

His hands bobbed, detached in the water by his sides, rising and falling with the languid waves or his grateful breath… both.

Be still. Shut down. Stop. Silence the pain. Leave it. Float, float. Fade. Lean in, embrace. Drift and fade, drift and fade. The waves persuasive, pervasive, promising release, pestering him to join their endless murmurings. He could surrender. He was spent.

Ross lay back. With his head cradled in the stones, he no longer felt the light breeze. The beach was a welcome warm embrace by comparison to the waterborne numbness taking his feet and hands degree by degree. Was this what death felt like? The soil offering a last caress to its progeny? Calming, soothing, a mother holding her offspring one last time before it leaves the nest; for the mother's benefit or for that of the child? The earth gives life, and in the end gives solace. Is this why we bury our dead? Not for the benefit of the bereaved, but to ease the passing of those going on before us?

It would be easy, so easy. Just, let go.

But he couldn't. Not now...

He mentally worked backwards through what he could remember.

Lungs and throat burning.

Breaching the surface, so desperate for breath that he was taking great gasps even before he was fully in air.

The car door finally opening like the mechanism on an expensive hi-fi, slowly, too slowly.

He'd stood on the inside of the opposite door, the one now lying in the mud and rocks of the loch bottom, arms locked, using the last remaining strength of his legs; only the faint light of the surface beyond the window had told him which way was up.

Before that, desperately clawing at the seatbelt latch as the car gracefully ended its tumbling, rocked ready to roll further, balanced on one side like a gymnast spoiling a perfect routine at the last flourish by almost taking one more step.

Seconds, or maybe hours earlier, the dashboard lights, every warning illuminated, being diffused one by one as the silted water of the loch claimed each, until their colours coalesced into a rippled spectrum of indistinct brightness. He'd watched in fascinated horror, reminded first of the Viking's Rainbow Road to Valhalla, and consequently the half-Swede, all-bastard Kris.

Sudden, unexpected, even in retrospect as though he'd shut his eyes at the scary part of a film he'd seen before, the impact of the water, first on the wheels, then the broadside of the car, and Ross was folded around the seatbelt by the sudden deceleration. The momentum of the car became a roll, roof first, into the dark, unbiddable waters of Loch Fyne. Ross had pressed his hands to the ceiling in reflex, perhaps to brace for whatever impact was coming next, or in supplication to God... he was the wrong way up for that.

The weight of the engine canted the Audi nose down, water hissing to steam on its hot surfaces. The sideways roll slowed but still rotated the car on its long axis, almost gently like a washing machine slowing at the end of its cycle. As water had started pouring in through Ross's partially open window, the air trapped in Miranda's side gave temporary buoyancy, holding the car on its side for its inexorable transit to the bottom. The pressure of the water damped the roll, but clutched the doors tight.

Even before the lazy descent through the water, his personal time slowing to a crawl as the car's slither down the steep shale slope into the loch gathered pace; jolts and buffets marking the few rocks solidly fixed into the otherwise mobile surface. Every bounce threw the contents of the car around like dice in a cup. CDs launched themselves from the dashboard and skittered around like startled

271

birds; Ross felt he could have reached out and plucked one from the air. To him, they drifted lazily past his face as feathers on a breath.

And further back to Miranda. She'd plucked the hard drive from Ross's unresisting hand, and was clutching it tight to her bosom with one arm, a fire and brimstone preacher with an heirloom bible; she was already out of the car, standing uphill, watching, tugging at her bottom lip.

Her face. Ross could see her at the end of his pleading, outstretched hand.

Her face.

Her face.

The jolt that had set the car in motion; the hesitant, stop-start as the tenuous friction between the loch-side scree surrendered. He'd watched her lean out to him, replicated in miniature in every raindrop on the side window. Had she stretched to save him? Or merely overbalanced as she'd let go of her lip, and shut the door?

# Chapter 37

"Ross!" Michael staggered backwards into the hallway, then rebounded through the doorway to hold Ross tightly to him, a gesture he hadn't made since Ross was 12 years old.

"Son... I've been worried sick... why didn't you call? I've been that... well... look..." His dad stepped back again, and shook Ross firmly by his unresisting hand.

"Dad... can I come in?"

"What? Oh, yes... sorry. I mean... it's your place and all." Michael stepped out of the way.

Ross slouched across the wooden floor, shucked off his jacket, dropped it in the hallway and lurched, partially with the loss of the load and partially with long overdrawn exhaustion, into the living room. It was tidy. He barely noticed the now-visible space on the floor, the fact that his shoes didn't try to adhere to the carpet, the freshening breeze soughing the curtains now open at either side of the window. He fell into the sofa, tipped his head back and closed his eyes; they felt gritty under his eyelids. His hair was greasy to the touch.

Michael stood to his side. "Ross. You look like something the cat dragged in." Even with his eyes closed, Ross could sense the look on his father's face; part reproach, part relief. "What the hell happened? Could you not have let me know you were OK?"

Ross didn't raise his head or open his eyes. "Dad... I'm far from OK. I wasn't OK. I won't be OK. I don't even know what OK means anymore." He heard the armchair take his father's weight, felt him lean closer.

"Look at the state of you. Did you get mugged? What did they take?" Michael was inspecting the damage to Ross's face and clothes.

The boy turned to look at his father, opened his blooded eyes, took two breaths and began. He skipped the details of the software itself, Michael wouldn't understand, but outlined what he knew of the side effects of its functions; the power to make and destroy money and institutions alike, and the power those capabilities seemed to wield over those that came into contact with it.

He regurgitated, like a school boy reciting a tediously memorized poem for a class, in a monotone, what he'd already told Miranda about the two Americans, snippets of their recorded conversation, the mortgage crisis and the Greek collapse. He had no emotion any more. It was as though the first act of recounting the story had shifted the details from the part of his mind that felt, and into the part of his mind that dealt.

Maybe it was the sheer exhaustion, perhaps the familiar surroundings of his own flat, a childish comfort gained from the presence of his father which rendered the events of the last days and weeks unreal. There was a low-resolution graininess to the replay experience. Until he reached Miranda; he recalled the widening of her eyes when she heard of the life-changing potential within her reach, how she'd taken the hard-drive as she'd watched Ross slide towards the loch in the commandeered Audi. That's when the feelings flooded back.

Ross keened like a broken animal and watched his father fade and blur with the tears filming his eyes until all he could see was a smear of colour where Michael sat just feet from him. He flinched as his father gingerly touched his knee, unexpected.

"Son… son… shhh… it's OK. Yer dad's here…" Embarrassed, he heard himself. "Daddy's here… daddy's here… it's OK."

It wasn't the fact she'd sent him to his death, although of course, in time that would come to hurt too. It was that, for a moment… for a brief, iridescent moment… it was all going to work out. He'd seen her face light up when he'd suggested they could make it together. Everything else just faded away to background behind the glimpse into a future full of promise and possibility. Hope had given despair a blade with which to cut him.

But she hadn't wanted Ross. She wanted the money… the hard drive, the audio files, the code. She'd weighed him against a piece of software and found him lacking; software he had written. The dystopian world of science fiction was here and now; he'd been destroyed by his own creation.

He was worth less than a sequence of tiny magnetic fluctuations on a hard drive. And just as easy to erase.

Michael watched helpless as Ross sobbed and bawled, rocked forward, arms clenched across his stomach. He could barely make sense of the few incoherent words bubbling from Ross's mouth, punctuated with heaving sniffs as his son struggled to control himself. How had the human body evolved such that a grief so all-encompassing was so debilitating? What was the evolutionary advantage in being effectively disabled by utter despair? Perhaps, as your tribe lay around you dead and dying, the last vestiges of fight evaporated when all hope was gone; the final passing all the easier for offering no resistance.

Ross's weeping subsided to a whimper. Finally, he looked up. His father recoiled subtly at the sight of his son's bloodshot eyes and snot bubbling at one nostril. Ross gathered himself for a sentence. "You know what's really fucked up, though?"

Michael shook his head. After all he'd heard how could anything be considered as *really* fucked up in comparison?

"What's fucked is… she… " Ross almost giggled. "She risked it all for fuck all."

"I thought you said she'd got the drive? That she'd disappear and live the high life?"

"Yeah. She got the drive." Ross reached into his jacket pocket. "But there's sod all of value on it... and the laptop is at the bottom of the loch!" He forced a triumphant grin as he held his headphones up to his father's face. "I blue-toothed the lot to the headphones' memory when we were in the car, then overwrote the hard drive."

Michael stared, his focus flicking from the headphones to Ross's eyes. He didn't understand.

"Dad... it means all she's got her hands on is a useless hard-drive. There's no way she can get any of it back... maybe a few emails floating around some accounts somewhere, but nothing useful."

"But... what are you...?"

"I've got the lot here... or as much as would fit anyway." Ross threw the headphones onto the sofa beside him, leaned back and rubbed his ribs. His gasps for breath between sobs had reawakened the pain.

Michael puffed his cheeks and blew out through pursed lips, slapped his knees and stood. "So you're saying... she's on the run... attempted murder." He pointed at the wreckage of his son. "Accessory after the fact." He counted off two fingers. "Perverting the course of justice." He tapped a third finger, then a fourth as he ran out of offences, and clenched his fist instead. "She's done a runner from all that for nine tenths of fuck all?"

"That's about the size of it, dad."

Michael stared out of the window at the dishwater coloured sky. Five floors below, Glasgow continued to churn through its day as it had done for many before. He reached a conclusion. "Well... she fucking deserves it, that's for sure."

Staring hard at the headphones, brow furrowed, Michael asked the obvious question. "So what are you going to do with that now?" He ploughed on. "To be honest... I'd delete the whole lot if I were you. It's brought nothing but trouble... it'll just make your life a bloody misery... money can't buy happiness."

Ross watched the headphones, half expecting them to melt into the sofa like the slag from a nuclear accident. "True, dad. It can't buy happiness… but you can rent it for a while."

"C'mon, son… do the right thing. Tell me you'll just wipe it all…"

Ross cocked his head to one side, but kept his eyes on the headphones. "Yeah, dad…" *Probably.* He added to himself.

Michael patted Ross's shoulder as he headed for the door. "Cup of tea? There's nothing stronger in the house." Ross just nodded.

Over the tinkle of two cups being loaded with sugar and the kettle starting to rumble, Ross followed his father into the boxy kitchen, leaned on the door jamb and stared at the back of his bulldog neck.

A skitter of high heels cut through the kettle's boiling rumble. The front door still stood open, the rattle of stilettos echoed on the stone landing.

Michael remained bent to the task of putting fresh teabags in the cups. He didn't look round. "If that's that wee tart come back for forgiveness, tell her to fuck off. After everything she's put you through?" He picked up both cups and thrust them back on the counter with a bang.

There was a tentative knock. Ross turned to the front door as a waft of *Eau des Jardins* shimmied up the hall way. His eyes widened. There she stood, shredding a tissue, mascara slicing through the rouge of her cheeks.

"Emmm… dad." He didn't look away. "That's mum here to see you."

# Chapter...

The whine becomes a howl becomes a scream

The thrill of barely restrained potency; the surge.

A moment of indecision as gravity and aerodynamics tussle over the craft; it escapes, clambers upwards and away.

The saccharin sweet linger of kerosene in the cabin, sipped away by the ventilation system.

A young woman, releases her held breath, and eases the seat-belt looser.

In a moment or two, she will reach over, and pull a brand new laptop from her bag, freshly purchased, duty-free. She will attach an external hard-drive. She'll settle back, ask the first class steward for another glass of first class champagne; first class... after all, this is a one-way flight. She will open a folder labelled 'K-R Finance Project'; she's been putting this moment off, to savour and enjoy... like caching a favourite chocolate to compensate for the bitter taste of something less palatable.

She waits for the screen to refresh. Puzzled, she sees only a single icon, daring her to select it. She tugs her bottom lip, leans forward.

Instead of a document, application or batch of files, a media player will open, dancing waves indicating audio playback in progress; audio she has no chance to hear over the rumble of wind around the fuselage, being chewed up and spat out by the vast turbofans.

Fumbling in her bag for headphones, she makes the connection.

The song "Sunshine On Leith" proclaims judgement: "You saw it, you claimed it, you touched it, you saved it..."

She stares, her eyes misting over, at the purged folder... her ticket to untold riches... She saw it, and claimed it... touched it...

Nothing left.

Nothing but a single song, and fourteen hours flight time to figure out how to save herself.

Printed in Great Britain
by Amazon